Mandy Sutter is an award-winning poet, writer and hypochondriac who met her partner of ten years via Internet dating. They now live near the famous Ilkley Moor with a large black dog called Fable.

Mandy went to school in Nigeria and has co-written several part-fact, part-fiction books about the lives of Somali women. Two were published in 2007 and another two are in the pipeline.

She spent several years as Writer-in-Residence at Leeds General Infirmary, working with patients and staff.

Mandy also writes a successful blog, Reluctant Gardener, about her dad, who at the age of 87 took on a new allotment.

'Stretching It' is her first novel.

STRETCHING IT

Dear Ade

Hope you enjoy it!

Lots of love
Mandy

MANDY SUTTER

Ubley Nov '13

Indigo Dreams Publishing

First Edition: Stretching It

First published in Great Britain in 2013 by:
Indigo Dreams Publishing Ltd
132 Hinckley Road
Stoney Stanton
Leics
LE9 4LN
www.indigodreams.co.uk

ISBN 978-1-907401-96-1

Designed and typeset in Minion Pro by Indigo Dreams.

Cover design by Dru Marland: drusilla.marland@btopenworld.com

Printed and bound in Great Britain by Imprint Academic, Exeter

*Papers used by Indigo Dreams are recyclable products made from
wood grown in sustainable forests following the guidance of the Forest
Stewardship Council*

This novel was written as part of a Writing MA at Sheffield Hallam University

For my mother and for all mothers and daughters

I should like to thank the following people for their invaluable help: Jane Rogers, Caroline White, Alice McVeigh, Ronnie Goodyer, Dawn Bauling, John Griffiths, Dru Marland, Lesley Glaister, Marion Urch, Annette Green and last but not least Tim Morris, who kept the cups of tea coming

STRETCHING IT

1. *Cream tea*

Huddersfield station was a Grade One listed building described as 'a stately home with trains'.

Jennifer sat on a stone bench outside its imposing entrance, careful to make her green plastic Primark handbag visible on her lap as promised. A breeze tousled the tops of the city's trees but didn't trouble her hair, which was welded into a natural look with hairspray.

She was looking for a tall, slim man wearing a trilby. But of the people who surged out onto the steps with each train arrival then trickled gradually away, none wore hats of any description.

Then a tall man in a Barbour coat came out. He was wearing a leather hat with a wide brim and flat top. Jennifer surveyed it. Was this a trilby? She didn't think so. On the other hand, the man was tall. But was he slim? While she was trying to work it out, he walked straight past her without so much as a glance and flagged down a taxi.

She breathed out again. She tried to read the paper she'd brought. But her eyes wouldn't even take in the headlines. Was she going to be this nervous all evening?

'Jennifer?' asked a voice at her shoulder.

She looked up. A tall man held out a leather-gloved hand. He was wearing the kind of hat you would take off by pinching the two sides of the crown together, also a tie and a smart dark raincoat. He was very handsome in an old-fashioned way.

Having not expected any of these things, she felt flustered.

'You must be Alec,' she said, standing to take his hand. 'And that must be a trilby. How very nice to meet you both.'

She laughed.

He didn't.

But neither did he seem to be flinching at her size, something that, at four stone overweight these days, she sometimes saw people do.

'The pleasure is all mine,' he said in a cut glass BBC accent. Then he took her elbow and propelled her back into the station.

'Where are we going?' she asked.

'All will be revealed.'

He deposited her by the bookshop and joined the queue at the Ticket Sales window. She was glad of the chance to study him from a distance. As he advanced in the queue, brandishing an expensive looking wallet, she saw decisiveness in his posture as well as in his manners. He was immaculate: the belt of his raincoat had probably been ironed.

In short, he was totally out of her league. He came back, folding notes into his wallet. Only then did she wonder about the transaction he'd just made. On the phone, he'd been very insistent they meet at the station itself, even though there was a perfectly good hotel with a bar next door.

'Are we going somewhere?' she asked.

He held up two platform tickets, little things in thick pink paper, like something from the last century.

'I'm surprised you can still get those,' she said. Then, when he didn't say anything, 'I thought you were spiriting me away.'

'No. I work in Churley. It's in the opposite direction.'

Did he mean Chorley, a town on the Lancashire border? And in the opposite direction to what? Before she could ask, he had taken her elbow again and was steering her through the sliding glass doors and down the platform, towards the station buffet, the Head of Steam. It seemed odd. This was an open station and there was an entrance to the buffet on St George's Square.

He held the door open. 'Here we are. The refreshment room. You've been in here before, I expect?'

They passed into the dark interior. 'Well, no,' she said. 'I'm not a great user of stations. I drive, you see.'

His face fell. He headed straight for the bar without asking her what she wanted to drink. She slid onto an upholstered bench at a dark wooden table and glanced around. The place was a cosy cross between a pub and a café. Men huddled over pints at the bar, while solitary women with cases sipped coffees.

He came back with a pot of tea and a plate of scones flanked by little dishes of jam and cream. It was odd food for seven o'clock in the evening.

'Er, thanks,' she said. Had she told him she liked cream teas, on the phone? She couldn't remember.

'Fresh,' he said, indicating the scones. 'Or so she says. Although if these were made this morning, she's Shirley Temple.'

'Shirley Temple?'

A glass of water stood on the tray. He pushed it towards her. 'For your eye.'

'My eye? What do you mean, my eye?'

'There's a piece of grit in it,' he said.

She blinked, but couldn't feel anything. She checked the corners of both eyes with a finger. 'There's nothing there.'

But he leant across the table, and took hold of her chin. His hand was cool and slightly rough. He tilted her head towards the light. 'Look up,' he ordered.

'But … .'

'Now look down.'

He stared into her right eye. She felt his breath on her cheek.

'There really is nothing there,' she said.

She glimpsed a white handkerchief then suddenly she was jerking back from the shock of having had it poked into her eye.

'Ow! What are you doing?'

Her eye stung and watered. She searched her bag for a tissue.

'Hope that didn't hurt too much,' he said. 'I killed two patients this morning. Matron's very displeased with me.'

'What?'

'I don't dare go back to work.'

He laughed and she realised he was joking. She returned his smile as best she could with one eyeball on fire. This was getting weirder and weirder. She turned to the cup of tea to calm herself down. Perhaps she should try to steer the conversation more – launch into self-disclosure, and tell him about the microscope factory she worked in or her last papier-mâché sculpture, a giraffe-cum-forklift truck – get the conversation onto a more normal footing.

'I do apologise,' he said suddenly.

She lowered her cup. 'What on earth for?'

'For boring you with long medical words.'

'What? 'Matron' and 'patient'?

He was producing two bars of Cadbury's Dairy Milk from his pocket and talking about going to the pictures. She stared at him, baffled.

'Of course, you know what's happening, don't you?' he asked.

'I wish I did.'

'I've fallen in love with you.'

All the rope she had been allowing him ran back suddenly onto its reel.

'I beg your pardon?' she said. 'Excuse me for a few minutes, would you?'

In the Ladies, she put the toilet seat down, sat on it and took several deep breaths. She was on a date with a weirdo. The very kind of thing the personal ads were known for. The very kind of thing her friend Nyesha had warned her about, and said she was inviting by placing an ad. Well, a judgement about that would have to wait. She wondered if she should ring the police. But it wasn't a criminal offence to go on a date, even if you were insane.

She studied the toilet window. It was too small and high up for a person to climb through, a person of her size anyway. She would have to think of another way.

Back at the table, he was pouring her a second cup of tea.

'Alec,' she said, resolving to sit down only briefly. 'I'm afraid I can't stay out much longer.'

She was ready to tell him about her mother – say there was a problem. But she didn't have to.

'I know exactly what you're going to say,' he said

'You do?'

'I know what you feel about this evening. I mean, about the sordidness of it.'

Jennifer was startled. 'It hasn't been *that* bad.'

'You're going to say that it isn't worth it.' His tone was getting increasingly passionate.

'Alec,' she said, 'calm down. Let's be sensible about this.'

He gave a harsh laugh. 'It's too late now to be as sensible as all that. It's too late to forget what we've said and anyway, whether we've said it or not couldn't have mattered.'

Jennifer stared at him. She'd heard those words before. In fact, come to think about it, there was a ring of familiarity about several things he'd said this evening.

'The feeling of guilt and doing wrong is too strong, isn't it?' he said.

Jennifer frowned, trying to place this utterance along with the rest of them.

'Too great a price to pay for the happiness we have together,' he added.

Realisation arrived like a veil snatched suddenly away.

'Oh, God. I get it,' said Jennifer.

'Of course you do. How could you not?'

The loudspeakers announced the departure of the eight forty to Sheffield. Alec turned his face away. 'I can't look at you now. I know this is the beginning of the end. Let's be very careful; a sudden break would be too cruel. Shall I see you again? Next Thursday? I ask you most humbly.'

Jennifer tried to remember the end of the film, her mum's favourite. 'I'm not sure what I'm doing next Thursday.'

It didn't sound much like David Lean's classic script. But Alec didn't seem bothered. He was rattling along, on his own track.

'I'm going away,' he said. 'Johannesburg. They're opening a new hospital. I haven't told anybody. I couldn't bear the thought of leaving you. But now I see it's got to happen. It's happening already. Couldn't I write to you?'

Jennifer hesitated. But he didn't need an answer. 'Forgive me. For everything. For meeting you in the first place. For getting a piece of grit out of your eye. For loving you.'

His eyes shone with tears.

She was unable to stop tears, of fright but also of pity, coming into her own. His eyes looked so sad. He was expecting her to say something. If only she could remember Celia Johnson's final lines.

Then his lips moved, saying something silently. On the platform, a guard's whistle shrilled. His lips moved again, prompting her.

'Cats cause rain?' she tried. 'Dad's a drain?'

He frowned.

'That's your train,' she said.

Relief flooded his face. 'Could you really say goodbye and never see me again?' His lips moved silently with the answer.

'Yes,' she said, following. 'If you'd scalp me. I mean, if you'd help me.'

He rose to a crouch, picking his hat up from the table. Time stood still. Jennifer, heart pounding, prayed that he really was going to leave, not pull a gun out of his pocket and shoot her in the head, before massacring everyone in the café and then turning the gun on himself.

But with a final, heartfelt look, he straightened and walked to the door.

Jennifer sat for a few moments, just being alive.

Her gaze fell on the two bars of chocolate. In the old black and white film chocolate came in silver foil, with a paper sleeve. Today you got sealed plasticised envelopes. It wasn't the same. Nevertheless Jennifer opened one and ate it. Then she opened the second one and ate that too.

When she finally stood to leave, it was to knowing nods and sympathetic glances from all around the bar.

2. *Bad Apple*

Jennifer lived with her mother, Alicia, on an estate of fifties semis in North Leeds. Outside, the pebbledash and paintwork looked sorry for themselves. Inside, there was further evidence of low-income living: the house was furnished with junk shop finds.

Nothing matched. In the cramped hall, two golden cherubs held up a vast tarnished mirror. In the sitting room, a chandelier was staffed by energy saving light bulbs. Alicia's health hadn't been good for years, and Jennifer had no time or money to spend on giving the place a facelift.

But tonight, as she let herself in, she was as glad to see the place as she'd ever been. She was also glad that Alicia was still at her weekly *Times of our Lives* evening at the local community centre and that Nelly Sykes, the neighbour who came in to help out, had gone.

She sank down on the hall stairs, her usual phone perch, with a large glass of Merlot.

'Can you believe it?' she asked her friend Nyesha.

'Hardly,' said Nyesha. 'Even worse, you had this guy down as one of your top prospects. This would never have happened if you'd used the Internet – you could at least have seen his picture then. Or let me look at all those letters.'

Jennifer wasn't so sure about this second option, Nyesha's track record with being men only marginally better than hers.

'I couldn't do that. Letters are private. Imagine how you'd

feel if you'd written one. You wouldn't want it handing around and analysing.'

'Self-preservation is what I'm talking about here,' said Nyesha. 'Not moral niceties. I knew the letter-writing thing was bonkers, anyway. No wonder you're attracting crazies.'

Jennifer was still grateful to Alec for not being fazed by her weight. Best not mention that though, unless she wanted a lecture on self-esteem.

'I wanted something personal. I wanted to see their handwriting. Anyway, it's time letters made a comeback. It's time people reconnected with the joy of indecipherable scrawl and spelling mistakes.'

There were other reasons Jennifer had wanted letters, but it was best not to mention those now.

'Look, it could have been worse,' she added. 'What if he'd been expecting me to re-enact *Anna Karenina*? I might have had to throw myself under the nine-fifteen to Barnsley.'

'Why is it, every time something bad happens to you, you just end up grateful it wasn't worse? Why not stop people taking advantage of you in the first place?'

'Don't worry,' said Jennifer. 'The next date will be fine.'

There was an incredulous pause. 'You're not going to go *on* with this crazy thing? Oh, I should never have left Leeds.'

Jennifer sighed. 'What else can I do? You know what it's like, working at that factory. And Mr Right is hardly going to march up to the front door while I'm sitting watching telly with Mum.'

Nyesha grunted. 'I know. But I don't like the idea of you putting yourself in danger.'

'Don't be daft. One bad apple and all that. Besides, I couldn't bear to throw away all the work I've done to get to this stage.'

'So when is it? Your next date?'

'Next Tuesday, when Mum's out at *Times of our Lives* again.'

'And who's the lucky psychopath this time?'

'Barry. He's a solicitor at a big Leeds law firm.'

'And?'

'I don't know much more than that, to be honest. We only talked for a few minutes because he was in a rush. He sounded interesting, though – a bit brusque maybe, a bit alpha male, but crisp and sparky.'

'Why doesn't that make me feel even a tiny bit better?' asked Nyesha.

As Jennifer went into the sitting room with the rest of the wine and a bag of kettle chips, she admitted to herself that it was indeed a worry that so many hours, days and weeks of work had produced only six dates. It was the kind of inefficiency they would have jumped on her for at work.

She'd surfed the Net and scanned the back pages of the papers for days before she'd plucked up the courage to write an ad for the local paper. Then there'd been the task of studying all the letters that came in reply, trying to read something into people's handwriting and the sort of paper they'd used.

Letters had been transferred from one shoebox to another and back again: Absolute No's (bulging); Faint Possibilities (half full); Probable Yeses (scanty). Then there'd been hours on the phone. And now, one of her hard won prospects had gone down the pan in less than an hour.

'Oh dear,' she said, aloud.

And then she switched the television on and turned her attention to a documentary about earthquakes that made her problem seem as insignificant as a flea on an elephant.

3. *Tuna Melt Panini*

Greg Bond wasn't good looking: he was freckly with tightly curled carroty hair and flesh bulging over the top of his waistband. He was the kind of bloke who would have been called ginger-nob at school. But it didn't seem to matter. His confidence was like magic glue, making everything about him stick together and add up to someone who signified.

The morning after Jennifer's date she was settling down to a cherry scone and what passed for a latte from the office coffee machine when she was startled by the sight of him approaching her desk at top speed.

Before she'd had time to think, he'd thrust a piece of paper under her nose. 'What do you call this?'

She looked down at the email he'd printed off. Printing out emails was frowned upon, but this was definitely not the best moment to mention it. The email was from her and it was a complaint to a local printer.

'Hi R,' it said. 'The leaflets were fantastic, but we think they're a bit pricey. Any chance of a teensy rebate? Hope you don't mind us asking.'

'What's wrong with that?'

He came round and sat on the edge of her desk. His thigh was an inch from her mobile phone; an odd, distracting intimacy. He jabbed at the email.

' "R"?, "Teensy"? "A bit pricey"? "Hope you don't mind"? Is that appropriate language with which to address one of the firm's suppliers?'

'Well, I talk to him on the phone so much, it'd feel wrong to be formal.'

'Even so, that's not the only problem. Saying his leaflets are fantastic isn't exactly paving the way for a refund.'

Jennifer felt caught out. 'But they looked great. He did a marvellous job considering it was only two-colour. And he's only a small business. He's feeling the pinch what with the credit crunch. It would be awful if we contributed to putting him out of business.'

A muscle moved in Greg's cheek. Was he mulling it over?

It seemed not. 'This company could be one of the big players in the semiconductor industry,' he shouted, 'if only it wasn't full of people who insisted on running it like the village sweetshop.'

Heads turned all over the office. That was the trouble with open plan: any incident got broadcast all round the factory and repeated back within the hour, usually involving a sexual perversion.

And Greg wasn't tactful. He'd made a lot of enemies since he'd arrived from Head Office a month ago, not least among the factory workers whose redundancies he'd called for. Having said that, he was supposed to be saving the company from ruin, so perhaps tact wasn't high on his list of priorities.

'Sorry,' she said.

She wished they could gel better. This wasn't her first telling-off.

'I really am sorry,' she said again. 'We must seem very old-fashioned to you.'

'Look,' said Greg. 'You've been PA to the Marketing Director for some time, haven't you?'

Jennifer nodded. Every weekday morning for the past ten years she'd driven her pink roofed Mini around the Ring Road and turned right just before the Seacroft roundabout. Every morning she'd walked through the factory, a one-story building carbuncled with add-ons, to her workstation in the huge open plan office where Derek from Finance muttered over the sales team's expenses at one end and the sales team jabbered into their phones at the other. Every morning she'd sat down to a view that had become almost as familiar as her own thoughts.

'Well,' Greg said, 'What did Ron Sandle have you doing in all that time?'

'He didn't like to bother me with too much secretarial work.'

'Bother you with secretarial work? What else was he supposed to bother you with?'

'He thought of me more as a ... personal helper.'

'What?'

'Well, making his travel arrangements.'

She hesitated.

'Fair enough,' said Greg. 'But what else?'

The wrong sort of thing sprang to mind, like the time he'd asked her to clip his nose and ear hairs, or renew his subscription to 'Big Jugs Monthly'.

'Er, watering his plants,' she said. 'Buying cheese and wine for board meeting lunches. Ordering flowers for his wife's birthday.'

Greg looked incredulous.

'He preferred me not to get involved on the business side,' she said. 'Anyway, he was a face-to-face sort of man. He agreed things down at the golf club.'

In fact, Ron had spent more time down at the golf club than at work. He had retired to Spain, where he was probably even now practising his swing.

'He would rather have prised his eyeballs out with a rusty screwdriver than let me write a letter or email on his behalf,' Jennifer said.

Greg held up his hand. 'I've heard enough,' he said. 'Listen, Jenny. Attitudes in this company have to change. We need to start looking like a cutting edge, professional outfit. We need to *be* a cutting edge professional outfit, of course, but that's going to take longer.'

Any minute now he would start talking about being accountable for the end product.

'We need to be accountable for the end product,' he said. 'And the end product in your case is the impression we make on the outside world.'

He stopped. She snatched her gaze away from his leg, now actually touching her mobile phone.

The muscle in his cheek twitched again. 'You haven't the faintest idea what I'm talking about, have you?'

'Oh! Well, I hear your words. But I'm not sure how they translate into actual things I should be doing.'

The muscle worked overtime. 'You're not helping me, Jenny. Time we had a talk. Looked at the, well … options. Not today, obviously. Or this week, come to that. I'm busy as fuck. Say, end of next week.'

'Options?' said Jennifer. It sounded ominous.

'Don't worry about it now. We'll discuss it then. Over lunch, let's say. The Frog and Newt.'

Jennifer brightened again. In all her years of working for Ron Sandle, he'd never treated her to so much as a cup of coffee. Her thoughts flew to clothes. What would she wear? Her blue striped blouse, perhaps, with the black skirt? But the skirt was warm for summer. On the other hand, it was smart and a size twenty-four, which meant she could definitely get into it.

'Hallo?' said Greg. 'Anyone home?'

'Sorry!' she said. 'I mean, yes. I'd love to go to the Frog and Newt. It would be fantastic.'

Greg looked taken aback. 'They knock up a reasonable tuna melt panini, I grant you. But don't get that excited.'

He stood up, making her mobile phone skid across the desk. As he moved away, he ran his finger around the inside of his collar, as if it was suddenly too tight for him.

When she got home, she found a dozen elderly people in the sitting room, all talking at once. Alicia sat among them holding court, erect and tiny in her most recent Oxfam shop bargain, a pale blue silk blouse, which she wore buttoned to the neck despite the day's warmth. Pepe, her poodle, lay next to her on his back, his neat purplish balls displayed proudly like figs on a platter.

Alicia had been forty when Jennifer, her only child, was born, so Jennifer was used to the occasional old person about the place. They didn't usually appear in such a high concentration per square foot, but belatedly Jennifer remembered something about a get-together to celebrate someone's hip replacement.

She hesitated in the sitting room doorway, hoping she could get away with a quick hello then disappear upstairs. She tried to catch her mother's eye. But her mother did not allow her eye to be caught.

Sighing, Jennifer advanced into the room, manoeuvring past occasional tables bristling with teacups and plates of pink cake and biscuits. She breathed shallowly, trying not to inhale the scent of floral perfume laced with aroused poodle.

Alicia was still engrossed in conversation, so Jennifer sat down next to a man in an auburn toupee who was holding forth on the Homeless. White heads nodded in agreement but Jennifer tried and failed to listen. She grazed absentmindedly from all the plates and bowls within reach, clocking up three Hobnobs, a piece of carrot cake and a handful of Minstrels.

What would she and Greg talk about at the Frog and Newt? She couldn't imagine him sitting still long enough to eat a meal. But it was a definite Development. He would be practice for her dates. Or perhaps her dates would be practice for him.

'A minute on the lips, a lifetime on the hips,' said a voice, and Jennifer turned to see a wagging finger.

She hid her annoyance with a smile. She wasn't ignorant about calories. In her teens and early twenties, she'd counted them to control her weight. But these days it seemed like too much trouble.

'The fat gets inside, you know,' said the woman. 'It lays all around the heart and kidneys. And then – boom!'

'Right,' said Jennifer. 'Are you a friend of Mum's?'

'Mum's been dead thirty years.'

'Not your mum,' said Jennifer. 'Mine. The one over there, in the blue blouse.'

The woman peered myopically across the room.

'Them ones with dogs is what gets my goat,' said the auburn-toupeed man. 'There's one outside t'Dennis Healy centre who gets a hundred quid a day, by all accounts.'

The woman gripped Jennifer's arm. 'Who are you?'

'I'm Alicia's daughter.'

'I expect you're the cook,' said the woman. 'Cooks are always fat as butter. I'll have a cup of tea, dear, if you don't mind. Two sugars. And not too much milk.'

Familiar feelings about the futile nature of human existence gripped Jennifer as she heaved herself from the sagging armchair.

The kitchen was a square, sunny room, recently resuscitated by Nelly's husband Ernie and a tin of yellow emulsion. Nelly stood at the sink in her apron, up to her elbows in suds. 'Cut some more Battenburg for us will you, love,' she said by way of greeting.

Jennifer sliced the pink and yellow checked cake and arranged it on a plate. She put the kettle on to boil.

'And take your mother's new pills in, would you,' added Nelly. 'See if you can get her to eat a bit of summat with them. She won't have had a thing, despite sitting there surrounded by cake all afternoon.'

Jennifer knew exactly what her mother would say when pressed. Something like, 'Don't fuss, dear. We're not all addicted to carbs.'

But she dutifully emptied two red and white capsules into a saucer, plus a segment of pills from the tablet organiser. Pills of varying hue and shape lay next to each other. It was like a garage for miniature spaceships.

Nelly eyed them. 'Them new ones any good?'

'We don't know yet,' said Jennifer. 'She's only been on them a week. And they're only temporary.'

'Waiting for her latest test results, is she?'

It wasn't a question that needed answering. Alicia was always waiting for her latest test results.

'I do think she's marvellous, your ma, the way she copes,' said Nelly. 'Especially when she's so often in pain. She's a lesson to us all.'

'She certainly is,' said Jennifer.

'What'll she do if it all comes to nowt again?'

'I suppose it'll be back to keying words like 'polyp' and 'fistula' into Google again.'

'You what, love?'

Jennifer picked up the tray, complete with cake, pills and tea, and braced herself for a return to the room of old folks. 'Nothing. We'll be back to Dr Ganguly again, I suppose. To see if he'll refer us to another consultant. Specialising in another part of the human body.'

'Are there any left? Body parts, I mean?'

Jennifer laughed. But Nelly's face was serious.

'Sorry,' said Jennifer. 'I expect there are. The spleen, perhaps. Or the sigmoid colon. I don't think we've ever investigated those.'

4. *Rancid butter*

A week went past, a week in which Jennifer tried unsuccessfully not to cling, life-raft style, to the idea of her next date.

When Tuesday evening finally came, it was hard not to shove Alicia out of the house.

'Gently, dear,' said Alicia as she was helped into her jacket. 'I mustn't be manhandled, you know. Narendra says I bruise easily. I'm still recovering from that dreadful jolt last week when you nearly crashed the car. I'm sure you've given me whiplash.'

'A child ran out in front of the car. What did you want me to do – run him over?'

Alicia applied pearl lipstick in the mirror. 'I've half a mind not to go this week. All that jollification. As if being old makes your IQ diminish to the level of a three-year-old.'

'But you enjoy it when you get there,' said Jennifer, too quickly. 'What are you doing this week, anyway?'

'Oh, Macramé, I expect. Gilbert and Sullivan. Brain surgery.'

At last Jennifer was helping Alicia down the drive and onto the hydraulic step of the minibus. She felt guilty. But there was no point in telling her mother anything before there was anything to tell, was there?

Half an hour later, having run back into the house, flung on a clean blouse and a smear of pink lipstick, Jennifer was sitting at a table near the door in the Frog and Newt.

As she sipped the contents of a little bottle of Pinot Grigio, she gazed at the couples out for the night and the office workers whose after-work drink had extended into the evening – women on bar stools easing their heels out of their shoes; men stuffing ties into pockets – and scoured the pub as casually as possible for a lone blond man, five foot eleven and wearing a pinstripe suit. Barry had said he was twenty-nine, so she expected someone of about thirty-five.

But there was no one like that yet, even though he'd planned to finish work at seven on the dot and be in the pub by seven-thirty. 'It'll make a change. You should see the hours we do. There's so much pressure to make partner, no one wants to be the first to go home.'

He said he'd rather meet than waste time forming a false impression. Jennifer had appreciated his clarity but now found she had no impression of him at all, false or otherwise.

She sat on, keeping her eye on the door.

Several lone males arrived, and she held her breath as their eyes searched the tables. But all alighted, with grins or nods, on faces other than hers.

Ten minutes went by, then another ten. People who had been standing at the bar drifted over to the tables, deciding to make a night of it. Jennifer tried to enjoy the ambience, but it was hard when your head jerked up every time the door opened.

She finished her first little bottle of wine and started on a second. She flipped open the clamshell of her phone to see if there was a message. There wasn't, just Pepe's demented face lighting up as usual. The time, quarter past eight.

Something had obviously gone wrong.

Had he been held up at work? It was possible.

Had he got the date wrong, or the pub? There was a chance.

Had he had crashed his car, and been taken away in an ambulance? It wasn't out of the question.

Then again, it didn't seem exactly likely.

Fighting feelings of disappointment, she held out for another ten minutes before draining her glass and standing up. As she passed the bar, a group of pinstriped men fell silent. She opened the heavy oak door of the pub. One of the men raised his hand in a mock salute. The door closed on the moist atmosphere of beer and people; the sound of laughter.

In the morning, Alicia was tetchy. She moaned about the fact that Nelly had bought sliced bread, making the toast too thick. Then she said the butter was off, though it smelt fine to Jennifer. Now she was attacking the marmalade.

'It's absolutely ghastly,' she said. 'Look at all these great big lumps of peel. They make me positively gag. It's not good for my acid reflux.'

Jennifer was not in the mood. 'Try that,' she said curtly, handing her mother the lemon curd.

Alicia was being awkward because she was suspicious. Jennifer had got back well before her last night and changed into leggings and a sweatshirt, but an unsettled atmosphere had pervaded the sitting room.

Now her mother waved the curd away. 'You know I can't bear that stuff. Yellow pap! If only Nelly would buy something decent. I do wish we had a Harrods in Leeds.'

'Why do you want a Harrods? We couldn't afford to shop there.'

'I disagree. Sometimes a small exquisite item of food – a jar of marmalade made with Sicilian lemons, for example – is worth its weight in gold. Besides, I should feel better just knowing it was *there*, even if I never went in.'

'When we got Harvey Nichols you said the prices were daylight robbery made worse by the money going straight to London.'

Alicia sniffed. Her lipstick had bled to the rim of her lips. 'I'm sure I never said any such thing.'

The sound of savaging came from the hall.

Jennifer found Pepe subduing two items of post on the

30

doormat. One was a small brown envelope, like the ones the paper had used to forward the lonely hearts letters. Jennifer had disliked them: their pale brownness conferred a seedy quality to the whole venture. But this one seemed to have something inside it. Jennifer, not in the mood for such things, shoved it into the pocket of a nearby jacket on the coat stand and immediately forgot all about it.

'Anything for me?' called Alicia.

'No.'

'No *Understanding Parkinson's?* You're sure? It hasn't gone under the mat?'

Jennifer opened the second envelope on the way back into the dining room. 'It's only a bill.'

'By the way dear, will you buy me a large bottle of aspirins today?' asked Alicia. 'Own brand will do.'

'Are you planning an overdose?'

'That's not funny. No, I want you to mash them up for me. You can put them in a plastic bag and bash them with a rolling pin. Added to shampoo, they work wonders as a cure for dandruff, apparently.'

Alicia had taken to DIY beauty treatments recently. But Jennifer was only half listening. She was staring at a long list of phone numbers. Trying to save money, she'd recently switched them to a new phone provider, who obviously itemised the bill.

With unusual agility, Alicia leant over and snatched it. 'What are all these phone codes?'

Jennifer tried to take the bill back, but Alicia's hand pinned it to the tablecloth.

'That's the code for Harrogate. And who do we know in *Wakefield*? And this looks like the code for Glasgow.'

Jennifer hid behind her teacup. Glasgow had been Tim, the vet who sounded lovely but lived too far away. 'Since when have you been an expert on national dialling codes?' she asked weakly.

'Oh, they had us learn some of them at the old folks' club,' said Alicia. 'Keeps the numerical memory ticking over. Not one of our more stimulating sessions.'

Jennifer remembered all the phone calls, the men with their different styles: jokey, earnest, cool, charming. Some who'd interviewed her assiduously but told her almost nothing about themselves. Others who'd told her so much she could have made them her specialist subjects on Mastermind.

'You owe me an apology,' said Alicia.

Jennifer sat down. It would have been better to tell her mother freely, rather than get cornered like this. Still, things didn't always go according to plan.

She straightened her Houses of Parliament place mat and swallowed. Her mouth was suddenly very dry. Her palms sweated. Nevertheless, she tried to go on.

'You're right. I do. Listen, I'm really sorry you had to find out like this. I wasn't *planning* on keeping it from you. It's just I was worried how you might react.'

She stopped. This was harder than she'd imagined. She took a couple of deep breaths. She felt the details of her confession begin to form themselves into sentences, ready themselves to be spoken. And behind this confession were other confessions, about how she felt these days, about how she'd felt for years.

But her mother cut her off before she could continue. 'There's no need to get emotional, dear.'

'What?' said Jennifer.

'Don't say 'what' dear, say 'pardon.' I *agreed* to switch phone providers, if you remember. Of course I remember a conversation about the reliability of these new companies, and who took which side. But now that my point has been proven, and we'll be going back to BT, I don't think there's any more to be said on the subject.'

'Uh?'

Alicia folded her napkin and fed it back into a tarnished silver napkin ring.

'This brain may be getting old, but it still works. However, one has to allow one's children to make their own mistakes. Or else, how do they learn?'

'I'm hardly a child, Mum,' said Jennifer. 'I'm thirty-two.'

'You're still *my* child,' said Alicia. 'And now you know that although established companies may be more expensive, they don't send you other people's phone bills by mistake. That's the difference.'

An unexpected feeling washed over Jennifer as she realised her secret was safe. She'd felt it last night in the pub when Barry had failed to show: crushing disappointment.

She wasn't looking forward to telling Nyesha about the latest debacle. But at lunchtime the next day, her friend rang her at work, eager to hear what had happened. And when Jennifer had told her story, cupping her hand around the phone so no one on the sales desk could hear, Nyesha, true to form, was outraged and unsure whether to blame Jennifer or the shittiness of life in general.

'Are you just picking dodgy blokes or is this a representative sample of Yorkshire's single men? The first one's a crazy man and the second stands you up. Weren't there any clues in their letters?'

'Well, no,' said Jennifer. 'All the Probable Yeses wrote decent letters.'

'What do you mean, decent?'

'I mean not obscene, not mentioning deranged and possibly dangerous ex-wives, and not making themselves sound boring or sad. Plus they all had ordinary names. No Geffrons, Hawks or Filberts. Just plain Andys, Johns and Steves. They had ordinary jobs, too. No astronauts, human cannonballs, or special agents. Just lawyers, businessmen, photographers – well, one was unemployed, but I let him in because he likes dolphins. And they all showed taste in their choice of writing paper and pen. No ragged pages torn out of notebooks, no block mailings, no blotchy biros.'

Silence from the other end of the phone.

Then, 'Are you sure your criteria were ... .'

Jennifer interrupted. 'All I can think is that letters and phone calls only show certain aspects of people. Like the way a jacket emphasises broad shoulders or a tie brings out the colour of someone's eyes. You get those little bits of information and your imagination fills in the rest. You know you shouldn't, but you do.'

'*You* do, you mean,' said Nyesha. She sighed. 'I'm sure I shouldn't be encouraging you but go on, who's the next fantasy projection?'

'Lawrence. The photographer. He used recycled stationery.'

Despite everything she'd just said, Jennifer couldn't help brightening at the memory of their conversation. 'He sounded really great. Not formal, like Alec, or brusque like Barry, but ironic and downbeat. A bit like Jack Dee. I bet he wears dark jeans and a charity shop overcoat. He seemed authentic, too. True to himself and his feelings.'

'Oh God,' said Nyesha. 'But you're right. You've got to see them all now. I mean, it can't get any worse, can it?'

5. *Free espressos*

Salvatore's Salon, where Alicia and Jennifer got their hair done, was in an upmarket parade of shops just off the Ring Road.

They drew up outside at eight-thirty on the Friday morning. It was four days until the date with Lawrence and there was also the impending but elusive lunch meeting with Greg to consider. He hadn't firmed up yet, and Jennifer didn't like to push, but she had dressed in her black skirt and blue striped Curvz blouse this morning, hoping he'd take the hint.

Sometimes, when helped out of the car, Alicia would clutch Jennifer's arm as if she was drowning and say things like, 'This car is so low to the ground. I do think you might have been more considerate when you bought it, and spared a thought for your poor old mum.'

But today she pushed Jennifer's arm away. 'Goodness, dear, I'm not an *invalid*.'

Jennifer looked across to the salon. Behind the smoked glass window, the hairdresser was drinking from a tiny cup and grimacing.

'Good morning, ladies,' he said as he let them in to the empty salon, opened early for their benefit. The draught pressed his shirt into the hard, concave shape of his stomach. It made Jennifer conscious of her own stomach, quivering beneath her skirt like a half-set jelly.

Salvatore smiled at Alicia. 'You are looking very beautiful this morning,' he said. 'A sight for the raw eyes.'

Jennifer was sure he spoke bad English on purpose. After all, he had lived in England for twenty years.

'Going to be another hot day, I think,' said Jennifer.

'I hope so, yes,' Salvatore said, winking at Alicia, who simpered.

He never flirted with Jennifer. In one way this was a relief. But it was a paradox how, as a fat person, you sometimes felt completely invisible.

He passed Alicia into the hands of Tony, his pimply assistant, saying, 'Gown up the lady,' in a tone of voice that made Alicia preen. She loved people being ordered about for her benefit. It was a relief when they had all gone over to the mirrors.

'My dear man,' Jennifer heard. 'You mustn't tease an old lady so!'

Salvatore looked around. 'Old lady? There is no one answer to that description 'ere.'

Irritated, Jennifer snatched up a glossy magazine. It opened at an article about self-esteem. It was full of bullet points. Trite rubbish, she thought. The glossier the magazine, the more fatuous the content.

Nevertheless her eyes skipped down the list of instructions: 'If you want the world to notice you, first you have to make yourself noticeable'.

Glancing at herself in the mirrored wall, her heart sank. Despite the smart blouse and skirt, it was easy to suspect that Barry had taken one look the other night and decided not to bother. Her face was okay, with large amber eyes, shapely lips and a small nose. But they were marooned in excess cheekage and chinnage.

Back when she'd first thought of lonely hearts, she'd known her weight might be a problem. She'd tried to take a philosophical view. But a philosophical view didn't protect you from feeling like shit in the event. She put the magazine down.

The other hairdresser arrived and turned the radio on.

Salvatore gyrated as he put foam rollers in Alicia's hair. 'I want your ugly, I want your disease,' he sang.

Eventually Alicia went under the heat lamp and Salvatore came back into reception where he flicked through his appointments on the computer, wincing. Then he made a phone call. Jennifer caught fragments of a conversation about a lack of customers due to the credit crunch.

She glanced around. It was well after nine now but the salon was still empty. She felt sorry for him. He was always so generous with Alicia, cutting her hair for below even his Senior Citizen's rate.

His phone conversation went on. Now he was talking about making someone breakfast and about some DVD it had been too soon to play. Finally he came over to escort her to the chair.

They both looked at her long straight hair in the mirror, hair that had been the same for years. 'The usual?' he asked. 'I trim the ends?'

Then he glanced at her smart outfit. 'Or perhaps today I do something different?'

She pondered. Would a new haircut really make that much difference? And could they really afford it?

As if reading her thoughts, he winked. 'I charge the low rate. I have no other customer for an hour.'

She hesitated.

'Go on! What-a you got to lose?' he said. 'Trust me. I make a something nice. Something ah, beautiful!'

'Beautiful? That might be stretching it a bit.'

But he smiled, as if beautiful wasn't the least out of the question and she found herself nodding, and walking obediently to the washbasin.

As well as having her hair done regularly, Alicia spent an hour in front of her mirror every morning. As far as the foundations, lipsticks and eye shadows on her dressing table were concerned, it was standing room only and her wastepaper basket was always full of flattened, squashed rabbits' tails smeared with different colours.

But now, in a car heady with a double dose of hair spray fumes, she made no comment whatsoever on her daughter's new haircut or the complimentary make-up that the salon's female junior had applied to 'complete the picture'.

Jennifer wondered if she was sulking about the wait. But she'd seemed happy enough, reading *Hello* magazine and drinking free espressos from Salvatore's Gaggia machine.

'What do you think then, Mum?' Jennifer asked eventually, as they slowed for the Moortown roundabout.

'About what, dear?' asked Alicia vaguely.

'About my new look, of course. You're always telling me I ought to smarten myself up; I thought you'd be bursting with comments.'

Alicia sighed, as if she couldn't imagine anything less interesting. But she did eye her daughter up and down. She pressed her lips together.

'Well?' asked Jennifer.

'Oh, I don't know. The whole thing is rather – how shall I put it – *tarty*.'

The comment stung, but Jennifer didn't rise to the bait. 'And does tarty suit me?' she asked.

Alicia blinked. 'Oh, really,' she said, and turned to look out of the window.

Mother: 0, Daughter: 1, thought Jennifer, suppressing a smile.

6. *One steak, medium rare*

It was gone ten when Jennifer arrived at work and crossed the car park at a trot. She hoped Greg wouldn't mind. Even though the office worked on flexi-time, you were meant to get permission to arrive this late.

On the plus side, her head felt as light as candyfloss. Eric from Packing shouted at her as she passed his shed. She smiled. There was something downmarket about being fancied by a man who had naked women gaffer-taped to his walls, but you had to take compliments where you could.

The sight of her new head, first in Salvatore's mirror and then in glimpses in her own rear view mirror, had been startling. She expected the security guard to look up and exclaim. But he remained glued to The Sun. The company's founders, men from the previous century and the one before that, didn't react either, just frowned down as usual from the corridor walls.

She headed for the Ladies, and the mirrors.

She opened the door to see Jocasta Jardine, the firm's only female – and only successful – salesperson, leaning on the washbasin smoking, strictly against company rules; against any rules. Smoke, toilet freshener and the perfume that she'd obviously just sprayed everywhere made a choking cocktail of smells. Jennifer headed for the toilet, where there might be more fresh air.

But Jocasta put an arm out to stop her.

'That's a belter of a new image.'

Elfin women always made Jennifer feel like a St Bernard next to a Chihuahua. And Jocasta was trendy to boot. Today she was wearing a red mini skirt and a figure-hugging black sleeveless top that showed off toned bronzed arms.

'The make-up's a bit over the top though, don't you think?' said Jennifer, her eyes stealing to the mirror.

Salvatore had cut loads of hair off – she'd seen it on the floor – and done something with his mousse and his hairdryer to make what was left full of life. It looked wonderful, as if it had been scribbled on side to side with a thick brown crayon.

But the make-up was less convincing. On top of her old face was a new one thick as parchment. Its cheeks were pink, its lips crimson, its eyelids green. Its skin was as smooth and uniform as a pair of tights. Salvatore had said it brought out her true self. Jennifer had nodded to be polite. But it wasn't her idea of a true self.

'I think I might take it off,' she said now. 'Some of it anyway.'

'There was a little sizzle as Jocasta ran the tap onto her cigarette. 'You do right. In the meantime don't creep up behind anyone, unless you're trained in cardiopulmonary resuscitation, that is. By the way, Greg's on the warpath. He's noticed you're late.'

'Oh no!' said Jennifer. 'I'd better go and show my face straight away. The make-up can wait.'

'If I were you ... .'

But Jennifer was already out of the ladies and hurrying to her desk. She dumped her bag and in an effort to look efficient, grabbed some post and set off upstairs to Greg's office at a run. But at the top, a closed door confronted her and there was no reply when she knocked.

She pressed her ear to the door, but it was so soundproofed up here on the director's corridor there might have been a thrash metal band rehearsing on the other side for all she knew.

She scanned the post in her hand. It was to do with a big

electronics show in Zurich that Greg wanted the company to attend and that the firm's managing director, Wally Walton, desperate to save money, did not. Things like this kept landing on her desk since the publicity manager had left and not been replaced.

Perhaps Greg wasn't in his office. She could leave him a note, just to prove that she was at least on the premises now. She turned the handle and walked in.

There, perched on the spare desk like a huge muscular budgie was Wally Walton. In his fifties, he was as fit as a fiddle and held a mug of tea in a hand that looked as if it could squeeze the life out of you in an instant. He never normally noticed Jennifer but as she came into the room now, he stared.

'Sorry,' said Jennifer, backing out. 'I'll come back later.'

'It's all right,' said Greg, shovelling papers into a pink file that Jennifer recognised as the kind they used in Human Resources. 'We're about done here.'

He stuffed the file into his desk drawer, looking grim.

Walton stood up, biceps straining shirtsleeves. 'Do what you've got to do, Bond. Though I won't pretend I like it.'

He left the room giving Jennifer a nod so minimal it was almost imaginary.

Jennifer sat down before Greg's desk. 'Jocasta said you were looking for me.'

Greg swivelled irritably in his chair.

'Sorry I'm late,' she added. 'I got held up by a can of hairspray.'

But he didn't laugh, just fumbled in his jacket pocket, not meeting her eye.

'I've got a few queries to go through with you,' she said.

'That will have to wait,' he said. He found the car keys he'd been looking for in a trouser pocket and stood up. 'I'm afraid we can't put this lunch off any longer. Perhaps on the way you can tell me what the bloody hell you've done to your face.'

As they drew up outside the Frog and Newt, Jennifer had to suppress her memories of being stood up by Barry. The pub stood a mile or so down the York Road and was an old building whose identity had been thoroughly refurbished out of it. The latest atrocity was in the garden: a big plastic tree stump with a face on it.

Jennifer also still felt hurt and annoyed with Greg, despite wanting not to.

'You've made yourself unrecognisable from the neck up,' he'd said in the car, as they sped through Seacroft, past cafés with grilles over the doors and the 'Town Centre' sign where someone had changed 'Town' to 'Nowt.'

'That amount of make-up doesn't suit anyone, let alone a woman like you,' he'd added.

It was the 'woman like you' bit that had stung the most. She'd been intending to wipe some of the make-up off in the pub toilets, but Greg's remark made her keep it on, out of sheer bloody-mindedness.

'What'll you have?' he asked now, as they entered.

She peered at names written in different coloured chalks on a blackboard.

'Sex in the Bath,' she said, defiantly.

'Oh!' said Greg. 'Well, all right. And what about eats? A panini? Steak and chips? Chicken curry with poppadoms?'

Jennifer glanced at the menu. The thought of eating in front of him was daunting. 'A salad sandwich, please.'

'Is that all?'

'I'm not a big eater at lunchtime,' she lied.

They went through to a garden at the back, inhabited by more plastic trees with faces, and sat down at a wonky wooden table. The sun bounced blindingly off concrete. Her drink was turquoise, more like a swimming pool than a bath, and tasted very sweet. Her make-up was starting to melt. She wiped the red lips off on a serviette and felt cooler.

'Now then, Jenny,' said Greg. 'As we said the other day, you've been in the department a long time.'

He ran his fingers over the rough wood of the table. 'Seen a lot of change in that time, not just in your job but in the company itself. A necessary thing, change. To keep a company competitive, to keep it supple.'

'Yes,' she said, not sure where this was going. 'We have to keep pace with technology. When I first started, we made ordinary microscopes. Now we make machines that measure to a fraction of a micron. It's amazing.'

He looked taken aback. 'We? Yes, well, your loyalty does you credit. But you're aware the company's made a significant loss for the past five years running?'

'Yes. But we have to invest in R&D in our line of business. The semiconductor market moves so rapidly.'

He steepled his fingers. 'Well, yes.'

He swigged from his pint and ran his finger around the inside of his collar. The blue diamonds on his tie matched his eyes. She hoped she wasn't starting to fancy him.

'We also have to begin promoting our products more aggressively,' he said. 'Attend the big industry shows.'

'Zurich, you mean?'

'Yes, Zurich. But the money has to come from somewhere, Jennifer. And here's the thing.'

The thing? She hadn't realised there was going to be a thing.

'We have to make cuts. Not just in the factory,' he said.

'One steak, medium rare! One salad sandwich!'

A waitress bore down on them brandishing plates, and minutes were taken up in the polite distribution of knives and forks, serviettes, salt and pepper and little sachets of ketchup.

'What do you mean, cuts?' asked Jennifer. She wondered if he was going to tell her that the publicity manager was definitely not going to be replaced. Or perhaps it was something worse than that. Her mind swam. She glanced down at her anaemic sandwich with its icy-looking slices of cucumber and wondered how she was going to swallow any of it.

But Greg didn't reply. He hacked a triangle off his steak. It was rare: blood soaked into his chips.

'Look, Jenny, let me ask you a question. What brought you to this company in the first place? I know your job was different, under Ron Sandle. I expect it was more in your line then, was it?'

This sounded ominous. But Jennifer couldn't help feeling pleased that he'd asked her a personal question.

'Well, it *was* more varied. I ran a car boot sale of all our old microscopes once. People rang up from all over England and I had to take them up to the stockroom and show them what we had.'

Greg seemed unimpressed, so she cut it short. 'But I still love working for the company. Even now you've arrived. Sorry. That sounded terrible. But you know what I mean.'

Greg didn't look as if he did.

'I'd rather be at work than at home, sometimes,' said Jennifer, in a last desperate attempt to prove her point.

But Greg just looked grim. 'Yes, Walton told me there were problems. An ailing mother.'

'Wally Walton was talking about me?' said Jennifer.

'Yes.'

'Why?'

'Never mind that now. Look, are you your mother's carer or not?'

Jennifer extracted a thin cartwheel of tomato from her sandwich and nibbled on it. 'Yes.'

Greg sighed. 'You've got financial help, though, at least? Your father's pension?'

'No,' said Jennifer. 'She didn't qualify for that. They, well, they were never married.'

It was a fact she still stumbled over, even after all this time.

'Really?' said Greg. 'That's hard on you.'

Jennifer frowned. Pity was the last thing she wanted, especially from him. She put the piece of tomato down.

'Look, it's not a problem. I'm used to it. And I get loads of help from our neighbour, Nelly.'

'Even so … .'

'You asked what brought me here. Well, the need to earn a living. After my 'A' Levels, I went to secretarial college. I thought that would be the most useful thing to do. So I spent a year coming last in speed typing tests and writing down things in shorthand I couldn't decipher later.'

Greg frowned.

Too late, she realised this was another example of her being too honest, not image-conscious enough.

'Right,' said Greg. 'And what *were* your 'A' Levels? It doesn't say, in your file.'

'French, German, English and Art.'

'Four? That's a lot in anyone's money. Didn't you want to go to Uni?'

Jennifer put down her sandwich. 'Yes,' she said.

Without wanting to, her thoughts went to a moment that was still vivid in her mind, twelve years on: the moment she'd opened her unconditional offer to study Interior Architecture at Brighton. She could almost feel the paper in her hand again, hear the call of a collared dove from the garden, see the reflection of her own flushed face in the hall mirror.

'But it doesn't matter now,' she said. 'Anyway, I did an HND in Fine Art at evening classes instead. I designed a café for my final project. It had seating on different levels, and the windows had poems etched in the glass. The lighting was like a fountain.'

'Not that that's remotely relevant to anything,' she added.

'At evening classes?' asked Greg. 'For fuck's sake. That must have taken forever.'

'Seven years, what with all the different modules. I finished last year.'

Greg seemed about to speak, then didn't. He pressed his thumb and forefinger to his brow. There was a long silence. Then he pushed his plate away, grabbed his jacket and stood up.

Jennifer was baffled. 'Are we going back already?'

'Yes, Jenny, we're going back, via the printer's. Meanwhile I'll try and figure out what to do. I'm not sure whether this puts a new complexion on things or not.'

'A new complexion on what things?'

But he didn't answer: if there were beans to spill, it didn't look as if he was going to spill them now. This was perhaps a good thing. But as Jennifer followed him out to the car, she had the feeling that she had once again failed obscurely in the mission of every good Personal Assistant: Making your Boss's Life Easier.

7. *Orange Club*

Stebbing Print was housed on an industrial estate further round the Ring Road. Greg said Jennifer could stay in the car if she wanted to, but she'd opted to come in so now they were standing in a reception area staffed by three parched Yucca plants.

As a sixty-something man with bouffant hair, a silk cravat and a tweed jacket with leather patched elbows swept in, Greg stepped forward and held out his hand.

Jennifer blinked. Although she'd spoken to Robert numerous times on the phone, they'd never met and he wasn't the way she'd pictured him.

He stared at her too, as if the feeling was mutual.

She wanted to say she didn't always look like she did, but Robert was already ushering them into his workshop. 'Before we sit down and submerge ourselves in the peculiar sort of dreariness that only a business meeting can induce, let me give you a whirlwind tour.'

He marched them round the small unit, where leaflets churned rhythmically from a big machine, and towers of printed and neatly parcelled work stood waist high.

At the guillotine, they watched while a lad trimmed business cards for a Mr Brian Kelly of BK Packaging and shovelled the excess card into a skip full of psychosis-inducing misprints.

Jennifer, who loved all things papery, was finding the tour interesting. 'I love that smell. It's like opening a new exercise book on the first day of term.'

'Ah, you liked school,' said Robert. 'Not the case for all of us, sadly.'

He opened a door onto a tiny, cluttered office and fished out a couple of folding chairs for them to sit on. The lad brought three coffees in, on a bent tin tray, and a plate of Jacobs Orange Club biscuits.

'Real china!' said Jennifer. 'How lovely! Porcelain is ... .'

'Now then, Stebbing, about the Opticheck instruction manual,' interrupted Greg. 'Our green-obsessed managing director wants it bound without using chlorinated compounds or varnish.'

Before he had died suddenly of a heart attack when she was seven, Jennifer's father had spent his days prescribing antibiotics, advising people to exercise, and referring any interesting illnesses to the hospital. His evenings he'd spent making paper in the garden shed.

Among the ordinary shed stuff – the columns of plant pots, the shelf of hammers and screwdrivers, old margarine tubs full of nails and screws – his papermaking tools still stood: the picture frame he'd used as a mould, the food processor he'd used to blend the pulp, even the old washing up bowl he'd immersed the frame in.

His paper had been beautiful. She still had some sheets of it. But it was these old unglamorous tools that reminded her most of him. Perhaps that was because he'd always let her help with the papermaking: let her press the button on the blender, stir in the liquid starch, wiggle the frame side to side in the paper pulp until the top was even.

More excitingly, he'd let her contribute to the actual materials, unravelling pink wool from her old jumper, collecting chrysanthemum petals from the garden to stir in. He'd welcomed grass cuttings from the neighbour's lawnmower; tin foil stolen from her mother's kitchen drawer; sunflower seeds picked

48

carefully off the loaf in the breadbin. Once, she'd brought him toenails, clipped from the dog. Into the blender the dark crescent moons had gone, to produce a paper full of spikes, impossible to write on.

After she got home from work, she sat down at the workbench. She kept her own tools here these days: pliers, a roll of chicken wire, old saucepans, plaster of Paris and piles of her mother's old magazines: *Arthritis News, Colon Cancer Concern, Respiratory Disease Now.*

She glanced at her latest project, a sturdy skeleton of chicken wire, waiting for its skin. One evening soon she would get to work on that, breathing in the perfume of the night-scented stocks from the garden, watching tiny summer insects gather in a cloud around the shed light.

For the moment, she contented herself with wiping her make-up off with spit and an old rag, peering into the little cracked mirror hanging by the door.

When she'd arrived home, Nelly had gripped her shoulders with slippery yellow Marigold hands and told her she looked like a man in drag. It had been a new low. 'It just isn't *you*, love,' she'd said.

Jennifer, extracting herself from the berubbered grasp, had wondered what everyone took to be 'her'. Normally she might as well be invisible, for all the attention anyone paid. Now, because she'd changed something, everyone was falling over themselves to utter the definitive judgement, as if she was the latest portrait of the Queen.

As she watched her real face emerge again from the smooth tan mask, it looked even blander than usual, like the thing her art tutor had always warned her against: a design that had tried to be all things to all people and had failed.

8. *No Appetite*

Jennifer's papier-mâché sculptures were not cutesy. They were strange, unsettling marriages between beast and machine. Nyesha's leaving present, for example, had been a massive elephant-cum-cement-mixer. Nelly owned a large toad/tractor with eyes the same nicotine yellow as her husband Ernie's fingers.

Jennifer tended to give her creations away. Partly because there wasn't room at home to display them – Alicia's hideous collection of china shepherd boys and girls saw to that – but partly because she liked to think of them out there in the world.

But not everyone liked the sculptures, or knew what to do when they were given one.

'What the fuck is this?' Jennifer's cousin Jane had screamed on her wedding day when the wrapping paper fell to the floor, revealing a camel crossed with a double-decker bus.

'At least it'll scare off the Jehovah's Witnesses,' said her new husband.

So Jennifer's models generally got relegated to the less public areas of a household. A meter reader, on his way down basement stairs, might jump as he glimpsed a creature that was half polar bear, half ice cream van, lurking in the shadows. An elderly aunt, staying in a spare bedroom at Christmas, might smile when she found a tiger-cum-golfcart on the top shelf of the wardrobe.

Dr Ganguly, however, was made of sterner stuff. He displayed his own hippopotamus/hot air balloon in his surgery, in full view of all comers.

It was late the following Monday afternoon, and Jennifer and Alicia sat in front of his desk while he shuffled through papers. On the filing cabinets, the hippo's ears, like knotted handkerchief corners, seemed to swivel above its inflated belly.

Dr Ganguly pounced on a computer printout and held it up triumphantly. He read quickly down it, repositioning a strand of hair over his bald patch while he did so.

'Nothing out of the ordinary there ... or there.'

He looked up and beamed. 'Alicia my dear, you're in perfect working order. There's nothing here that causes me the slightest concern.'

'But what about the pain above my left eye?' asked Alicia. 'And this terrible buzzing in my ear? It's got so loud, it drowns out Jeremy Vine.'

Dr Ganguly managed to look grave, compassionate and yet gently discouraging all at once. 'All I can suggest is persistence with the tablets. Get some fresh air, perhaps? Lack of activity does us older folk no favours. And you might try eating a bit more.'

Alicia sighed, as at a terrible disappointment. 'Oh, I've no appetite, Narendra,' she said. 'None whatsoever.'

'I understand, my dear,' he said. 'But try, eh? Just try.'

Alicia put on the smile that conveyed bravery in the face of great difficulty. 'If you say so, Narendra. If you think it will help.'

'That's the spirit,' said Dr Ganguly.

Jennifer sighed inwardly. She'd heard all this before. Delving in her pocket for a tissue, her fingers brushed something hard. She frowned then remembered the envelope that had arrived the other morning and that she'd stuffed into a random pocket.

Alicia, meanwhile, was on a new tack. 'Perhaps we should try a nerve man? Jennifer ran some stuff off for me the other night, from the Internet. About MRI scans. Apparently they're an absolutely marvellous diagnostic tool. I mean, perhaps I have a schwannoma.'

Dr Ganguly's eyes darted nervously, as if he had forgotten what a schwannoma was. 'Well, yes, the MRI is useful. Non-invasive too, which is a big plus.'

Alicia leaned forwards. 'I read your article in The Lancet, you know. The one about tuberculosis in turkeys. They found me a copy in the library.'

It was true that Alicia, with a large medical dictionary balanced precariously on the arm of her chair, had struggled through the entire piece. Whether she had understood any of it was another matter. What on earth was in this envelope? It was obviously from the local paper and connected with lonely hearts. But her fingers could make no sense of it.

'Goodness me,' said Dr Ganguly. 'That old thing. Well, well.'

'Anyway, we've taken up quite enough of your time,' said Alicia, beginning to get up. 'I shall leave it with you, about the MRI. Of course, I shan't hold my breath. I imagine there's quite a wait for these things.'

He cleared his throat. 'These tests cost the NHS a lot of money. And in the absence of any other symptoms … .'

Alicia swayed and seemed in danger of falling.

Dr Ganguly, moving surprisingly quickly, came round the desk and put his hand under her elbow.

'I'll see what I can do, my dear,' he said, resignedly.

'You *do* look after me, Narendra,' said Alicia. 'I simply can't tell you how much I appreciate it.'

He escorted her slowly to the door. Halfway there, she lifted her stick and pointed it at some dusty yellow plastic roses in a vase. 'You must let me bring you some fresh blooms. I'll get our gardener to cut you some.'

Jennifer snorted, unable to let this one pass. 'Gardener?' Nelly's husband could barely support himself around their small lawn by holding on to the ancient Flymo, let alone do any gardening. Alicia threw her a dark look.

Dr Ganguly turned. 'Before you go. A word.'

When Narendra Ganguly had arrived at their local medical practice ten years ago, it had been Nelly who'd recommended him.

'But isn't he a coloured gentleman?' Alicia had asked.

'Aye. But he's a lovely manner about him. Attentive. Not like that Dr Rawlings, yawning over your bunions.'

'Oh, I don't know. I mean, don't they have a different medical system in India? What do they call them, charkas? Or is it Mediterraneans?'

'You're thinking of the Chinese, love. Bruce Lee and all that. Don't you worry, there's nothing exotic about Dr Ganguly. He treated my Ernie's boils with common or garden antibiotic ointment.'

Alicia had resisted for another fortnight then reluctantly made an appointment. To say she'd taken to Dr Ganguly was an understatement. She was impressed by his Oxford education, and the fact that he still published articles. But it was more than that. His gentle encouragement brought out the little girl in her.

'Narendra says I'm doing ever so well,' she would cry, as if he were a teacher, and she his star pupil. She would bring him little things from the garden, daffodils in spring, a maggoty apple or two in autumn.

Now, when Jennifer had installed her mother in the waiting room and gone back to his office, she found him standing at the window, studying the large oak outside. She sat down on the edge of the chair. What was so drastic that it had to be said in private?

'I'm afraid I shall be retiring,' he said to the tree.

Jennifer let out a long breath. 'Oh, thank God.'

He turned, startled.

'I'm sorry,' said Jennifer. 'I thought you were about to tell me that my mother had some incurable disease.'

'Ah,' said Dr Ganguly. 'Not that. But the fact of my leaving will pose certain problems for your mother. You'll be getting a Doctor Lethem.'

'I see,' said Jennifer, seeing nothing.

Behind him, the oak's bark was thick and furrowed. From somewhere, she remembered that the first papermakers had used bark a lot, but nowadays it was considered a problem in the manufacturing process.

'Retirement is retirement. But one never likes leaving one's longer standing patients to the administrations of a new broom. One becomes fond of them, you see.'

'Well, the feeling is mutual,' said Jennifer. 'Mum thinks the world of you.'

Dr Ganguly gave a polite smile.

'No, really,' said Jennifer. 'You've become very important to her.'

'Ah! That's kind, most kind,' said Dr Ganguly, looking marginally taller for a few seconds. 'It is always gratifying to know ... . ' He stopped himself. 'But I'm afraid all this is rather beside the point. The point is that Dr Lethem may take a different line with Alicia.'

'A different *line*?' said Jennifer.

Doctor Ganguly returned to his desk, leaving the oak to its own devices.

'Yes. Modern chap. May send her down to Jimmy's. Delicate business. Psychiatrists.'

Jennifer felt as if someone had punched her in the stomach. 'Psychiatrists?'

Dr Ganguly tented his fingers, almost as if he were praying. 'Indeed,' he said. 'May have a point, but she won't see it that way. Cleaves to the old ways, your mother, if I may say so. Very private. A lot to be said for it, in my view.'

'You mean ... you think her illnesses are psychosomatic? What about all the tests she's had over the years? And all those thousands of tablets?'

The doctor inclined his head. A momentary closing of the eyes. 'They may have been helpful. Maybe not. Her symptoms, as

I'm sure you know, are genuine enough. But hypochondriasis is a complex condition.'

Jennifer stared at the kindly, worn face. She had always appreciated his dishevelled looks, interpreted them as a sign of unworldliness.

'This is a bit of a shock,' she said.

'Come now,' he said gently. 'Is it really?'

She looked down. To be honest, it wasn't. The thought had crossed her mind many times: she'd have been a fool if it hadn't. But she'd become used to sidestepping the issue, pretending not to see the way Pepe did when he passed a cat in the street and thought he might be required to chase it. She'd become used to sacrificing truth to preserve the status quo.

'No,' she admitted. 'It's just the fact that you're saying it out loud.'

'Indeed,' he said. 'Indeed.'

A conspiratorial look passed between them. It was quickly gone. He stood up. 'You'll forgive me for leaving it there. The practice manager has us all on a new regime. Seven minutes maximum.'

'Of course,' said Jennifer, standing up quickly.

'Oh, one thing,' he said, as she put her hand on the doorknob. 'Looking at your mother's medical records, her health problems began in the late nineties, about ten years after your father's death. Did she suffer some kind of trauma, an emotional one I mean, around that time? Sometimes difficulties like hers can be traced back to such things.'

Jennifer stared. On the filing cabinet, the hippo, with its tiny enfolded eyes – red beads from one of Alicia's old necklaces – seemed to wink.

'Is anything the matter, dear?' asked Dr Ganguly.

'No,' said Jennifer, faintly.

Dr Ganguly held up both hands in a gesture of surrender. 'No matter, then. Just a thought.'

'Yes,' said Jennifer, recovering herself. 'Well, I expect we'll be seeing you before the summer's out. I'll save my goodbyes till then.'

9. *Lentil gloop*

Although she was only seventeen, she felt as if she'd been waiting a million years for something like this to happen. It was the week before her last ever school holidays and she was the only person at the bus stop when he appeared, walking like a cowboy in jeans smeared with oil. He had oil on his face and hands, too, and a leather jacket despite the fact it was summer. His hair was curly and dark.

'There a bus to town from here?' he asked.

His jacket was all rips and zips. Nothing like the boys at school, who all wore baggy jeans and combat boots.

'Mm,' she said. 'They all go into town from here. Except the number forty-two.'

He grinned. 'My bike's broken down.'

'Oh.'

'Thing is,' he said, winking at her, 'I've no cash.'

He turned out his pocket to show her. The lining of his jacket was smoky blue paisley. 'Lend us a quid?'

She felt a prickle of uncertainty. Perhaps it was a ploy to get her talking then drag her off into the bushes at gunpoint. She glanced at him again. He didn't look to be concealing a gun. She noticed a pewter ankh on a leather thong around his neck, like a soft note in a loud song. But maybe that was just a decoy. And maybe he'd already hidden a gun in the undergrowth. She stared up the road, willing the tall lurching oblong of the number fifty-six to appear.

'Fair enough,' he said. 'I bet your mother's told you not to talk to strangers, hasn't she? Look, I'll walk it. Nice meeting you.'

The mention of her mother made her frown. She dug in her bag and brought out her pink sequinned purse.

On the bus, he followed her to the raised seat at the back. The engine's vibration made the flesh at the top of her leg tremble and she hoped he couldn't see it, through her thin school trousers. They were pale grey, not the most flattering colour for a girl already having trouble squeezing into a size sixteen. But he wasn't looking at her leg. He was gazing out of the window. As the bus gathered speed on the dual carriageway, she took in little glimpses of him, like sips.

'What do you do,' she asked, 'when you're not cadging bus fares?'

He laughed. 'I've just finished at Leeds Uni.'

'I'm hoping to go to Uni. Not Leeds, though.'

'Right.'

They both looked out of the window then, at the low white building and playing fields of a school they were passing. Girls in short navy skirts ran here and there, clutching hockey sticks.

'This isn't your school, then,' he said. 'Seeing as you're still sitting here.'

'No,' she said, wishing she could think of something clever to say.

He wasn't bad looking, actually. Apart from an attempt at sideburns and a hint of moustache on his top lip. And she liked the fact he wasn't trying to chat her up. She didn't like being chatted up. It made lads say stupid things. More stupid than normal, that was.

'What subject did you do at Uni?' she asked.

'Engineering.'

They rode on. She chewed her bottom lip.

'Did you know,' he said, 'it took three years to build the

58

foundations of Brooklyn Bridge? And when it was built, they got Barnum's Circus to take a herd of elephants across, to show how strong it was.'

'Really?' she said. 'That's amazing!'

Then she couldn't think of anything to say, so she said nothing. Another mile went past. The bus driver seemed to be trying to break the land speed record.

'It's my stop in a minute,' she said.

'Right.' He grinned. 'So this is the part where I ask you out, is it? And you tell me to fuck off?'

Her pulse quickened at the swear word. 'I don't know.'

He grinned and fished out a pen. 'Look, write your number on the back of my bus ticket. Then you can tell me to fuck off from the comfort of your own home.'

She crammed the number into the spaces between the purple printed fare, hoping he'd be able to read them later. She got off the bus and walked down it on the outside while other people got on and paid. She glanced shyly up to where he sat, hoping he was looking.

He was. 'What's your name?' he mouthed.

She mouthed her name.

'What?' he mouthed back.

She licked her finger and began to write it in the grime on the outside of the bus window. But the bus began to move off, so all he got was a backwards J.

They spent that summer biking out along the back roads to Dales pubs. It was an adventure, dismounting bandy and stiff legged in different village squares like cowboys arriving at some far-flung border town. When there wasn't much traffic, they rode back without their crash helmets. The speed turned her hair to whips. She buried her face in the back of his jacket, intoxicated by the wind and the cheap pub wine and the prospect of a long slow kiss on the doorstep.

At the end of August, he invited her to the Womad Festival. By some miracle Alicia agreed, but only because she thought they were going in a group.

The sun blazed, the day they rode down. Bobby kept the bike at a constant speed all the way down the A1 to Reading, and it was like riding a pneumatic drill. But when they arrived to fields of brightly coloured tents and tepees and a collision of different musics, Jennifer forgot her tiredness.

They pitched his tiny two-man tent and went to get a bottle of Newcastle Brown and cardboard trays filled with lentil gloop, which they climbed up a grassy slope to eat. It looked like sick, but Jennifer loved it.

Then they sat in the sun and listened to sitar music floating over from the main stage. People wandered by in grungy clothes and further down the slope a woman peeled off her top. Jennifer watched with envy. A few minutes later she was peeling off her own top and bra too, quickly before she lost her nerve, like pulling off a plaster. The sun felt like fire on her chest. Her breasts looked white and huge, like bread dough after a night in the airing cupboard. When Bobby tried to roll her down the slope, she laughed till she nearly wet herself.

Later, lying together in the tent, he picked off all the bits of grass that were still stuck to her. They had zipped the blue and orange caterpillars of their sleeping bags together and lay on top of them under the slanting orange ceiling. She breathed in his scent of motor oil and patchouli. He kissed her. His lips were soft.

She had already gone to the clinic.

Too scared to go for the Pill or the coil and have the evidence on her medical record, too embarrassed to talk to him about condoms, she had gone for the old-fashioned option: a cap.

She had experimented several times with the off-white rubber dome, squirting silvery cream round the rim then pinching the sides to make a figure eight shape. But now she felt his naked thigh against hers, she was overawed by the significance of what they were about to do. She drew back.

'You okay?' he asked.

She nodded. They kissed again, and she felt his hand snake down to the top of her thigh.

She wriggled out from under him. 'Sorry. I'm not sure I can do this.'

He sighed then shifted his position, taking her head into the crook of his arm.

'Are you cross with me?' she asked.

'Look, it's not supposed to be an ordeal. We'll wait till you feel like it. And if you don't, then we won't do it.'

'Are you sure?'

'Yeah. It's good just being here, not having to count the minutes before your mam sends out a search party.'

He was asleep in seconds. But Jennifer lay awake, listening to the distant sounds of the late night band and trying to feel the cap inside her, the spermicide dissolving in the heat of her cervix, unused. She decided things would be different the next time they tried.

And things were.

The next afternoon, the whole experience was so novel that she forgot to feel desire. It didn't hurt, exactly: it just felt strange to have a part of him inside her and when he came, with a lost, startled sound, so out of character with his normal confident self, tears of wonder rose to her eyes. When they lay, warm and close afterwards, in the tent's orange light, it was like being an animal in a pack: snug and safe.

That evening, they watched the bands. He was knowledgeable, and talked a lot about who was in each band and which bands they had been in before. She just counted the moments until they were in the tent together again, close.

When they made love again, he tried to make her come, but she wriggled away from his fingers.

'I want it to happen naturally,' she said. 'With you inside me.'

Bobby raised his eyebrows. 'It's not always that easy.'

Her face fell. She hated the knowledge that he'd had past girlfriends.

'Sorry,' he said, pulling her head into his chest. 'Tactless. And I keep forgetting you're just a baby.'

She didn't reply.

'Hey,' he said. 'You might not've liked me if I was some speccy geek who'd never been out with girls and had just stayed at home playing with my slide rule.'

'I would have liked you,' she said. 'I would have liked you loads.'

'Well, I might not have liked you. I might only have liked girls who knew the value of pi to nine decimal places.'

'I'd have had to show you my equilateral triangle, then.'

He laughed. He always did when she made a joke, no matter how bad it was. Feeling that low buzz against her ear was the best thing. Better than any music played by any musician who had ever been in any band, she thought, as she drifted off to sleep.

The journey back to Leeds passed quickly. All too soon, they were turning right at the bottom of Jennifer's road and riding up the concrete slope that led to the empty garage.

But even before Bobby had turned the engine off and hoisted the bike back onto its stand, Jennifer had a funny feeling.

'Something's wrong,' she said, putting her helmet down on the drive.

'What?'

But she was already making for the front door. Inside, her voice rose as she went from room to room, calling.

She went upstairs, looked in all the bedrooms and came back onto the landing. 'She's not here.'

Bobby had brought the helmets in. He put them on the hall table.

'Don't put them there,' she snapped. 'You'll scratch it.'

'Calm down, J. Listen, she's probably out shopping.'

'She wouldn't just go out. Not when she knew I was coming back. There's no note anywhere.'

Jennifer walked slowly back down the stairs. Everything felt skewed and odd.

'Maybe she's gone next door,' said Bobby.

Jennifer shook her head. 'No.'

'What do you mean no?'

'I just know something has happened.'

'How can you know? Look, my mam's a widow too. Doesn't mean she drops dead every time I go away for a few days.'

'Your mum's different. She goes on coach trips and plays the piano.'

'What?'

'Your mother's *normal*.'

She sat down on the stairs and burst into tears. She felt Bobby's hand on her shoulder. 'Where's the phone?' he said. I'll start ringing round.'

They located Alicia at Leeds General Infirmary. She had been taken in on Saturday night with suspected meningitis. At the hospital, they walked down long corridors in the late afternoon light. The staff nurse looked at them over the top of her spectacles.

'Ah, Miss Spendlove. We've been trying to get hold of you all weekend.'

'Didn't she tell you I was away?'

'I'm afraid she was rather disorientated when she came in.'

'Oh, but I'm nearly always here,' said Jennifer. 'Why did this have to happen the one time I go away?'

'Don't distress yourself. She's sitting up in bed now, and she managed tea and toast half an hour ago. As I say, she was quite poorly when she came in, but the crisis is over now.'

'So it wasn't actually meningitis?' asked Jennifer.

The nurse shook her head. 'No. We don't think so, not now. A mystery virus, we think. The doctor may tell you more. Your mother's tired, and rather low. Don't expect too much.'

Jennifer's heart sank. A few steps down the corridor towards her mother's bed bay, she stopped and turned to Bobby.

'I think it's best I see her on my own.'

'Yeah?'

'If she's feeling depressed.'

'Sure,' he said.

But as he walked away, in the leather jacket that had somehow come to represent all that was safe in life, she felt physically depleted, as though she might fall down onto the sticky, bleach-smelling lino floor. She realised she'd wanted him to say he was going with her, no matter what.

She walked on, and there was her mother, smiling wanly from a high white hospital bed. A bag of clear fluid hung fatly from a stand and a plastic tube was pinned into the back of her small hand. Her pink fluffy mules stood side by side at the foot of her locker, helplessly out of their depth. Her free hand flew out across the bedclothes as Jennifer sat down.

'I've been so frightened!' Alicia cried. 'So lonely. So afraid I was going to die without having had a chance to say goodbye.'

'Oh, Mum!' said Jennifer, offering her hand, submitting to her mother's grip.

She sat there for what seemed like ages, while her mother cried softly.

That had been the start. The headaches, sudden and disabling, had gone on. NHS investigations had proved fruitless, so Alicia had paid for a series of consultations with different specialists, an expense that ate savagely into their limited savings. And by the end of the summer, Jennifer had stood up and sat down in so many waiting rooms she'd felt she was in an endless game of musical chairs.

The evening she told Bobby that she'd decided to defer her place at Brighton for a year they were sitting on the torn brown vinyl sofa at his shared house. She kept picking at a cushion, extracting bits of stuffing.

He looked at her in shock. 'But what about us? What about all the jobs I've applied for down there?'

'Well, you wanted to go south anyway. And it's only for a year. I'll visit you at weekends.'

He stared at his feet.

'You don't really think I'm going to let my Mum come between us, do you?' she said. She tried to push some of the stuffing back into the sofa.

'But what if she's not better in a year?'

'Then I'll bring her down with me. She can move in with us.'

She laughed at his horrified face and eventually he laughed too.

And at first, it seemed as if things might work out. When he got a job as a trainee technician for a civil engineering company in Portsmouth, Jennifer told Alicia that like it or not, she was going down on the train to see him every fortnight and he was coming up to see her on the weekends between. And he came, first on his bike, later in his Ford Orion.

But Alicia's headaches didn't go away. And new problems raised their heads. There was talk of a heart murmur, then a scare about ovarian cancer.

When Jennifer told Bobby she was deferring her place again, he seemed unable to understand why.

His visits grew farther and farther apart. There was never a moment when their relationship came officially to an end. Rather, it was a slow letdown, something travelling gradually to its vanishing point.

And Jennifer had kept his photo, a print of a curly haired young man in filthy jeans, wearing a pewter ankh and smiling at the camera as though he loved the person holding it. It lived in an

65

old shoebox under her bed amidst her most prized possessions, a stained Teddy, a reply to a fan letter she'd written to Roald Dahl and a sheet of paper her father had made out of rose petals.

10. *Squares of Chocolate*

The night after the visit to Dr Ganguly, Jennifer tossed and turned in bed, getting tangled up in her outsize men's pyjamas and feeling as if the Sword of Damocles was hanging over her. What was going to happen when Dr Lethem arrived in January, brandishing his new broom?

She must *do* something. But what? She'd tried discussing it with Nyesha, but her friend, whose own mother had died when she was a baby, had changed the subject.

Anyway, it was Alicia she should really be trying to talk to. But talk had never been one of their specialities.

And this latest topic was more taboo than the lot. It was also complicated. Jennifer knew from the Internet that an applied hypochondriac was capable of producing symptoms so acute and physically debilitating that the medical profession had no option but to take them seriously.

Alicia's symptoms, though changeable, were genuine. Her latest problem, the eye/ear thing, made one side of her face droop noticeably and she swallowed painkillers by the bucket load. Once or twice she'd even passed out from pain. At *Times of our Lives*, they'd used old-fashioned smelling salts to revive her. At home, they'd resorted to Ernie's hair-restorer.

Jennifer glanced at the clock. Ten to two. She must sleep. She was meeting her next date, Lawrence, tomorrow night. Never in her entire life had she felt less like going on a date. What good was romance, when your whole life was about to fall to pieces?

Three o'clock came and went and her mind was still drifting back to the unknown Dr Lethem. Would he make her mother go into therapy, and become even more self-obsessed than ever? Or would the threat of exposure produce new symptoms so dramatic that Jennifer would have to enter '999' on the phone's one-touch-dial memory?

When she finally did manage to drift off, it was into a dream about her mother, talking knowledgeably over the breakfast tea and toast.

'Darling,' her mother said in the dream. 'You can hardly expect me to behave like a normal mother. The psychotherapist has made me realise that I come from a dysfunctional family.'

And she went on to talk about her psychological traumas in exactly the same way she'd always talked about her physical ones.

The next morning at work, Jennifer felt like a zombie. Two cheez 'n' sausage surprises from the sandwich delivery service and numerous lattes from the coffee machine helped, but still it was hard to concentrate on work. A ream of expensive stationery got fed into the printer the wrong way up, an important client got cut off in mid-conversation, and finally a cup of coffee toppled and fell onto a signed contract Greg had brought down to her.

He rolled his eyes in disbelief. 'It's all very well your having qualifications, but if they're not accompanied by a bit of common sense, what use are they?'

'I'm sorry,' she said. 'I'm not sleeping well.'

If she'd been hoping for sympathy, she didn't get it. He seemed to want to go on telling her off.

'Apparently you told the sandwich girl you'd do the lunch orders on the directors' lunch order if she was too tired to get up the stairs.'

'Sorry. But she wasn't feeling well. She gets terrible migraines.'

'For goodness' sake! If she has to go off sick, then the caterers will send a substitute. It's not up to any members of my staff to fill in for her. And another thing: this coming in late every other Friday morning has got to stop. I know you have to take your mother to the hairdressers, but can't she get a taxi back?'

'That might be tricky. She's very nervy at the moment. The sight of furry dice might push her over the edge.'

Greg stared at her, the muscle in his right cheek working, then turned on his heel and walked away.

Jennifer's heart sank. What she'd really wanted to say was that there was no need to treat her like a child; that if she came in late, she could be trusted to make up the time. But every time she opened her mouth in front of him, something that sounded stupid or genuinely was stupid came tumbling out.

She watched helplessly as he headed across the office then veered off in the direction of the sales desk.

For a fat person, eating was a bit like poking about on the 'reduced' shelf at Tesco's: best done when no one was looking. But as Greg talked to Jocasta Jardine, Jennifer saw his bad mood lift. She stuffed several squares of chocolate into her mouth, and followed them up with more before she had even finished chewing.

Half an hour later, Greg arrived back at her desk again.

'I've got a job for you,' he said. 'Something even you can't mess up.'

The remark stung. He led her upstairs and they entered the marketing department stockroom, a large, light room next to the staff sitting room. Once upon a time, so Eric from Packing said, it had been a canteen, where actual meals got cooked. But now it was filled with teetering columns of cardboard boxes and graphics panels, and there were papers and old photographs all over the floor. They made a shiny, colourful sea.

'This lot has obviously been here since the year dot,' said Greg. 'It needs sorting. And putting in some kind of order. I can't believe it's been left like this.'

She tried not to feel that this was her fault.

He kicked a dusty box. 'Anything current needs saving and sorting. Any rubbish – brochures for obsolete products for example – can be thrown. Keep a copy of everything for the archive. Think you can manage that?'

His tone was brisk. She nodded. You had to be tough, Nyesha said. Some men let power go to their head and behaved like wankers. And who cares what wankers think of you? But Jennifer did care, that was the trouble.

'Don't stand there looking as if you're about to burst into tears,' he said. 'Get on with it. And put an overall on. There should be one somewhere in the company that'll fit you. Try down in the Machine Shop. They're all big blokes down there.'

When he had gone, she looked about her. She walked over to a rusting filing cabinet, peered into a cracked old envelope. He was right, the stuff in here hadn't been disturbed in decades. At the far end of the room lurked a big stack of tubular metal poles, like scaffolding. There were some old bits of microscope here and there, too. There was even an old overall on the back of the door.

She put it on and found it fitted just fine. 'So there, you wanker!' she said.

The next few hours were hard work but made her feel a lot better. She forgot Greg; she forgot Alicia and Dr Lethem; she even forgot her impending date with Lawrence. She'd left her mobile at her desk, so had no clock. But when the factory workers clomped to the sitting room, complaining about the continuous flushing system that Wally Walton had installed in the men's urinals, she knew it was about twelve.

She didn't bother with food; kept putting it off till later. But suddenly it was later. A knock came on the door. Outside the sky was growing dark.

'You've not spent the whole day on it, have you?' said Greg. 'It didn't merit that kind of ... fuck!'

Jennifer turned to share his perspective.

The boxes of current brochures were stacked in a neat row against the wall. She had resisted the temptation to colour-coordinate them and had sorted them in date order, the more recent ones nearest. Rubbish was separated into piles for recycling. The bits of old microscope were sorted and cleaned and laid on the windowsill. The whole room was tidy. Basically, it now made sense as a stockroom.

But Greg wasn't looking at any of that. What he was looking at stood in the middle of the cleared floor space.

'What the... ?' he said.

'It's an old exhibition display system,' said Jennifer, nodding at the tubular poles she had spent an enjoyable half hour putting together.

'It's called the Omega. I found the instructions at the back of one of the filing cabinets.'

He walked up to the construction, which was the size of a small car. 'How did you set it up?'

'It all fits together with an Allen key,' said Jennifer.

'A what?'

Surely he had heard of an Allen key? She handed one to him and he turned the small tool over in his hand, peering at it. 'What's it made of?'

'The Allen key? I dunno. Steel?'

'No, not the key, the display system.'

'Oh. Aluminium, I think. It's very lightweight.'

'Hm.'

'Is the room okay, Greg? I've worked really hard on it.'

'Uh?'

'Have I done what you wanted?'

But he couldn't take his eyes off the structure. He gave it a violent shove. 'This is a sturdy beast.'

Jennifer sighed. The faint hope that he would actually be pleased with her tidying job dwindled and died.

'Is it okay if I get off home, then?'

'Uh? Yes, yes, off you go.'

He was still muttering to himself as she left the room. She walked slowly down the stairs. At least he wasn't *dis*pleased. But it seemed to her suddenly that this was cold comfort, very cold comfort indeed.

11. *Chardonnay*

In the Frog and Newt, all the seats were taken. There were also people standing and leaning.

'Huh,' said Lawrence the photographer, 'you can hardly hear yourself think.'

He and Jennifer had recognised each other in the car park, courtesy of the green plastic handbag. Jennifer had arrived half an hour late, due to Alicia's sudden and unexpected demand that she pick up a prescription for her before the chemist shut. Lawrence was equally late. Jennifer didn't mind: she just felt grateful that he'd turned up.

He looked a lot neater than she'd imagined. The charity shop overcoat she'd envisaged was absent, along with the ironically worn tie. Instead, he wore a blue denim shirt tucked into jeans of exactly the same shade. A neat dark beard, pointed leather boots and a substantial belt buckle completed the Wyatt Earp look.

Jennifer wore the navy suit. It had seemed fine with Alec, but next to Lawrence and his cowboy garb, she felt like a department store manager.

He went to get the drinks, while she looked for somewhere to sit. There was one free table left, in front of a fruit machine where three lads punched buttons. It would have to do. Jennifer sat down. At least the whooshes and bongs coming from the machine would keep her awake.

Lawrence arrived, clutching a pint of lager and a quarter bottle of Chardonnay.

'They stung me three fifty for your drink,' he said.

'I'll get the next round,' said Jennifer.

This dating business was costly.

She glanced at Lawrence again. He might look like an extra from High Plains Drifter, but he was quite attractive. There was a period of adjustment you had to go through, at the start of these dates. A period where you kissed goodbye to the imaginary picture you'd formed and embraced reality. It was the same for him, she knew. 'Curvy' owed a lot to poetic licence.

Clinking glasses in an ironic sort of way, they spent a few minutes exchanging pleasantries about the pub and the area.

He asked her about her job, and she answered, taking care not to get onto any hobbyhorses.

It seemed to go okay. But then she asked him about his job. He worked for the local paper. When she said that must be interesting he said, 'It's mind-numbingly, coma-inducingly, suicide-provokingly boring.'

Jennifer had once seen a newspaper press in operation and found it fascinating. It had been incredibly noisy, as if the news was being shouted as well as printed.

'But all that information you provide for everyone,' she said.

'Information, shminformation.'

'And surely you get to meet a lot of people?'

'People are overrated.'

Questions began to flood out of her then, but they didn't come out in her normal voice. They came out all upbeat.

Deluged with positivity, Lawrence soon began staring into his pint and repositioning it minutely on the beer mat.

The lads at the fruit machine cheered as coins clinked into the tray. Jennifer heard herself ask why he didn't go for a job on a national newspaper.

He put his pint pot down and looked at her. 'You women come to these things armed with lists of questions, don't you? Perhaps you're right. I mean, why go through hours of chitchat?

Why not just cut to the chase?'

Jennifer tried to defend herself and her gender. 'Well, there *are* questions. At the back of one's mind, that is. But I wouldn't call them a list. I wouldn't call them an armoury.'

Lawrence waved dismissively. 'What you really want to know is: am I humper, a dumper or a thumper? Am I a drinker, a thinker or a stinker? Am I a sucker, a mucker, or a ... .'

'Look, there's no need for that. I'm sorry if I've offended you.'

Lawrence rolled his eyes. 'But surely you want to know whether I've ever made a woman pregnant? Or been a practising homosexual? Have I ever been sectioned? Am I an alcoholic, in or out of recovery? Do I suffer from obsessive-compulsive disorder? Intestinal parasites? Genital warts?'

'I want to get to know you, yes. But ... .'

'Is my salary above or below the national average? Do I make regular contributions to a reputable pension fund? Have I been inside? If so was it for some pardonable and even vaguely heroic offence, like breaking into an animal lab and releasing twenty cages of semi-paralysed mice onto the North Yorkshire Moors, or was I caught at a bus stop, masturbating onto a packet of Bird's Eye Fish Fingers in a pensioner's shopping bag?'

He sat back. 'That's the kind of stuff you women really want to know, isn't it?'

The date was brought mercifully to a close by the landlord switching on the PA system and announcing a pilot pub quiz night. As the barmaid began squeezing between the tables distributing pencils, Jennifer and Lawrence stood up as one.

'Right,' said Lawrence, at the door. 'This is where we shake hands and say, "How lovely to meet you, I'll be in touch again." Or some such bollocks. Then we walk away and never see each other again.'

'Yes,' said Jennifer. 'That's about it.'

12. *A few bits of bread*

What with the disappointing dates and the problems at work, Jennifer's phone calls to Nyesha had become more frequent. She was wearing a groove in her bum from sitting halfway up the stairs out of Alicia's earshot. On the plus side, she felt closer to her friend now than when she'd lived down the road in Chapeltown. Now that Nyesha had accepted the dating thing, she was being quite supportive.

Tonight, Lawrence was first on the agenda.

'Sounds like the guy's simply done too much dating,' said Nyesha, when Jennifer came to end of her story. 'I can understand that.'

'Yeah,' said Jennifer. 'And I can't really blame him. His world-weariness got to me. I behaved like a Blue Peter presenter on speed.'

Nyesha laughed.

Jennifer went on. 'It's strange. However good a man looks on paper or sounds on the phone, sometimes the two of you just don't gel.'

'Do you think you might have got on better given more time?'

'There is no time on these dates, Nesh. Well, officially there's two hours. But things get set in concrete in the first few minutes. And now I'm halfway through my Yeses! I had no idea it was going to be like this. Perhaps I should have arranged to see more than six.'

'You still could.'

'True. But if these are the best, what are the rest like?'

'When's the next one? Next Tuesday?'

'No, it's tomorrow, Thursday, early doors after work. I'll have to tell Mum I'm working late. I'll stay on half an hour, so I'm not totally lying. But John couldn't make a Tuesday, said he always goes to Manchester then. He was mysterious about it, actually. Said he'd tell me when he saw me.'

'This is the company director, right?'

'Yeah.'

'Well, he's probably got fingers in all sorts of pies. Talking of which, how's Greg?'

'Oh God. Wait till I tell you what happened today.'

Nyesha had used up her tolerance on Lawrence and had none to spare for Greg. 'This man might be good news for the company but he's bad news for you,' she said when Jennifer finished the stockroom story. 'He's damaging your self-esteem. Probably fancies you.'

'Don't make me laugh,' said Jennifer. 'I think he wants to fire me rather than anything else. And there are simply no jobs around at the minute. How would Mum and I survive? Her state pension goes nowhere.'

'Look on the temp sites.'

'Not my scene.'

'You're really wedded to that place, aren't you? I can't imagine why. Perhaps it's you that's in love with him?'

'Huh, I'm not even sure I like him. Anyway, he's married.'

'You don't not fancy someone just because they're married,' said Nyesha.

'Really?

Nyesha was silent.

'You'd better tell me about your week,' said Jennifer.

Nyesha and Jennifer had met a year ago, when Nyesha was filling in for Wally Walton's PA. Jennifer had admired the striking British Jamaican woman instantly: she had a figure as rounded as Jennifer's, but carried herself in such a way that before the word *fat* could so much as beg for house room, the word *sexy* had already got its feet up on the table and was pouring itself a drink. And Nyesha admired Jennifer for looking after her mother.

'Bless you!' she said when she found out. 'You're behaving like a real woman and putting family first.'

But their time together was short lived. When Wally Walton's PA came back from maternity leave, Nyesha hit thirty and decided to make her long anticipated move to London.

And she was happy there.

Jennifer wouldn't have wished her friend otherwise. But Nyesha's new job was hectic, and left little time for visits north.

Jennifer had gone down a month or so back.

'You wouldn't believe how much there is going on here,' Nyesha had said as they sped through the West End in a taxi. 'And it's going on all the time, not just on Saturdays like in Leeds.'

Jennifer tried to ignore the little green numbers on the taxi's meter, increasing steadily.

'You can walk down the street and there'll be a bunch of people playing steel drums in the park, or something. It's bustin'! I went to a Gary Younge talk the other day.'

'Who?'

'You know, the journalist. And it was only a Wednesday.'

'There's little things that bother you, of course,' Nyesha added.

'Like what?'

'Well, the flat's so small I had to chuck out all my Forever Friends figurines.'

Jennifer rolled her eyes.

'And the pensioners on my street have to go to the post office in pairs to cash their Giros because they keep getting robbed.'

'Now that is bad.'

Nyesha shrugged. 'That's London. Your trouble is, you lead too sheltered a life. If you lived down here, you'd grow a tougher skin. You'd have to.'

A tougher skin sounded a great idea. Jennifer would have liked one, and a visit to Nesh every month would have been a start. But there was no way she could afford it. In the restaurant, she'd volunteered to pay for their meal – a few bits of bread, hummus, olives and sun dried tomatoes – then nearly died when she saw the bill, the same as a week's worth of shopping at Leeds outdoor market.

'Oh well,' she'd said. 'We're only going to your church tomorrow, aren't we? Presumably that's free.'

'Yeah. Apart from a pound for the collection plate.'

It was only money. Even so, when Jennifer's coach began winding its way north from Victoria Coach Station, she felt relieved. In London, money vanished from your purse like a conjuring trick. One minute there was a fifty-pound note, the next minute there wasn't. On her low income, she couldn't help feeling like one of those beleaguered pensioners: robbed in broad daylight.

13. *Tomato plants*

The next morning, Jennifer was at her computer looking at a site called *stopwhingeingstartliving.com* when Greg passed, clutching a torn-open envelope and giving her a look so cold it could have frozen the fires of Hell.

'Greg ... ,' she began, but he was already walking past her and heading off through the swing doors that led onto the factory floor.

She waited anxiously for a few moments, bending a paperclip in and out of shape. Derek from Finance approached, yellow checked shirt bulging above worn brown cords. He was holding a sheaf of grubby looking papers.

'They're all urgent, these.'

'I'll do them right away,' said Jennifer, trying to see past him.

'That's what you said last time. Finance Department's the poor relation in this sodding company, pardon my French. It's all marketing this and sales that, these days. Brochure this and mail shot that. Hey, don't walk off when I'm talking to you!'

Jennifer caught up with Greg in Goods Inwards, or rather saw him go out of the factory and in to the Packing Shed. She followed. He was in a huddle with Eric and Eric's assistant, pointing at a graphics panel showing one of the company's products superimposed over a sunset. Eric was gesticulating with his staple gun and sucking his breath through his teeth in the time-honoured manner of workmen everywhere.

Jennifer took a few steps nearer and a volley of shots went off that nearly gave her a heart attack. She looked down; she had trodden on some bubble wrap. All three men were looking at her.

'Hello, love,' said Eric. 'By, but you're a sight for sore eyes.'

'Jennifer,' said Greg.

From the look on his face, it was obvious that she had done something very, very wrong. She felt weak and scared.

'I can see you're busy,' she said. 'It can wait.'

'No, it had better not.'

He barked out some instructions to Eric and walked quickly towards her, neatly sidestepping the bubble wrap. 'Follow.'

Without returning Eric's blown kiss, Jennifer followed Greg back through Goods Inwards and into the factory. They passed the clean room, a freestanding sterile room that stood in the dusty factory like a time machine visiting from the future.

They walked past the glass-walled software engineers' office, with its bearded faces. They passed the sick room. Jennifer glanced in at the bed with its neat pile of charcoal coloured blankets and felt she couldn't walk any further.

She stopped. 'Greg, what have I done?'

'Hmm,' said Greg, avoiding her eyes. 'I'm not really sure how to broach this, Jenny. Let's just say I received some rather unusual post this morning.'

Jennifer realised suddenly that he wasn't so much angry as embarrassed. Her mind raced. Was it a complaint from a customer about her?

He reached into his pocket, pulled out a crumpled ball of paper and handed it over. Jennifer smoothed it out and read the words aloud. They were staggered down the watermarked cream paper in gold ink.

'It is a truth universally acknowledged, that a single (or married) man in possession of a good fortune must be in want of a shag.'

'Looks familiar, does it?' asked Greg.

'Familiar?' said Jennifer. 'Well, yes. It's from Jane Austen.

Except for the bit in brackets and the last word, that is.'

'Jane who? The general manager's secretary? Why would you try to pin this on her?'

'No. Jane Austen. One of the most widely read novelists in the English language, famed for her wit and acute social commentary.'

Greg looked blank.

'From the nineteenth century. Wrote Sense and Sensibility. And Pride and Prejudice. You know, it was made into a series with Colin Firth. He jumped into the lake wearing a white shirt and when he came out, it was clinging to his ... .'

'You mean it's a quotation? Well, whatever. It hardly matters who wrote it originally. Who's written it now, that's the question – and sent it to me, signed 'J.'.'

He looked piercingly at her.

Belatedly, she realised this was her own initial. All the strength went out of her legs. 'You mean, you think I sent it?'

'Jenny, you're not an unattractive woman. Nice eyes. And if you could get yourself in shape, lose a bit of ... but anyway, that's beside the point. I've heard on the grapevine that you're into lonely hearts dating. And this note, well, it smacks of the same thing.'

How on earth had he found out about the dates? Though she shouldn't really be surprised. It was impossible to keep anything secret in this place.

'What do you mean, "same thing"?' she asked.

He looked awkward. 'Well, anonymous. Cowardly, in a certain way.'

'Doing lonely hearts isn't cowardly,' cried Jennifer. 'You'd know that if you'd sat in a station toilet for half an hour figuring out how to cut short a date with a psychopath. But even if it is, aren't cowardly people entitled to love as much as brave ones?'

'So you admit it? Sending this?'

'I didn't say that.'

'Oh, come on, you must think I'm an idiot. Who else could it be from? Who else goes around "being herself" and treating the workplace as if it's nothing more than an extension of her own personality? Who else sits at her desk all day, thinking about sex and romance instead of doing an honest day's work?'

'Most women, I would have thought,' said Jennifer. 'But if you're looking for someone beginning with J, then Jocasta Jardine. Though I wouldn't have taken her for a Pride and Prejudice fan.'

Greg eyes widened. The certainty drained out of his expression. Further expressions followed: disbelief, amazement and finally a sort of dazed wonderment.

Jennifer held the paper out to him.

He took it without a word, then turned and walked back up the factory floor.

Jennifer stood for a few moments, staring into space. Then she went into the sick room, closed the door and sat down on the bed. She pulled a tissue from the box on the small table, and pressed it to her eyes.

She could cope with working with people she had nothing in common with. It happened. She could cope with a boss who didn't recognise her strengths. Ron Sandle had been a good case in point. But working closely, day after day, with someone who stood ready to pounce on her every move was just too much.

A sob came, then another. Finally she tipped over onto the bed and let the tears flow until the thin sick room pillow was soaked with them.

The rest of that day, Jennifer worked as never before. She cleared her in-tray. She didn't bother with chocolate or scones; didn't even bother with coffee.

Derek was smug. 'Wasn't so hard, was it?' he said, picking up ten perfectly presented letters and sauntering back across the office, picking his nose.

When she had finished all her other work, Jennifer opened a new document in her Personal folder and worked on that. She printed out the letter – on the firm's best stationery, naturally – slotted it into an envelope and wrote Greg's name on it. Normally, internal communications were done by email. But this, like the letter Greg had received this morning, was different.

As soon as Greg had gone home, she went upstairs, overtaking the catering franchise girl, who was going from office to office distributing leaflets.

Greg's office was such a bare room now. Ron Sandle's battered directories had been removed from the shelves, his tatty wall planners taken down, his geraniums and tomato plants ousted from the windowsills. In their place, rows of new books about marketing theory, bare clean walls, executive toys.

The room was all about work. Work, and nothing but work. There was the picture of Greg's wife, stunningly beautiful and an alcoholic if you believed what you heard on the factory floor, but that was about it. The room held no ornaments, nothing that might be accused of existing purely for its own sake. The Marketing Department was turning into a barren, utilitarian place.

Jennifer sank down into the chair in front of Greg's desk, making it exhale slowly. This room was the only director's office to have two windows. She sat listening to the hum of rush hour traffic, watching the leaves of a beech tree flutter.

There was a knock. The catering girl came in.

She glanced at the envelope in Jennifer's hand. 'Are you all right? You look like shit.'

Jennifer liked the girl, a Goth who was doing the job as a filler. They'd shared conversations about each other's minor problems and triumphs. In fact she was probably the one who'd grassed about Jennifer's dating. But this was too big a thing to tell her.

'I'm fine,' said Jennifer. 'I'm just thinking.'

Greg always cleared his desk completely before he went home. Jennifer waited, gazing at its polished wooden surface while the girl delivered her leaflet, which looked to be about a price increase.

And then the girl left, and Jennifer went on sitting there.

The Frog and Newt was quiet at six o'clock. It had been tempting, at the sight of the grinning plastic tree stump, to drive past. The road led to York, and beyond that to Scarborough and the sea. Jennifer, not in the mood for a date, would have liked to drive and drive to where the vertiginous drop of the cliffs, the wheeling gulls and the roar of the chill, turbulent North Sea would have driven her problems out of her head.

But she didn't. She stood at the bar until a barmaid appeared and she was able to order one of the interminable little bottles of wine and sit down at what was becoming her usual table, nearest the fireplace.

And then a man with a dark blue jacket, faded jeans and a confident walk came in. Jennifer did a double take.

The man strode over. He had clear, grey eyes and a nice smile. Nothing looked to be receding, drooping or spreading.

'John?' she asked.

'Hi!'

He gripped her hand. His eyes took her in and seemed to like what they saw. He had a firm, warm handshake. His voice was deep.

'Good to meet you. I'll get myself a drink.'

Jennifer sat back in a state of bewilderment.

When he came back with a gin and tonic, he sat opposite her, turning his chair slightly sideways so they wouldn't be eyeballing each other. He had nice hands, she noticed, with clean, straight-cut nails.

She smiled. 'You found it okay, then?'

He glanced round. His jacket was beautifully tailored. 'Oh

yes. Used to drink here twenty years ago, when it was a proper boozer. I see they've given it a facelift. Or what passes for one, these days.'

They shared a grin.

'And you?' he said. 'Is this your local?'

'It has been, recently.'

'Ah. Many dates?'

'You're my fourth,' she said.

He grinned again. He had teeth like a toothpaste advert. She had never seen such a well-groomed man up close.

'Had quite a few replies to your advert, I expect?' he asked.

'Nearly a hundred.'

'I'm not surprised.'

The way he looked at her as he delivered this compliment made her neck go hot.

She collected herself. 'You sound as if you've had some experience of this kind of thing before.'

He smiled. 'Let's just say I'm not exactly a stranger to it.'

'Oh,' she said. Somehow that wasn't the reply she'd been expecting.

They moved on to talk about work. When she talked about hers, his eyes moved restlessly around so she cut quickly to asking about his. He answered her politely enough. But his answers were brief and she got the feeling he wanted to cut to the chase. That was fine by her. Emboldened by the success of the date so far, she decided to lead the way.

'So, when you've answered ads before, have you ever met anyone you've really liked?'

He laughed. 'Oh, I've met plenty of pretty girls.'

'Oh?' she said. She sipped her wine. 'No one you've wanted to start a relationship with, though?'

John swilled ice around his glass. 'As in a committed relationship? No. But then, surely people don't come to these things expecting to meet the love of their life?'

'Well, some people do,' said Jennifer. 'I suppose there could be many reasons why ... .'

'Look, let's not beat about the bush. I can see from your figure that you enjoy the, um, sensual pleasures of life.'

'Sorry?'

'You have appetites.'

From the way his eyes moved up and down her body, he wasn't just talking about food.

Jennifer wished she smoked. Scuttling outside with a packet of fags and a lighter would have bought valuable thinking time. A tube of Murray Mints was not a good substitute.

John was leaning closer, dropping his voice. His breath smelt of gin and mouth freshener. 'How often do you get to indulge those appetites?'

'Pardon?'

'You heard.'

But hearing wasn't the problem: it was believing.

'You mean ... have sex?' she asked, wincing that he'd made her say it.

'Mm.'

She was too flustered to dissemble. 'Not very often.'

He smiled. 'Would you like to change that?'

Her mind raced to a hotel room rented by the afternoon. A mini bar, underwear strewn across the carpet, a king size bed with crisp sheets. Sex with a stranger – something she would never do, of course.

'What, with you?' she managed to say.

He crunched a sliver of ice. 'With me,' he said. 'But perhaps also with others. I'm talking about clubs. Clubs where people like you and me go. People in our circumstances. People with needs.'

And there it was, the big, black, shiny fly in the ointment. She remembered their conversation on the phone; how he'd been out when she called, and had rung her back from the bath. She'd thought it was because he was a busy man. She sat back in her chair and sighed.

He leant forward. 'Something pure about it, when there are no emotional ties. Something joyful, something innocent.'

And now he was talking about a place in Manchester he went to on a Tuesday night and how he would drive her over there and how she would have no expenditure whatsoever.

'All you need do is wear something pretty,' he said. 'Stockings, suspenders with a bit of lace on, maybe. You'd get to meet all sorts. Nice people. Broad-minded. You'd have to make sure you were clean down below, though.'

Jennifer couldn't help picturing ageing, slack bellied men with hairy shoulders, shambling around in their Y-Fronts. She had a sudden vision of the Tuesday night cup of tea with Alicia. Alicia would talk about how Mrs Farquharson's false teeth had fallen out into her cup of coffee and Jennifer would describe how she'd given Mr Entwhistle a hand job while his wife pleasured herself with a nine-inch dildo nearby.

'Do the men take their socks off?' she asked.

John's eyes narrowed.

'Look, it's kind of you to invite me,' she said. 'But I've got an elderly mother at home. What I mean is it just isn't the kind of arrangement I'm looking for.'

'Bring a friend along with you the first time then, if that'd make it easier.'

'My friend lives in London,' said Jennifer.

'London to Manchester is nothing, on the train,' said John. 'We could pick her up at the station.'

He was a tryer. You had to give him that. Jennifer thought of Nyesha sitting in her underwear with a drink with a pink umbrella, being stared at by men with ear hair.

She laughed again, louder this time.

John glanced, embarrassed, at the few other customers now in the pub.

But a whoop broke out of Jennifer, followed by a gasp.

She had to retreat to the Ladies, where she stood clutching her bag in the privacy of a cubicle and gulping with a strange, painful laughter that was close to crying.

14. *Space for a coffee machine*

The next morning, Greg was waiting at Jennifer's desk when she arrived. He looked shamefaced.

'My office, please, Jenny. If you don't mind.'

Nodding, she dumped her bag.

Derek in Finance, perhaps sensing serious intent via body language, had stood up to get a better view.

'That man could sniff out a story in a sensory deprivation tank,' muttered Greg.

Upstairs he didn't bother to sit down, but bounced around the room on the balls of his feet, like a boxer. The post toppled in his in-tray and the sound of car horns drifted in from the Ring Road. He picked up one of the balls on his Newton's Cradle and let it fall. A rhythmic clicking began.

Jennifer, also standing, got ready to deliver the sentence she had been rehearsing since yesterday: about the soul destroying effect of working with someone who seemed to think she came lower down Darwin's evolutionary scale than a nematode worm.

But she didn't get the chance. 'Sit,' he said.

Like a trained dog, she obeyed. She opened her mouth to speak but he got there first.

'Listen, Jenny. Before you start, let me say what I've got to say. I need to clear the air. It seems I owe you an apology for yesterday.'

'Well, yes. You made me feel ... .'

'Point is I jumped to conclusions.'

'You don't seem to have a very high opinion ... .'

'I hold my hand up: it was wrong of me.'

'It's hard working with someone who ... .'

Greg stopped pacing and eyeballed her. 'You may also have gathered I was thinking of putting you on the redundancy list.'

'No,' said Jennifer, startled.

He set off on another lap of the room. 'It's true I was considering it. But my thought processes have moved on since then. That day in the stockroom, the thought occurred to me that the PA job isn't exactly playing to your strengths. I've been slow acting on it – I've got a lot on my plate just now – but there are more interesting duties I could put your way. Not managerial work, obviously, but arty stuff like dealing with brochures, liaising more with the printer on the creative side of things, thinking about the company's exhibition attendance. Think you could hack that?'

He went straight on without waiting for an answer. 'If so, you'll save the company money. And saving the company money equals saving your job, never mind all that bollocks Walton spouts about getting people to re-use staples and wipe their arse on both sides of the toilet paper.'

He began talking about the cost of exhibition stands and contractor fees. Jennifer listened politely, assuming he would come back to the point sooner or later.

And eventually he did.

'Which is where you come in,' he said. 'Think you could knock up a quick stand design out of that Omega system? On the cheap, that is. Then show the sales team how to put it up?'

'Whoa!' said Jennifer. Her mind flew to the booking form she'd filled in for Zurich.

'It's a major show, isn't it? And we've booked a big space.'

'Yes. Meaning?'

'Our stand will be very visible.'

'Come on, all you'll have to do is build a rough structure;

chuck a few chairs here and there, find space for a coffee machine, lob on a few graphics panels and Bob's your Uncle.'

'I think there'll be more to it than that.'

'Okay, okay. But how about if we get the FD's PA to take over Derek's work for a bit, give you a bit of space? What if the salespeople started preparing their own quotes? I mean, how hard can it be? It's only a question of inserting a few numbers in a standard document. Frankly it's outrageous that they don't do it already.'

Jennifer thought of the tedious job, which often ran to pages. She imagined Jocasta breaking her nails on the computer keys.

'Ah! You like the cut of my jib on that one, don't you?' said Greg. 'So, you're up for it, then?'

'Well, maybe,' said Jennifer. 'But you do realise that I've never actually designed a … .'

'Never mind that,' said Greg. 'What I need to know is will you now?'

It was all happening far too quickly. Jennifer felt as if she had jumped on a bus without knowing what number it was. And now the driver was speeding up the road while she stood, wobbling and fumbling change out of her purse. She stared at him, unable to come up with any sort of answer.

'Come on, come on,' he said. 'I've a nine-thirty to get to. Yes or no?'

She nodded, slowly. 'Well, yes. Yes. And thank you.'

'Splendid!'

He had never looked this pleased with her. As he swept out of the room, she could swear he was smiling.

She sat for a few moments, fingering the resignation letter still in her pocket. She'd decided last night that she wouldn't quit just because the going had got tough.

That made what had just happened all the sweeter.

She held the letter up and tore it into little pieces then let them flutter gently, like falling cream petals, into his bin.

15. *Stale Bourbons*

In the kitchen, Pepe huddled in his basket, consuming stale bourbons. Nelly must have been shopping: four full bags stood on the work surface. One bulged with vegetables and in another Jennifer could see the distinctive livery of Heinz tomato soup, Alicia's favourite.

She unpacked the bags, enjoying the simple task.

It was amazing that twenty-four hours could bring such a sharp turnaround of events. It was a pity Nyesha didn't share her optimism.

She'd laughed about John, but to the story of Greg, she'd said, darkly, 'A leopard cannot change his spots. Neither can the Ethiopian change his skin. Jeremiah 13, verse 23. Don't agree to anything. And certainly not without a pay-rise.'

'Too late,' said Jennifer. 'I already have.'

Her friend's pessimism couldn't dent her good mood. The new duties sounded interesting – exciting, even. Humming, Jennifer folded an empty carrier bag for reuse and lifted out a value bag of bananas from the second one.

She blinked.

Underneath the bananas was some pink fabric. She plunged her hand in and touched silk. She pulled it out – it was a dress. It had a full skirt, the kind you would wear a net petticoat underneath, and a strapless boned bodice. The colour held other colours within it, like mother of pearl.

She pressed the dress against herself, smoothing the skirt

down to see the length – mid-calf – and twisting this way and that, trying to see her reflection in the microwave. It was so feminine. It was of course much too small for her, the way most feminine things were. She laid it aside.

But there was something else in the bag: a pair of high-heeled shoes, the same colour as the dress. Unlike the dress, these might fit. Jennifer took off her sturdy lace-ups and slipped her right foot in to one. It was like stepping into a cool pool. She turned her foot this way and that. Then she put the other shoe on and teetered across the kitchen.

'I see you've found 'em then.'

Nelly, in her blue and white striped apron, had come through the back door.

'They're beautiful, Nelly,' said Jennifer. 'Are they yours?'

Nelly went to the sink and ran water into the bowl. 'When I saw you the other day with your hair and that, I went home and dug everything out. It were my going-away outfit, you see. Thought I looked the bees' knees in it.'

She drew a photo from her apron pocket.

It took Jennifer a moment to recognise Leeds Town Hall and Nelly with a mass of curls and only one chin. A smart-looking man stood next to her.

'So that must be Ernie! He's got hair. And just look at that double breasted suit.'

'Oh aye, he were a sharp dresser in them days.'

'And were you madly in love?'

Nelly laughed. 'Get away with you. He grew on me, though. Anyway, I've got those lamb sausages your mother likes, from Jubbs. The potatoes aren't English, but that can't be helped.'

Jennifer stepped reluctantly out of the shoes. 'Thanks for showing me, Nelly.'

'Showing you? I'm giving it you. Consider it a belated birthday pressie.'

'But my birthday was eight months ago.'

'All right, it's your early Christmas.'

'But it's your special outfit.'

'So? I shan't be getting into that dress again anytime soon.'

'And you think I will?'

'Get along on with you,' said Nelly, handing her a paring knife.

Jennifer would have liked to say more, but Nelly was looking embarrassed so smiling to herself, she took the knife and began peeling potatoes.

Perhaps it was the effect of sorting out one problem that made Jennifer want to sort another. Or perhaps the letter about the MRI scan was to blame. It had arrived, delighting Alicia but giving Jennifer an unpleasant jolt. Whatever, that evening when they were sitting over their empty plates in the dining room, Jennifer heard herself say, 'Mum. Can we talk?'

Alicia waved her stick. 'Can't it wait, dear? Narendra will be here in twenty minutes, and I haven't touched my hair since this morning. Or my face. Some of us take a pride in our appearance, you know.'

Jennifer let this pass. 'What's Dr Ganguly doing, coming round?'

'Don't fuss, dear, it's to do with a little committee I said I'd be on: The Patient's Voice.'

'Right. But I really do need to ask you something.'

Alicia sighed, but put her stick down.

Jennifer took a deep breath. 'Could you and Nelly manage if I went out more in the evenings?'

'Well, you do go out. And we seem to manage then.'

'Yes. Good. Though what I really mean is, could you manage if, for example, I had a boyfriend?'

Alicia sat up straight. 'By which I take it you've already got one.'

'Hang on,' said Jennifer. 'There's no need to jump to

conclusions.'

'And that's where you were the other Tuesday night?'

'No,' said Jennifer. 'Though it is true that … .'

'And when I asked you where you'd been you just mumbled and said you'd been out with the "usual suspects". I suppose you're going to tell me next that you're in love?'

'No, I'm not. In fact, I'm not telling you anything more until you calm down.'

'Calm down? Calm down? Why should I calm down, when my own daughter makes barefaced lies into articles of everyday coinage?'

Alicia's hands began to tremble. Images Jennifer had been trying to resist flashed into her mind: hospital corridors smelling of disinfectant; a white face in a white bed; a quavering, hysterical voice. And that was only her own.

'Mum, don't upset yourself, please. I'm only talking hypothetically.'

'Oh, I'm upsetting *myself*, am I? It isn't that my only child, once so lovely, so *pure,* the very child Terry Wogan once admired in the pram outside the BBC Look North Studios when he came up to Leeds, has been casually deceiving me for days, perhaps weeks?'

'I haven't,' said Jennifer.

'I suppose you're pregnant, are you? Well, that wouldn't surprise me, knowing the modern lack of self-control. And planning on bringing up baby in this house, perhaps. Not something even you can keep secret. Though I'm sure you'd try.'

Alicia's hands were shaking violently now. The sinews of her neck were standing out and her breathing sounded shallow and rapid. She really did need to calm down.

'Mum!' said Jennifer. 'It isn't anything like that. Not remotely. Now please compose yourself. Take deep breaths. Think of something relaxing: an Alpine stream; a summer meadow; a calm moonlit sea, waves gently lapping the shore.'

Before Jennifer could think of any more scenes from nature, the doorbell rang.

Alicia's hands flew to her hair. 'Oh, dear, dear, dear. You've got me into a state, just when I need to be at my most professional. Narendra wants composed, objective people on the panel, not emotional wrecks.'

Her hand pecked around weakly for her stick like the claw of a lucky dip machine. Jennifer picked up the stick and fitted it into her grasp.

Alicia gripped the table with her free hand and heaved herself up. 'What a sight I must look.'

'Dr Ganguly must see a lot worse.'

'Charming!'

'I didn't mean it like that. Look, I'll take him into the front room and entertain him while you get ready. I'll bring your hairbrush and lipstick down here.'

Alicia pushed past her, quite roughly for an ailing woman. 'Narendra's a doctor. He hasn't time to be *entertained*, as you put it.'

She went into the sitting room. Jennifer waited for a few moments then went into the hall to let Doctor Ganguly in. But as the diminutive GP nodded and beamed, and was let into the sitting room to be received by a surprisingly serene-looking Alicia, Jennifer realised it was she, not her mother, who was seething with a strange mix of emotions and who badly needed to calm down; who needed to visualise Alpine streams, summer meadows and moonlit seas.

As her mind was too agitated to conjure them, she went into the kitchen for the next best thing: a large glass of Sauvignon Blanc and a bag of sour cream and onion Kettle Chips.

16. *Hermesetas*

Inside the packing shed, a waist-high bench equipped with tools ran the length of one wall. Bales of bubble wrap and rolls of brown paper were stored at one end and at the other a battered filing cabinet supported a kettle and mugs.

The floor space was normally kept clear. But on the following Tuesday morning, various pieces of display system which Eric had carted down from the stockroom stood in an angular, clanking pile in the middle. Eric, so short and round in proportion to his waistline that he had to cut the legs of his overalls off at what would have been someone's else's knees, chucked the last piece on and bent over, hands on thighs, to recover himself.

Pushing his thick-lensed glasses up his nose, he accepted the plastic cup of tea Jennifer had bought him from the machine.

'How long do you think you'll be down here, then, building this stand?' he asked. 'A month or two?'

Jennifer shrugged. It was hard to say.

'Bound to take longer than you think,' he said, grinning and decanting his drink into a white pint pot that said 'I Love Tea'.

Jennifer glanced around the packing shed again, at the bare brick walls and filthy windows. Something had changed since her last visit, though she wasn't sure what.

'You've tidied up.'

Eric cleared his throat. 'Aye.' He looked embarrassed.

Jennifer realised what had happened. 'You've taken your

naked ladies down.'

He flinched at the word 'naked'.

'Mark of respect, intit? Anyway, too skinny, most of them birds.'

In their place was a shiny if sober row of postcard views of Spain.

'Thanks, Eric,' said Jennifer.

A stream of tea shot out of Eric's mouth and spattered in the sawdust. 'Is there sugar in this?'

'Well, yes. Three spoonfuls. I thought that was the norm for workmen.'

Eric pointed to the top of the filing cabinet where a little blue and white cylinder nestled next to a scruffy radio. 'Hermesetas. One. For future reference.'

He glanced at the tea again, which was the colour of David Dickinson's face.

'Bit strong for me too love, if I'm honest. Shall I brew us a nice drop of Earl Grey?'

That afternoon, Jennifer saw that the hardest working member of the packing department was indeed the kettle. Every task was tackled at a snail's pace. Official breaks got stretched like a sumo wrestler's waistband, and there were also plenty of unofficial breaks, to smoke under the 'No Smoking – Dangerous Chemicals' sign and read out headlines from the Sun.

Nevertheless, the work got done. Eric and his assistant could lift and bend, hammer and staple with the best of them. Miles of bubble wrap got wrapped around items of optical equipment, hundreds of polystyrene blocks got cut to anchor them in their crates, and millions of polystyrene beads got poured in to add cushioning in transit.

Jennifer's work seemed insubstantial by comparison. She looked up product footprints in technical specs, counted and measured bits of stand, considered bench heights and assessed optimum distances between products and customers. The smallest compartment would house an optical microscope the size of a mobile phone, the largest a scanning electron microscope the size of a small car.

And then she marked the stand dimensions out on the floor. Eric enjoyed watching her crawl around with her bottom in the air: he was there grinning and nodding every time she looked up, giving her the thumbs up, his eyes looming behind the thick convex lenses of his glasses like goldfish in a bowl.

But it was great work, more enjoyable than any amount of PA work could ever be. As usual, when she was absorbed, her personal problems shrank down to nothing, like minimised windows on the computer. She hardly even thought about her impending date that evening.

By three-twenty seven, which was when Eric took his overalls off, allowing three minutes' walk exactly to the clocking-off machine, the floor was completely chalked up, and Jennifer was standing looking at it, not a thought in her head except how great the stand was going to look when she finally got it built.

As a concession to Greg, Jennifer was now getting her hair done after work rather than before.

But at five-thirty, Salvatore's Salon was every bit as empty as usual. His mirror was a different story. Its edge was crowded with new photographs, all of him. Face down and naked, he lay on a sunny beach. In a tight black wetsuit, he straddled a jet ski. In the briefest of trunks, he hung upside down from the rigging on a boat. The real Salvatore, standing behind her, wore a diaphanous pale pink shirt, through which his nipples showed.

She felt completely surrounded by him. As he pinned her hair into sections and began to trim, humming tunelessly, it was difficult to know where to rest her gaze. Nerves about the approaching date were also beginning to get to her. She settled for perusing the bottles of lotions then moved on to the cup of coffee Tony had brought, which stood misting up the bottom of the mirror.

She realised with a jolt that he had stopped cutting and was giving her a penetrating stare. Since he'd done her makeover, his attitude towards her had changed, though she couldn't put her finger on how. It was unsettling.

'You go somewhere?' he asked.

'I'm meeting a friend for a drink, yes,' she said, noncommittal.

'You know this friend long?'

'No.'

'You' mama know this friend?'

Jennifer tensed. This morning, Alicia had eyed her suspiciously when she said she was going to get her hair done after work. Jennifer had been on the verge of blurting out the truth then making a run for it. Not a mature strategy, but better than nothing. She hadn't had the chance, though. Nelly had come in and begun ranting about the council and the blocked drain.

'Well, no, she doesn't.'

'Don' worry,' said Salvatore. 'I won' tell. Is friend you never met before, yes? Who is?'

Jennifer sighed. She supposed there was no harm in Salvatore knowing. After all, weren't hairdressers the world's unofficial confessors, keepers of a thousand secrets?

'His name's Trevor. He's a crime writer.'

'A writer? Is good!'

'You think so?'

'Of course! Is perhaps famous. Where you meet 'im?'

His enthusiasm was gratifying.

'At the pub,' she said.

'And 'ow you recognise 'im?'

Jennifer realised she had forgotten to ask Trevor about his appearance. 'It shouldn't be hard. He's going to sit at the table by the fire.'

By mistake, she glanced at the photo of Salvatore hanging upside down. A black, vertical line of hair led into his trunks.

He saw her looking. 'It was very 'ot that day,' he said.

But luckily the topic of the blind date held more appeal. 'So. 'Ow he recognise you? Do you mention your elegant hands? Your beautiful hair, your amber eyes? Will there be a lily pin to your breast? Or' – he appeared to concede to the English gardening calendar – 'a bloom of chrysanthemum?'

'No,' she said. 'I think I said more about my handbag than myself.'

Salvatore shook his head in disappointment.

'You must blow your own, 'ow you say, trombone? Or how else will a man know you are a person worthy of love and respect?'

'By the evidence of his own heart and mind?' Jennifer said.

But Salvatore had already turned the hairdryer on, drowning out her reply.

Trevor's letter had been well written. It had also been dynamic. He hadn't, for instance, asked 'shall we meet?' but 'when shall we meet?'. To add to the charm, his letter had been typed on an old manual typewriter, on masculine-looking pale grey stationery.

Jennifer knew it was foolish to set too much store by these sorts of things. Nevertheless, when she pushed open the door of the Frog and Newt later that evening, with Nelly's high heels making the soles of her feet burn like paper boats in hell, she couldn't help looking for a Daniel Craig figure with gold-rimmed spectacles and a serious smile.

So it was something of a shock when a man of about fifty, fat, bearded, dishevelled and diamond-pattern-sweatered, raised his hand in welcome.

Her eyes shot to left and right to make sure there were no other tables by the fireplace, tables she had perhaps missed in the past. But no.

She realised she was standing with her mouth open. She pasted on a smile and tottered over.

He stood up. 'Hello, Jennifer.'

He held out his hand. His eyes flickered to her shoes. Hers flickered to the tabletop, which held an empty pint glass, foam sliding down its sides. She realised what this meant: she could escape to the bar, which would give her time to adjust.

'Can I get you another?' she asked.

'Don't mind if I do.'

Jennifer walked quickly to the bar. How come he was so old? Had she forgotten to ask his age? She couldn't remember for the life of her.

For once she was grateful for the pub's slow service. By the time she arrived back at the table, she felt better. He might be twenty years older than her, but he was a writer. She had never met one of those before and the encounter was bound to be fascinating.

She sat down next to him on the upholstered bench, her dates so far having taught her the paradox that it was easier to talk when you weren't face to face.

'Sorry I didn't recognise you straight off,' she said. 'I'd pictured you differently. I've done that a lot on these dates – formed the wrong impression from people's letters.'

'Yes, that's the problem with the written word,' he said. 'But looks can be deceptive. It's what's on the inside that counts.'

Why did unattractive people always think they had great personalities? It was surely open to question. But perhaps in Trevor's case it was true. She must at least give him a chance.

'So, you're a crime writer?' she said. 'How interesting. What sort of crimes do you write about?'

'Well, murders,' he said, picking up his pint. 'The more sadistic the better. It seems to be what readers want.'

'Yes, I suppose one has to have a niche,' said Jennifer. 'But how do you come up with grisly plots? It must be hard.'

'Not really,' he said, opening a packet of nuts. 'All my nine novels so far have been based on true crimes. All local, too. Truth being, as they say, stranger than fiction.'

'Really?' said Jennifer. It seemed unlikely that there would be enough sadistic crime in Yorkshire to base a whole series of novels around.

'Absolutely,' he said, with relish. 'You'd be amazed. The public don't know the half of it. But my sources tell me stuff. They tell me the kind of stuff that never gets into the papers.'

She must have looked doubtful, because he gave her a penetrating look. 'Don't believe me? Where do you live?'

'North Leeds. On an estate of semis not far from the Ring Road. I've lived there most of my life.'

He leant forwards. 'Where, exactly?'

She wondered where this was going. But it couldn't hurt to tell him.

'Woodlands Avenue.'

'Case in point then,' he said, sitting back. 'Ten years ago there was a nasty murder a few streets away from you. A woman was forced to mate with the family Alsatian and then brutally killed in front of her husband and son. In Oak Grove.'

'Oh! And in Oak Grove? But I walk down there to get to the dentists.'

Trevor shrugged. 'The husband ended up losing his marbles: went up into the attic and hung himself from the roof timbers. After poisoning his son with anti-freeze, that is. I believe the dog remained unharmed. Re-homed to a family in Gildersome, as I remember.'

'Oh,' said Jennifer. She vaguely remembered reading something in the papers. But there had been nothing about shag by shepherd dog or annihilation by antifreeze.

'Surely a terrible murder like that is a one-off.'

'Hah! Of course not. It's going on all the time.'

'Maybe so,' said Jennifer firmly, 'but I'm sure *your* life's not

104

all rape and murder. You mentioned golf.'

'Ah yes,' said Trevor, draining his pint. 'I belong to a golf club at Eccup. I get down there when I can.'

Jennifer brightened. 'Oh, the club by the reservoir? How lovely. I take Pepe – Mum's poodle – for walks there sometimes.'

'Yes, it's a pleasant spot. But back to what we were saying just now, a golf course is an excellent place for a murder. We're not talking serial killer now, more industrial espionage. Business rivals, and so on. A friendly game, building bridges, then kapow! A well aimed shot to the temple proves fatal. Happened at Moortown Golf Club eight years ago. The police knew it wasn't an accident but they couldn't prove anything.'

'Yes, well, I'm not really into sport,' said Jennifer. 'The occasional game of table tennis is all I manage.'

'Oh well, you've got me there,' said Trevor. 'I can't tell you about any ping pong related murders. Though in theory you could suffocate someone by forcing a ping pong ball down their … '

'Look, might I have read any of your books?' asked Jennifer.

'They're widely available. In good bookshops, that is.'

'It's just that I can't think of a crime writer called Trevor.'

'Well, I write under a *nom de plume*.'

'Oh, really? What is it?'

He looked awkward. 'I'd rather not say if you don't mind. I'm quite well known and I wouldn't want it to get out about this dating thing.'

Jennifer was taken aback. She was out on a date with someone well known. On the other hand, she didn't know who it was. She felt a bit insulted by his secrecy.

'Of course if things progress between us then that's a different matter,' he added.

She nodded. 'Fair enough.'

And she supposed it was fair enough. But somehow now she couldn't think of anything to say. A silence fell, probably not that long in real time but seeming as extensive as the Lower Palaeolithic period, minus the invention of flaked stone tools.

Mercifully, Trevor went off to get more drinks.

'You were saying you lived with your mother?' he asked when he came back.

Jennifer fell gratefully upon the topic and talked for five minutes non-stop.

Trevor nodded and looked interested. Then he said, 'of course, the difficulty of the mother-daughter relationship is another great motive for murder. You might think it would be more natural for the daughter to do away with the mother, but there have been plenty of cases where Ma's the one up for manslaughter. In Roundhay, there's been a string of nasty cases involving kitchen implements.'

Half an hour later, Jennifer had heard all she would ever want to hear about what could be done with a potato peeler and a George Foreman grill.

Trevor saw her to her car and leant on the passenger window.

'Well, that went pretty well,' he said, suppressing a belch which nevertheless filled the car with a beery smell. 'Shall we do it again? Call you next week. And I might tell you my pen name next time.'

She did her best to return his smile, but her tyres gave her away by screeching as she pulled out of the Frog and Newt's car park.

She'd thought she might encounter one or two pitfalls during her search for love. The conversation might dry up, perhaps, or a man might talk all evening about his ex. But an obsession with gruesome crime? That hadn't been on her list.

As she sped towards home round the dark, lonely expanse of the Ring Road, she felt nostalgic for the time when she hadn't been actively trying to meet someone. Because then it had been easy to imagine that there was a kindred spirit out there. Now, she was seriously beginning to doubt it.

17. *Chicken legs*

Over the next couple of days, Jennifer used the Allen key so much it callused her hand. And she inhaled so many paint fumes and drank so much strong tea that the inside of her mouth felt as dry as burnt toast. But as always she enjoyed the physicality of the work, the feel of different materials.

By Thursday afternoon, tea drunk and a pall of cigarette smoke hanging in the roof space of Packing, the stand stood, painted in green Hammerite, the size of a small bungalow.

She walked all around it.

Eric stopped banging nails into a crate and came over to have a look, hammer slipped into his belt like a gun.

'Imagine products there,' she said, pointing at one compartment. 'And spotlights there. Sofas at the far end. And some nice plants dotted about. It still needs a theme, but what do you think so far?'

Eric peered and frowned.

'Not so close.' said Jennifer. 'Look at it from an overall perspective.'

Eric took a couple of steps back, but still looked troubled. 'It's a right munter if you don't mind my saying so love.'

Jennifer was startled. In her mind, the stand gleamed on a thick emerald carpet, light bouncing off in a dozen directions. The scanning electron microscope stood proud with a gaggle of admiring Japanese businessmen around it, all signing order forms that would turn the company's finances around and secure pay rises for everyone from the cleaner all the way up to Wally Walton.

'It's meant to be industrial-looking,' she said. 'That's the fashion.'

'Like t'Pompidou Centre?' asked Eric.

'Well, yes,' said Jennifer, surprised.

Eric shook his head. 'Sorry to disagree, love, but I reckon that look's a bit dated now. Folks have got over the excitement of that Rogers and Piano exoskeleton stuff. You could have got away with it in the nineties, maybe even the noughties, but Zeitgeist's moved on now.'

Jennifer stared at him.

'I can't see it representing the company abroad,' said Eric. 'Do more harm than good, I'd have thought.'

'Oh!' said Jennifer.

'Anyroad,' he said, looking at his watch. 'It's getting toward my clocking-off time. Think on, lass.'

And he and his assistant were away in their usual on-the-dot fashion, not a minute before three twenty-seven and not a minute after.

Eric wasn't the only one who didn't like the stand. The next morning, Greg jogged into Packing, stopped abruptly and wheeled round to face her, legs apart, hands on knees and chest heaving. If his pristine white trainers were anything to go by, this was the first time he'd ever exercised outside of a gym.

'Are you all right?' she asked.

'No. But never mind that. I don't like the look of your project. The way you've divided the compartments, for instance: they look uneven. Can't you make 'em more uniform?'

'Well, all the products have different footprints,' she said.

'I know that,' said Greg. 'But that doesn't mean the stand has to look like a dog's dinner.'

He surveyed it again. 'It just isn't right.'

'Any ideas how I can improve it?' asked Jennifer.

'Nope. That's your job,' said Greg. 'Sheesh kebab! This jogging thing takes a bit of getting used to. Have you written that press release for Electronics News yet?'

'It won't take long,' said Jennifer.

Greg slapped the fat around his middle. 'It's taken twenty years to accumulate. I doubt I'll get rid of it that easily. Listen, I know you've not finished yet with this stand design business, but I could do with bringing the sales team in, get 'em used to the idea that they're going to have to put the thing up in Zurich. Can you give 'em a quick demo?'

'What? When?'

'Just show them how the bits interlock.'

'But what if they don't like it, as you obviously don't? Can't the demo wait till I've come up with something better?'

Greg waved this objection aside. 'Credit them with a bit more imagination than that. Look, I'll bring them along later this morning. After the sales meeting. I'll do a bit of spiel to introduce the idea then hand straight over to you. Come on, don't wimp out on me. As a designer you'd have bigger presentations than that to do.'

'Oh God,' she said. 'Well, all right.'

An hour later Greg, the five salesmen and Jocasta entered Packing rather gingerly, not wanting to contaminate their suits. Jocasta was wearing a see-through white lace top and everyone's shoes gleamed like puddles in moonlight. Jennifer noticed that her own shoes were filthy.

The group took one look at the stand then shook their heads more or less in unison. The atmosphere was grim, like the final scene of a Shakespearean tragedy.

'So this is it?' said Jocasta. 'This is what you're expecting us to take to Zurich?'

Her Glaswegian accent made Switzerland's financial capital sound like the result of a session with Vicks Vapour Rub.

Greg cleared his throat. 'Yes,' he said. 'This is the Omega system. Jennifer here found it languishing in a far corner of the stock room and worked out, much to her credit, how to put it together.'

Jennifer stared. Had he just complimented her?

Various murmurs. A salesman clapped, but slowly.

'She's keen to pass the knowledge to you guys,' said Greg.

Jennifer tried to look keen.

Jocasta raised an eyebrow. The other salesmen shuffled. Greg soldiered on.

'Another great thing,' he said, 'is that you only need one tool to construct it: an Allen Key. Oh, and a modicum of common sense.'

He seemed to consider making a joke then decided against it. 'Have you got an Allen key to hand, Jenny?'

He took the key from her and held it up.

'Fuck!' said someone. 'It's one of those things you get at IKEA.'

'Is it going to be like putting up an IKEA wardrobe?' said someone else. 'What if we can't do it? We'll be a laughing stock.'

'We'll be a laughing stock if we can, and all,' said a third.

Greg looked ill at ease. 'Let's not lose sight of the end product. The end product is growth for the company's international sales platform. We're all accountable for that, and must all play our part in achieving it. If that involves a bit of mucking in at times, a bit of teamwork, so be it.'

'Nah,' said Jocasta. 'We're sales people. We need to spend our time at the show schmoozing clients, not fannying around with hardware. First you ask us to prepare our own sales quotations. Now we've got to build our own exhibition stand? It's not a productive use of our skill set.'

She said this so matter-of-factly it was hard not to agree. The other salespeople murmured their assent.

But then Jennifer heard herself speak. 'It's not really building,

Jocasta. It's more assembling. And it's easy. It's like a matrix: you just add bits on.'

Jocasta looked surprised at this interruption. But she didn't find it necessary to reply. She went on addressing Greg.

'Have you actually been to an electronics exhibition recently? They're incredibly high-tech. No one in their right mind would exhibit with a bunch of rusty poles like this.'

'It's not rust,' said Greg. 'It's discolouration. And Jennifer's going to give it a proper spray soon.'

Jennifer didn't like to say she'd already done this: twice.

'Anyway,' said Jocasta, 'if we're talking about Zurich, there's more chance of Lady Gaga appearing on our stand than the new scanning electron microscope. Word is that the software's not ready. Now, if it's all right with you guys, I've got clients to ring. I've got sales to clinch. I've got to help the company grow its international sales platform – which we can do perfectly well without erecting a pile of mouldy-looking scaffolding in Switzerland.'

And she walked out, leaving Jennifer and the circle of men clearing their throats and glancing in a bovine manner at each other. You had to admire her.

'She really liked it, then,' said someone.

They all laughed, except Greg.

When they'd all gone, Jennifer stood looking at her stand. She couldn't help feeling wounded by everyone's criticism. What did any of them – including Jocasta – really know? None of them had spent hours on YouTube as she had, looking at clips of electronics shows. Her design stood up brilliantly in that context. Well, it stood up. You just had to embrace minimalism as the guiding design principle.

But as she walked, yet again, around her structure, she realised that the imaginary Japanese businessmen who had clustered around it had stopped smiling and were walking away.

She came to a dispirited halt next to Eric's display of postcards. A beach scene; a mountain village; the Casa Batllo, one of Gaudi's buildings in Barcelona. Its windows, like holes in a membrane, reminded her of the story of Baba Yaga, the witch who lived in a house that stood on chicken's legs.

She spun round suddenly on her heel to see if the stand looked any better when you surprised it. But what she saw instead was that the stand, for all its clever structure, did indeed look more like something you would see on a building site and less like an international launch pad for a company at the cutting edge of technology.

Greg and the sales team would never be happy showing their clients around it. And nor would she if her first foray into the design world made her a laughing stock.

As she left Packing, she wondered how on earth she was going to make the stand look decent on a budget that the green Hammerite had already taken a hammer to. It was a major challenge, her chances of success probably as spindly as Baba Yaga's chicken legs.

She walked slowly back to her desk, trying not to feel discouraged. You had to be positive when it came to creative projects. You hit a block, and often that was the precursor to a really extraordinary idea. At least, that was what her tutors had said. Unfortunately, they had been less forthcoming about how you actually came up with the extraordinary idea.

18. *Coffee and carrot cake*

It had to be admitted that the dating venture hadn't been a success so far. Nevertheless, Jennifer rose dutifully the next morning, Saturday, to get Alicia breakfasted and settled for ten o'clock, so she could go off to meet her last date, Andy (unemployed, dolphins) for coffee. He'd said couldn't afford lunch.

Now she was near the end of the dating process, she wondered if it was worth trawling back through the Faint Possibilities shoebox. Then again, the idea made her feel weary. Perhaps she should give it a rest after Andy and try again with a new advert later in the year. Give Alicia more time to get used to the idea. At the thought of the whole thing being over, she felt mightily relieved. At least there would be nothing to lie about.

At ten past ten, saying she was going shopping, which was true in a way, she plucked her smart jacket from the coat stand. Putting her keys in the pocket, she felt something hard. It was the small brown envelope and its contents.

'Hah! I can't believe I keep forgetting this,' she said, pushing a foot into a shoe as she tore it open.

When she saw what was inside, she stopped with one shoe on, one shoe off. Something cool and smooth had slid into her palm, wrapped in a yellow Post-it note. It was a pewter ankh, solid and worn as an old coin.

Memories spooled in her head. He never used to take that ankh off, even when they were in bed together. Sometimes, when he was asleep, she would reach out and touch it, believing in its power as an amulet, thanking it for bringing them together. After all, it was one of the first things she'd noticed about him. She'd interpreted it as a sign of an inner self more gentle than the outer one, with all its ripped leather and stubble. She had been right, too.

'Oh,' she whispered.

She turned the Post-it note over. A phone number with a faraway code. A familiar code.

She stood staring at the ankh for a few moments longer, then closed her hand on it and held it, tightly.

The café, *Pied a Terre*, was at a crossroads in the student area. Jennifer stood outside while young people who looked as if they were still in bed drifted past. Hyde Park was just a few miles down the road from where she lived, but it was another country. Leeds was like that. Maybe every city was like that: intense pockets of contrasting life side by side.

As a skinny, feline-looking man in torn jeans crossed the road towards her she was already fingering the pendant and resolving to cut the date as short as she could.

'You must be Jennifer?'

She nodded. He had dark blond, tousled hair and brown eyes behind gold-rimmed specs.

The café wasn't to her taste, not because it was studenty but because it was so cramped. Five hefty pine tables jostled for space. Three were already occupied, so everyone's conversation was going to be audible to everyone else. Leaflets advertising yoga, crystal healing and Hopi ear candles eclipsed each other on a notice board.

Andy and Jennifer squeezed in opposite each other. Even a thin person would have felt claustrophobic with this arrangement.

'You found it all right, then,' said Andy.

'Mm. Is it your local?'

'Yeah.'

There was a pause.

'So, where do you live?' he asked.

'North Leeds.'

He drew his chair closer to the table. 'Um, where in North Leeds?'

She tried to edge back, but was jammed in by the table behind. 'Near Adel.'

'Where exactly?'

'Oh, an estate of semis. Pretty anonymous.'

'Which estate?'

It was Trevor all over again. Didn't any of these men have tact? 'You extract information pretty quickly, don't you?'

'Hey,' he said. He took a squashed handkerchief out of his jeans pocket and wiped his glasses.

She realised she'd hurt his feelings.

'Sorry,' she said.

She must make an effort, Bobby or no Bobby. 'It's just that we women aren't supposed to give out too much info on these dates, or so the paper says. You might be an axe murderer.'

He glanced at her handbag. 'So might you. There's room for an axe in there.'

She couldn't help laughing.

They ordered coffee and carrot cake.

'So, what do you do?' she asked, when it arrived. 'Oops, sorry. You're unemployed.'

'It's all right,' he said. 'It's a political statement. I'm a constructive anarchist.'

'What's one of those?'

By way of answer, he told her about a project he'd helped set up in an old church. He called it a 'reclaimed social space', talked about massive pots of vegan chilli cooked up to feed homeless people. It was quite interesting.

She told him about her job. She had to admit he was a good listener. He seemed to see through the words to the meaning of what was being said.

Still, when the waitress finally brought the bill, she was relieved. 'Well, it's been nice meeting you.'

'Same,' he said, grinning. 'So, er, do you want to do it again?'

She hesitated. 'Mm, not sure. Someone from my past got in touch this morning. Someone I was very close to.'

He held up his hand to stop her. 'It's cool. There's no need for excuses.'

She stared at him in dismay. 'No. Really. That *is* what happened.'

He pushed a tower of small denomination coins into the centre of the table.

'Whatever. That should cover mine. Sorry about the change.'

'No problem,' she said.

'Be seeing you then,' he said.

'See you,' she said. 'Listen, I ... .'

But he was already out of the door and jogging across the road with a long, loping stride, holding his hand up in acknowledgement to the cars that had stopped for him at the traffic lights.

And then there was nothing to do but leave too. She headed for the blackened church spire that signalled her parking spot. So, that was her dating venture completely finished. Not with a bang, either, but with a silly gaffe, an awkward little whimper.

Thoughts about her meeting with Andy plagued her for the rest of the day, and a couple of times she nearly picked up the phone to call him. But the cool hard presence of the ankh stopped her. She touched it repeatedly, letting its smooth contours spirit her away.

Later by the phone, she studied the Post-it note again. The glue strip had lost its stick and was covered with fluff and dirt.

But there was no other writing on it: just the number with the Portsmouth code.

Joanna Lumley, one of Alicia's favourites, was on TV, and the sound seeped through the closed sitting room door.

With her heart in her mouth, Jennifer picked up the phone and dialled.

It rang out at the other end. What sort of room was it ringing in, she wondered? She pictured a long hall with polished floorboards.

An answering machine clicked on. She breathed out, at once disappointed and relieved. She thought about hanging up, but didn't, because the voice message must surely be in his voice. But there was another click.

'Jackson Construction.'

Her stomach turned over. That gravelly northern voice: there was no mistaking it. But was this a work number? What was he doing at work on a Saturday night? She adjusted her mental picture to a Portakabin, Venetian blinds.

'Bobby?' she asked

'This is Bob Jackson speaking, yes.'

'It's me. J.' Odd to be calling herself that after all these years.

A missed beat. Then, 'So it was you, in the ad. I knew it. And you got my note.'

'And your ankh.'

Then they both spoke at once. 'It was a long shot ... .' 'I never thought ... .'

She laughed. 'You could have just sent it here. I'm still at the same address.'

There was a pause.

'Yes, still living with Mum,' she added, before he asked. 'But how did you get to see my advert? It was only in the local paper.'

'Ah, I always get the local paper when I'm up. I'm a sucker for stories about dogs digging up Roman coins in people's back gardens in Armley.'

'You've been up?'

'The M1 still goes all the way.'

There was a pause.

'You've got your own company now. By the sound of it,' she said.

'Ah, it's just an office in my house, don't get too excited. But yeah, I travel all over nowadays. Vancouver. Riyadh. Wapping. You? Are you working for some swanky design company now and developing a crostini habit?'

'I wish. I'm still a PA. Still working at the microscope factory, too.'

'What's going on? That place should have gone bust years ago.'

'It more or less has.'

They talked on.

She couldn't help thinking of slim hips, dark curls forever falling into eyes. He would have changed, of course, but without knowing how, she couldn't imagine it. Perhaps he had no hair at all, now. Perhaps he was four stone overweight, like her.

'I never thought I'd see that ankh again,' she said suddenly, interrupting a story he was telling about a big contract in the Far East.

There was another pause.

'I never was one for throwing things out,' he said. Look, it's a bit weird, talking to you on the phone.'

'Mm.'

'How about … why don't we meet the next time I come up?'

Even though this was what she wanted, she hesitated.

'I'm up in a few days' time as it happens,' he said.

'A few days?'

'You don't sound very keen.'

'Sorry! No, of course I'm keen.'

'If you want to leave it for a while, I'll be up again in two months.'

Two months sounded ages away. 'No, next week's fine.'

'Good. I'll give you a ring on Monday, once I know what I'm doing, sort out a time and a place.'

'Can we meet on Tuesday? It's easier, with Mum. It's her night out.'

A missed beat.

'You know how it is,' said Jennifer.

He didn't say anything.

'So … talk to you on Monday, then?' she asked.

'Sure. Sure. Monday it is,' he said, and then he was gone, and the conversation with the love of her life twelve years on was over and done, leaving her with an arrangement that had been easily made, as if seeing each other was the most normal thing in the world.

As she put the phone down and went into the kitchen to make Alicia a cup of tea, fear and excitement fluttered together in her stomach like moths rising out of a cupboard that hadn't been opened for years.

Although a few were printed out or photocopied, the letters in Jennifer's 'Absolute No's', 'Faint Possibilities' and 'Definite Yeses' shoeboxes were mostly handwritten.

Emptied out onto the shed workbench that Sunday, they made a varied pile, with their different shades and grades of paper, their blue, black, green and gold ink, their bold or tentative writing slanting this way and that.

I like to pamper and spoil a Lady.

I have sixty occupations. Vintner. Professional gambler. Film Director.

My name is Tron and I live at the House of Ping.

You lookin' at da man, watch me pull mah pants up, watch me do my dance, yup.

I am listed in Debrett's People of Today. My ambition is to produce a Son et Lumiere of the Kaiser Chiefs' music.

The variety and madness of the pile as a whole had both scared and fascinated her.

But looking at them now, she saw that they had one thing in common. They had all been written by people every bit as lonely as she was.

It had always seemed wrong to throw them out. And now she had an idea. She took a handful of letters, lined up their edges. Tearing decisively through the different thicknesses and textures, she rendered them into strips.

Soon the workbench was covered in a thousand fluttery, curly tongues.

She mixed wallpaper paste, took a brush and began sticking them, one by one, onto the wire skeleton that had been standing there now for weeks, waiting for its skin.

An hour later, she stood back to admire her handiwork.

Dear Jennifer, DEAR JENNIFER, Dear Jeniffer, said the animal's torso.

I have been described as very groomed, said the back of the head.

I always Support myself on my Elbows, said the bottom jaw.

Should now a possibility of a chance that we might meet, the likeness of both of us we need to see and kept, said the hindquarters.

When Jennifer closed the shed door on her sculpture, every square centimetre of its body was plastered with paper and words. It had a skin now. And that skin was imbued with as much hunger for touch as a real skin. It was a fitting tribute, thought Jennifer, to hope and longing. And love.

19. *Lime marmalade*

How soon work came round again. Some weekends, Jennifer was sure that Atlas, or whoever it was who held up the Earth, gave the planet an extra hard spin so that Saturday and Sunday merged into a blur and Monday arrived early.

She was standing in the hall eating toast and trying to prepare herself for the week ahead when the letterbox rattled. Two identical white envelopes fell onto the doormat, one addressed to her mum and one to her.

As soon as Alicia saw them she said, 'Ah, from the surgery. Sit down, dear. Eating standing up is deleterious to the digestion.'

But Jennifer had already opened her letter and was scanning it. Her stomach did a nosedive.

Beneath the turquoise and navy logo of the medical centre, it said: *We write to inform you that our senior partner, Dr Narendra Ganguly, retires at the end of December. While we are sorry to lose him, we are delighted to welcome his replacement, Dr Aloysius Lethem … .*

It just went to show: if you put off dealing with a problem long enough, in the end the problem came and dealt with you. She glanced apprehensively at her mother. But Alicia, although she had finished reading the letter, was merely helping herself to another slice of toast, a little smile on her lips.

'Have you read that letter?' Jennifer asked.

Alicia reached for the butter. 'Yes, dear.'

'Properly?'

'Of course, properly.'

Jennifer wondered if the two letters had been the same. But they must have been. She sank down into a chair. 'How come you're still looking so perky, then? Aren't you gutted?'

Alicia frowned. 'What an unpleasant expression, dear. One of – what's she called? - Nasher's sayings? This tea is delicious, isn't it? Nelly picked it out for me at Waitrose. Tippy Golden Flowery Orange Pekoe.'

Jennifer stared at her mother. Perhaps she simply had no idea what a change of doctor might mean. But it would be too cruel to leave her labouring under that delusion. Jennifer must at least *try* to prepare her.

'Mum. We need to have a serious talk.'

'Very well, dear. But pass me the marmalade first, if you will.'

Somehow, on the journey between Jennifer's and Alicia's fingers, the jar of lime marmalade managed to teeter on its saucer, fall onto the table then roll onto the floor, where it smashed on the floorboards.

'Oh! Clumsy me,' said Alicia. 'You'll have to get a dustpan and brush.'

'In a minute, Mum,' said Jennifer. 'I need to talk to you first.'

'No, now.' said Alicia. 'Or Pepe will cut himself.'

There was no arguing with this. Jennifer fetched the dustpan and went down on her knees, clearing up the mess with one hand and trying to stop Pepe licking up marmalade and broken glass with the other. It was not the best position from which to conduct a serious conversation. Nevertheless, if she waited till she was in a more vertical position, the moment might be lost.

'Does it occur to you,' she said from under the table, 'that the new doctor might not be able to see you every week? Might not want to?'

She finished picking up the bigger pieces of glass and began trying to brush the splinters into the dustpan. Pepe stayed at the edge of the scene, bobbing about like a cork on water.

'Has that dog cut his tongue?' asked Alicia.

'I'm trying to talk to you about something important,' said Jennifer to Alicia's knees.

'Oh, don't worry about the *surgery*. I'm one of their best patients.'

Jennifer crawled out from under the table with a dustpan full of sticky sharp mess. 'Mum, the best patients are the ones who never visit, not the ones who visit every week.'

Alicia had produced a little mirror and was applying fresh lipstick. She pressed her lips together, rolled them to distribute the colour then inspected her smile from all angles.

'Yes, dear. But Narendra will still be around. He only lives just around the corner. Plumtree Avenue. And with that nice black Honda Civic.'

'But he's *retiring*. He won't want to see you then. And Dr Lethem might take a different approach. An alternative approach. One you might not like.'

Alicia's lipstick smile showed no sign of faltering.

'Do you know what I'm talking about?' asked Jennifer.

'I think so, darling. Acupuncture, and so on. Rebirthing. Osteopathy. The one with the furniture – Chop Suey. We get them all, down at the community centre.'

'Mum! I don't mean alternative medicine. I mean, alternatives within the medical field itself. I mean psych ... .'

Alicia interrupted. 'That dog! He's got hold of the lid, darling. Don't you think you'd better get it off him? And by the way, can you get me some teething rings today? If you can spare the time, that is. Mothercare stock them. And Sainsbury's.'

'Teething rings? What do you want teething rings for?'

'You freeze them, dear. Marvellous for puffy eyes. You just pop them on. Like cold teabags.'

Jennifer stopped talking and stared at her mother. 'You're not up to something, are you?'

'*Up* to something?'

'Yes. Like making an arrangement with Dr Ganguly.'

'Arrangement? What sort of arrangement?' Alicia's eyes were blue and innocent.

'Oh, how do I know? To pay him privately after he retires, perhaps? Not that we can afford it. I mean, have you looked at your bank statements recently? There was £3.12 in your current account the last time I looked. That's not enough to keep him in Grecian 2000 or whatever it is men of his age wear.'

Alicia gave a gay little laugh. 'I don't know what you're talking about.'

'Hm,' said Jennifer.

And she took the dustpan and brush back to the kitchen, where she had to stand for ten minutes picking sticky sharp splinters out of the brush's bristles. Something was afoot. What it was, she had no idea.

But at least her mother wasn't upset about the letter. That was a blessing and would have to do for now.

If Jennifer had learnt anything from her lonely hearts venture, it was that the more you fantasised about something in advance, the more disappointing it was when it finally happened. But at work that day, walking around the exhibition stand and willing the light bulb in her head to burst into illumination, all she could think about was Bobby: Bobby, dressed in leather; Bobby, taking off his helmet and grinning at her; Bobby, not speaking, just beckoning her to get on the bike.

'Do you call this work?' asked Greg, as he entered the packing room and found her staring into space. 'From where I'm standing, it looks like slacking.'

'It might seem as if I'm doing nothing,' she said. 'But the wheels of creativity are still turning.'

'Wheels, my arse. There are four old instruction manuals on your desk. They need scanning and emailing to Russia. Some college out there is skint enough to buy up our old microscopes.'

He turned to go then turned back. 'One more thing. Might as well broach it with you sooner rather than later. The sales team have refused point blank to put your stand up in Zurich.'

'I gathered that,' said Jennifer, 'Wait till they see what I'm going to come up with.'

'No,' said Greg. 'I mean they won't put it up in any circumstances.'

'Oh.'

'We can't afford to pay an outsider to do it,' said Greg. 'And we can't take anyone off the shop floor: overtime payments would cripple us. So how about it?'

'How about what?'

'Coming out to Zurich.'

'Zurich?'

Greg rolled his eyes. 'Yeah, Zurich: largest city in Switzerland; home of cuckoo clocks and Toblerone; founded by Charlemagne's grandson, Louis the German; urban population of one million. Heard of it?'

'I thought we had to save money.'

'Don't be so bloody honourable. We need your manpower, sorry I mean horsepower, sorry, I mean input. And it'll be ten days on expenses. Derek in Finance will be complaining about you, not to you. Worth it for that alone I'd have thought. There's muesli, trams, snow, a watch museum, string quartets. You can eat fondue, go in a sauna. Not naked, obviously. What do you think?'

Before she could reply, he said. 'And if you're worried about your mother, we can cough up a few quid for the neighbour, all right?'

Breaking that particular bit of news to Alicia hardly bore thinking about. But it would be mad to turn Greg down.

'I'm in,' she said.

'Good,' said Greg. 'Welcome to Team Zurich! Our hotshot designer. Oh, and can you clean out my coffee machine? The hotplate's covered in brown gunk.'

As soon as Jennifer got back to her desk, and the manuals, the phone rang.

It was Nyesha. 'I've been ringing your mobile all day.'

'Sorry. It needs charging.'

'Why didn't you ring me yesterday? Come to that, why didn't you ring me last week?'

'Sorry,' said Jennifer, who had ignored Nyesha's messages for a few days now. 'I've just been really busy. Talking of which, guess what? Greg's just asked me to go to Zurich to put the stand up.'

'That's great,' said Nyesha. 'But listen, what was Andy like?'

'He was okay. Nothing special.'

But Nyesha was waiting for more.

'All right, he was nice,' said Jennifer.

'So you gelled?'

'A bit, I suppose. As I say, he was quite nice.'

'And?'

'There is no "and".'

'Why not?'

Jennifer sighed. 'The dates thing hasn't worked out, Nesh. That's all there is to it. In retrospect, I don't think it was ever really me.'

There was a pause.

'Fair enough,' said Nyesha. 'But you normally say more about the specifics. You bent my ear about Trevor for nearly an hour.'

'I'm not really in the mood today. I'm sorry.'

Nyesha sighed. 'I'm sorry, too. I really hoped this dating thing would work out for you.'

There was another pause, longer this time.

'There's something you're not telling me,' said Nyesha. 'Something's happened. What is it?'

Jennifer hesitated.

'Jen?'

'Mm … nothing's happened, not really. I'm sorry, Nesh, I've got to go: Greg's coming. We're not supposed to take too many private calls.'

'That's never stopped you before.'

It was true.

But more true was the fact that some things were too precious to tell anybody, even your best friend.

20. *Amaretto*

The afternoon of her date with Bobby, Jennifer was sitting in the printer's office in front of the slithering mass of papers that was his desk.

She'd called in a few times over the past weeks, liking the atmosphere of the place and liking Robert too, who was usually more than happy to bring out the china cups again and have a quick chin wag before she collected her box of brochures, or some business cards she'd had printed for someone back at work.

Today she had been keen to escape scanning the instruction manuals, a job that was off the scale tedium-wise. She also wanted to escape her own mind, where pictures of Bobby still seethed, his black curls peppered with grey, his body stringier but still strong. The quick conversation they'd had yesterday to fix up the details of their meeting hadn't helped.

Robert brought in a cafetière of coffee.

'Oh, that's nice of you,' she said. 'I hope I'm not keeping you from anything.'

The coffee grounds swirled then floated up to the surface in a thick, grainy band.

'Oh, what's to be kept from?' said Robert, who was wearing a red spotted bow tie. 'I shouldn't say it – it is my own business after all, but sometimes it's frightfully dull.'

She glanced around his office. It was even more of a tip than usual. Next to teetering columns of paper stood old lemonade bottles full of different coloured inks and powders. 'Been having a clear out?'

'Yes. Yuk! Old print gives me the heebie-jeebies.'

While he poured the coffee, Jennifer looked at a stack of billboard-size posters, hanging over the edge of a table so that they hid its legs completely. The paper curve reminded her of one of the Gaudi buildings she'd seen on Eric's postcards. In front stood a row of plastic bottles, reminding her of castle turrets. Such cheap, mass-produced things, plastic bottles, and yet they came in lovely shapes.

Robert handed her a cup of coffee. 'It's the thought of all that information that once seemed so *vital*, now completely redundant. Redolent of one's own mortality, I suppose.'

He began talking about how packs of business cards sometimes outlived clients then threw his hands up in horror.

'Hark at me! Getting all morbid when we've only just started our elevenses.'

But Jennifer was only half listening. She was still staring at the posters. Casa Batllo. That was the name of the Gaudi building.

Robert put his cup down on his desk, where it tilted recklessly. 'Are you all right, sweetie? You look a bit dazed.'

It was strange, the knowledge that you'd had a good idea. Strange, that the abstract thing in your imagination was more real and more exciting than any of the actual, solid real things in the room around you.

'Robert,' said Jennifer, urgently. 'Might you be able to let me have some boxes of waste paper?'

Robert looked puzzled. 'Well, it is the one thing we have in spades.'

'Anything would do. Newsprint, bank, bond. The size and colour wouldn't matter. And do you know where I could get hold of a load of plastic bottles?'

'Robert leant back in his chair and bounced his pencil against his teeth. 'As it happens, one of our most valued clients, a Mr

Brian Kelly, runs a firm called BK Packaging. They supply all manner of bottles for the fizzy drinks industry.'

Jennifer frowned. 'Oh, I don't think we could run to buying new stock.'

Robert smiled. 'No, dear. I haven't dealt with your company for five years without knowing that. I mention Brian because he often has waste stock. Bottles that haven't come up to standard. Perhaps he'd be willing to let some of those go, for a small fee.'

'Really? That'd be brilliant!'

'But what do you want them for?'

She hesitated.

'Well, it would be a way of … designing something.'

He waited expectantly.

She wondered whether to tell him or not. He was being so kind. But perhaps she ought to be circumspect for once in her life.

'Look, I *will* tell you,' she said. 'But I need to think it through first. And run it past Greg. And probably a few other people too.'

'Oh, spoilsport!' said Robert. 'I shall try to contain my curiosity.'

He sat looking at her for a few moments, playing the xylophone of his teeth with his pencil again.

'It's no good,' he said. 'Loyal as I am to that dear man who is your boss, I'm going to have to show you something.'

He sprang up, and went to the back of the room. He talked while he rummaged behind a cupboard.

'To be frank, you'd be better off running your design ideas past me than you would him. However blessed he is in the dynamism department, the poor love doesn't have a creative bone in his body.'

He brought out some artwork and laid it in front of her. It had been printed off from the computer and mounted on a board.

'Read, mark, learn and inwardly digest,' he said, brushing the

130

dust off his sleeves.

It took her a few moments to realise that the designs she was looking at were for her company's recently revamped logo.

Her eyes roved over the different suggestions. 'These are great! I love that purple one, with the magnifying glass effect. It's so clever.'

'Thank you,' said Robert. 'They were only initial roughs, of course. Our design associate, James, thought your boss could choose his favourites and we'd work them up into something decent. But we never got that far.'

Jennifer's eyes came to rest on the most staid logo of all. In fact, it could hardly be described as a logo: it was just a small triangle, then the company's name, written in Times New Roman. The format that, shortly after Greg's arrival, had come to adorn all their headed stationery and compliments slips. The penny dropped.

'He picked this one.'

Robert nodded gravely.

'I rest my case. Be careful, sweetie. When it comes to your design idea, be careful who you tell what to. And in what detail.'

Even a brilliant idea wasn't proof against the terrifying prospect of meeting the love of your life twelve years and four extra stone later. By the time Jennifer arrived at Salvatore's to get her hair done, her stomach was in free fall.

Tony let her in to the salon, his eyes roaming freely over her body.

'Can I use the toilet?' she asked.

'Boss don't normally let customers in there. Bit pongy. No ventilation, see.'

'I'll manage.'

He led her grudgingly to the back of the salon, where a door opened into a cramped passageway.

Going behind the sleek frontage of the salon was like going

backstage. The lino floor was grubby and planks of wood stood on end against the corridor walls. In a kitchenette, the Gaggia machine bowed down a worktop.

Opposite was the toilet. When she opened the door, Jennifer recoiled. Tony was right: it stank and the pan was brown under the water level. Fearing asphyxiation, she left the door open a crack as she sat down.

A sudden draught told her the back door had opened, and through the crack she saw Salvatore, carrying shopping bags. She should push the door shut. But she was struck by his face, serious and even a bit sad-looking when he thought no one was looking, as off-stage as the salon itself. She watched him put things away in the kitchen.

'Tony! 'Ave you been smoking?' he shouted.

Tony's reply was inaudible.

'I 'ave the video!' called Salvatore. A rattle, as he shook the box. 'You father, he show you nothing. I show you something.'

When she went back into the salon, they were still talking about Tony's smoking.

'You give it up,' Salvatore was saying. 'If you do this, I take you to gym. I show you the sit-up, the press-up. We do the interval training.'

He smiled when he saw Jennifer. 'Tony, fetch the lady the special drink.'

'I'm fine thanks,' she said, but nevertheless while Salvatore pinned up her hair, Tony went out and reappeared with a small glass of brown liqueur.

'Italian,' Salvatore said. 'Is made from the almond. No very strong. You like.'

Jennifer sipped the syrupy drink. Salvatore was waiting for a verdict. 'Lovely,' she provided. 'Warming.'

While he cut her hair, the alcohol plus his light touch made her relax and she was grateful. He kept very close to her, inserting himself between her and the mirror to do her fringe. By mistake, she looked down his shirtfront. She saw smooth brown muscles, dark nipples. She dropped her gaze instantly to his feet. His shoes were immaculate white, with gold bars across the instep.

'Ey, not so much the jerk about!' he said, taking hold of her chin and raising her head. 'Keep a-still!'

His eyes, velvet brown, were only inches away.

She shut hers and tried to think about something else. But she couldn't avoid his smell. Warm and musky, it burst through the citrus of his aftershave. It was impossible not to breathe it in, impossible too, despite everything else that was happening in her life, not to find it rather nice.

21. *Posh sandwiches*

The city was caught in limbo between the late summer day and evening. In McDonalds, people ate fries out of red cartons but most shops were closed, their big windows dark, their rows of clothes lonely and ill lit. Clumps of girls, barelegged despite the autumnal chill, began to claim the pavements.

Jennifer drove the Mini against the flow of traffic, heading for the city centre multi-storey. She drove up through eerie floors then made her way down the stinking stairwell to the main shopping street.

She walked past Harvey Nicks then cut through Marks and Spencer's, which was still open, and bought a pair of fluorescent pink tanga knickers just for the comfort of having something to do. The aura of her purchase lasted to the top of the street where the café they were meeting in stood. There, she had to hang on to a lamppost and take several deep breaths.

The Portobello, a trendy place that had sprung up before the credit crunch, was narrow but went back a long way. Leather sofas at the front gave way to a bar area which gave way to tables at the back. Jennifer headed for the tables. Sandwiches involving fruit seemed to be the order of the day: chicken and mango; Brie and pear. They flew by on white hexagonal plates the size of small protectorates.

Most of the men in here were too young to be Bobby.

Reaching the tables, she turned back to the bar. And noticed someone she hadn't seen before: a slender fortyish looking man, dark hair shaven at the sides, curly on top. He was wearing a black leather jacket.

Her heart turned over and yet again she regretted having chosen the sober navy blue suit to wear.

She stood for a few moments, pretending to herself that she didn't know what to do. Then, gripping the green plastic handbag hard, she walked up to him.

'Hi! Are you Bobby?'

The face turned laconically towards her. It was designer-stubbled and a gold earring glittered in one ear.

'Well, most of my friends call me Rob. And you are?'

Jennifer's heart sank. 'I'm not surprised you don't recognise me. I've put on a lot of weight since we last met.'

The man looked puzzled.

The barman seemed to be wiping the same nearby bit of bar over and over again.

'Can I help?' said another voice. Jennifer turned to see a plump, grey man in a plump grey suit, holding out his hand.

She took it, grateful for a friendly intervention, even if it was only from the café manager. But the plump man smiled into her eyes. 'I think it's me you're looking for.'

And then she saw that although his hair was the colour of aluminium, it was curly. And although his face seemed wider than it was long, his smile was a smile she recognised. His eyes were a colour she remembered, too: the colour of horse chestnuts.

'Oh,' she said, in relief, wonder and disappointment. 'Yes.'

'It was the leather jacket that threw me,' she said, once they'd sat down and ordered drinks.

Bobby stowed his newspaper in his briefcase. 'That bloke's jacket is in a lot better condition than mine.'

'You've still got it, then?'

'And the Norton. Though it's only a weekend mode of transport these days, I'm afraid.'

'You look so much cleaner,' she said.

'Is that good or bad?'

'Oh, good, I think.'

They grinned at each other. It was hard not to stare. She was amazed at how he'd changed. And how he hadn't. A waiter came over with their drinks, tilting a chrome tray this way and that.

They chinked glasses. 'It really is good to see you,' said Bobby.

Jennifer sipped Amaretto. 'I'm sorry there's so much of me to see.'

'Don't be silly. What gets me is that you're still living with your mother. And working at that factory.'

'Though I'm sure you've got your reasons,' he added quickly. 'But did you really never make it to Uni? You were so keen to go.'

'I know,' she said. 'But it all seems ages ago now.'

She hoped that didn't sound too sad.

His hair still fell into his eyes, and he had to keep sweeping it aside.

They talked about work. He described some of the projects he'd been involved in. He told her about the house he lived in, an old dairy that he'd converted. He talked about a trust he'd set up to encourage disadvantaged youngsters into the building trade. The life he described was a million miles away from hers: a life full of solid achievements that you could see and touch.

'Wow,' she said, 'it sounds as if your life's completely sorted.'

He dropped his gaze. 'Well, I can't claim that.'

'How do you mean?'

He hesitated. 'Well, no one can really say they've got it all sorted, can they?'

They talked about old times next, reminiscing about his old student house with the nylon carpet that crackled when you walked across it in slippers, the gas fire that singed your calves and left the rest of your body freezing and the emerald dragon that a previous tenant had painted on the sitting room ceiling.

They laughed. But Jennifer felt sad imagining the house modernised into anonymity, with stripped floorboards and neutral décor, the dragon eclipsed by halogen lighting.

They ordered fresh drinks. He produced a tobacco tin with a Zippo lighter. He began rolling a cigarette.

'Therapeutic,' he said. 'I know I can't smoke it in here.'

She watched him nurse the tobacco, back and forth, back and forth in the liquorice paper. Watching that was like hearing a song she hadn't heard for years: nostalgia came in a blast, bringing back all those times she'd sat, in cafés, at people's houses, on the grass in the sunshine on Woodhouse Moor, waiting while he smoked. It had been limbo time: five minutes here, five minutes there. She had always pretended to resent it. But in reality, their relationship had never got old enough for her to resent anything he did.

It was no good wallowing in the past. 'How come you've never married?' she asked, more abruptly than she meant to.

The cigarette stopped rolling.

'Sorry,' she said. 'Perhaps you *have* been married.'

He put the cigarette down.

'More than once?' she guessed.

He looked up. 'I *am* married,' he said.

The words hung. Her mouth had gone dry. *Am married.* Of all the answers he might have given to her question, she had not considered that one. She stared at his hands. The hands that had used to touch her body. Clean, these days, as cut potatoes. The café door opened and she gazed towards the brief, bright rectangle of light.

'I've got kids as well,' he said.

She felt a sinking sensation inside, as if everything good was draining away. 'Right,' she said. 'Well, how nice.'

A party of girls in short skirts and fluffy bunny ears came in and began giggling with the barman. Jennifer could happily have wished them dead. The music had got louder. The place was turning into a club. It made more sense, as a club.

'Tom's eight,' he said. 'Samantha's eleven.'

'Eleven?'

She did the maths in her head.

'But weren't we still together then? At least technically?'

'I know it sounds bad,' said Bobby. 'But Vicky – she's my wife now – worked for the same company, and ... .'

She could have done without the details. But he talked on, about how he'd begun to doubt that Jennifer was ever going to leave her mother and come south. About how Vicky had always fancied him, about how, one night after an office party, he'd given in to temptation, about how they'd both been horrified when they found out she was pregnant. About how they had wondered whether to keep the baby.

Jennifer sat, gripping her upper arms. Now he was talking about how it had never been right between Vicky and him, about how he got lonely and missed 'old friends'.

The expression made her suddenly furious. 'And that's the reason you got in touch with me? For old times' sake?'

'Well, yes.'

'Why didn't you just write to me? Or phone? As I said, Mum and I are still in the same house. Why send me your ankh, like that? It's such a romantic gesture. I thought ... well, it doesn't matter what I thought.'

He looked shamefaced. 'I've been on the verge of getting in touch loads of times. But you know what life's like.'

'I'm not sure I do,' she said icily. 'I have no idea what your life's like, anyway.'

'Oh, come on. You know what I mean. Time goes by. And it goes by in everyone's life, yours too. I didn't think you'd still be living with your Mum, not twelve years on. Look, I saw your ad, and acted on impulse. Was that really such a bad thing to do?'

She looked at his confused face. He always had been clumsy with feelings. But this was taking clumsiness to a new level.

She stood up.

'Where are you going?' he asked.

'To the Ladies.'

He glanced at the inch of wine she had left. 'Shall I get you another drink?'

'No, I'm fine, thank you.'

He checked his watch. 'You're probably right. Probably best call it a night.'

She suffered an unexpected jolt of pain. 'Oh!'

She stared at him. But if she was expecting him to beg her to stay he wasn't going to, and she marched off to the Ladies full of resentment and frustration.

It wasn't how she'd been hoping to feel on this date, she thought grimly as she stood at the row of stainless steel basins under lighting designed for people in their teens and twenties. She tried to compose herself. But the face that looked back at her from the mirror was miserable and confused. She didn't know how to be, with this new information.

They didn't linger over the last of their drinks and outside, on the pavement, their hug was stiff.

'I suppose we've finally reached the point where you tell me to fuck off out of your life for good,' he said. 'As you probably should have the day you met me at that bus stop.'

His self-deprecation wasn't attractive. And in a way, she did want to tell him to fuck off. But that was only part of the story.

'I don't know,' she said.

He took both her hands in his.

She couldn't look at him. 'Thanks,' he said. 'Thanks for not knowing.'

She shrugged, not trusting herself to say more.

He walked backwards a couple of steps, still holding her hands. Then he let go and smiled and turned. And then he was walking away. She stood, rooted to the spot. He reached the corner and she wondered if he would look back. But he didn't.

Still she stood, in the middle of the pavement, looking to where he had been. She wondered if she might run after him. But her legs started walking again, taking her up the hill back to the car park, back to the heart of the city.

22. *Cheese on toast*

She had heard of people throwing themselves into their work as a cure for heartbreak. But she had never done it herself. Until now, that was.

The next day she rang Greg's answering machine and said she was working at home all day and would not be available for calls. It was something he did regularly: that said, she wasn't sure he'd be happy about her doing it.

So she unplugged the landline and switched her mobile off, just in case. If he wanted her, he could drive round and get her.

The third bedroom at Woodlands Avenue was tiny. Any bed would have prevented the door opening, so inside there was just a desk and a PC. The room had good light and broadband though, neither of which took up any room. As a design studio it would do.

Jennifer spent the whole day in there, gazing fiercely at images on the Net, then kneeling on the floor over a large piece of sugar paper. Hours vanished in little pencil studies and extravagant sweepings of marker pen.

She hardly ate, apart from some cheese on toast and a cup of tea, and even those cooled on the windowsill while she worked. The idea for the exhibition stand took shape.

'You're not yourself today,' said Alicia when Jennifer went down to make her lunch. 'Surely, if one is well organised at work, there should be no need to work like this at home? I hope you're not being taken advantage of. I do worry about you sometimes, dear. You need to stand up for yourself more.'

'Don't worry, Mum,' said Jennifer. 'I'm all right.'

Perhaps if she kept saying it, it would be true.

But it wasn't true that night, as she lay tossing and turning in bed. And it wasn't true the next morning, when she got up and went into work early, carrying her drawings in a tube.

Eric was in Goods Inwards. 'There's some boxes arrived for you, lass. They weigh a ton, like.'

Glad of a distraction, she followed him to where twenty large boxes stood, sealed with Stebbing Print tape. Eric split it with his Stanley knife and they both stared at a great mass of paper off-cuts and misprints, ghostly off kilter images of magenta, cyan and yellow.

'What nob-head's sent you this shite?' said Eric.

'It's all right,' said Jennifer. 'It's shite I asked for.'

Her day of working at home hadn't gone down as badly as she'd feared, with Greg. He'd muttered a bit, but had backed off when she brandished the tube of drawings at him.

There was still work to do though, so she went up to the stock room, made an ad hoc drawing board from a couple of old dining room chairs and an old graphics panel and began on a drawing of the stand's rear elevation. Time passed as it had the previous day: slowly then in great chunks, as if someone was winding the clock forwards when she wasn't looking. She was grateful. The sooner this day was over, and a few more days besides, the better. In the absence of any other kind of healing strategy, the passage of time would have to do.

Two sets of footsteps came down the corridor.

'We should find those brochures in here,' said Jocasta Jardine, flinging the door open.

She was wearing thigh-hugging trousers and seemed to have nothing on underneath her jacket. Beside her, the salesman, one of the company's oldest, looked unfairly dilapidated.

'Oh!' she said, eyeing the drawing. 'What's that you've got there?'

'Nothing.'

But she came round anyway and peered over Jennifer's shoulder. Her perfume smelt like aftershave. 'It doesnae look like nothing to me.'

'It's only a sketch. You can't tell anything from it.'

But Jocasta stood there, cocking her head and looking amused.

'Will you take a look at this?' she said to her colleague. 'It's wild. Those things like mushrooms. And is that meant to be a window?'

The salesman came round to have a look but his face remained unmoved. Jocasta on the other hand, eyed Jennifer with something approaching interest. 'Bit of a dark horse, aren't you? On you go: we'll leave you in peace. We'll not interrupt the creative process. I wouldn't like to have that on my conscience.'

The room seemed to exhale when they'd gone.

Jennifer didn't cry about Bobby for nearly a week. She drove to work, stared at her stand drawings and her computer, then drove home, jollied Alicia and fed Pepe. She even talked to Nyesha on the phone, recounting the meeting with Bobby in a smooth voice that made her friend lapse into a suspicious silence.

Then one morning, there was a slithering thud as post fell onto doormat and Jennifer saw handwriting she recognised immediately. There was a card inside, with a picture of elephants walking across a bridge.

J, I'm heavier footed still, aren't I? Sorry. B.

'What are you *doing* out there?' called Alicia from the dining room.

'Nothing,' said Jennifer.

'You know, you can be quite selfish at times,' said Alicia. 'Standing reading your own letters while I'm in here waiting.'

Jennifer hardly heard her.

Alicia went on. 'I mean, there might be something important in *my* post. Another letter from the hospital about my MRI. Or something from the surgery.'

There was a muffled sob from the hall. 'Oh, for goodness' sake,' said Alicia. 'Don't tell me you're *crying* now. If you're going to overreact to every little thing I say, how can we communicate? I might as well be gagged and bound.'

The volcano of misery began to erupt.

'Dear, dear,' said Alicia. 'Making noises like that isn't necessary and it certainly isn't ladylike.'

But Jennifer was already out of the front door and in the car. She drove to the Ring Road, and joined the thick eastwards crawl of traffic, tears falling onto the steering wheel and filling her eyes so that the cars ahead of her blurred and leapt.

She cried for Bobby as she'd never cried before. She cried for love, as if with his departure there could be no love in her life ever again. She cried for the finished lonely hearts dates, for the fact that she should have seen Bobby first, and years ago, because that way she might have given other men more of a chance. But then she thought of Trevor and his wild beard, of Lawrence and his world-weariness and she cried even more, because all the chances in the world wouldn't have made things go any better.

And finally she cried for all of them because it seemed as if everyone was looking for love in the world and no one was finding it.

By this time, she was as late for work as she'd ever been. As her tears began to subside, her mobile went off. Through puffy eyes, she made out the word Unknown. That meant it was coming through a switchboard and was probably Greg. She had better answer it.

'I'm sorry,' she sniffed before he could even start. 'I can't talk: I'm driving. I'll be there in the next five minutes.'

"Allo, darling.'

It took her a few moments to recognise the voice.

'What the matter? Some bad naughty boy he has been upsetting you?'

'Uh?'

'Is terrible! You nice person, you not deserve. I can perhaps cheer you. What you think? I pick you at seven thirty. I take you for drink.'

'A drink?'

'Yes, you know. Gintonic. A pint of John Smeeth.'

'But, seven thirty when?'

'Tonight, my darling.'

As she stopped for the lights, she realised what he was talking about. 'You mean, tonight today? Salvatore, I can't possibly.'

'Tomorrow then. Thursday. Is my special night, sacred night, for drink with the boys. But for you, I make exception.'

She shook her head. What on earth was going on? And did she really care?

'Why, Salvatore? Why are you asking me?'

'Why? Why?' he mimicked playfully. 'Because you are very special lady, is why. Interesting. Because I like spend time in your company.'

'What will we talk about, for goodness' sake?'

'How I know what we talk about? I think, when it come to the talking, you women will never have a trouble.'

She took the phone away from her ear and looked at it. When she brought it back he was still there, saying something about Bacardi Breezers.

'I 'ave to go now,' he said. 'Cannot hang around all day doing the speaking. I see you tomorrow about seven-thirty. You will not regret.'

He hung up. As the lights turned green, Jennifer thought that the driver in front might as well get out of his car, climb up onto the roof and twirl his underpants around his head. She would not have found it any less bizarre.

23. *Cold pastry*

Twenty-four hours passed, during which Jennifer kept putting off calling to cancel the date. Then, when she might have called, the day suddenly got very busy. Plumbers were in the toilets all day installing spray inserts, Wally Walton's latest move to save water, and the staff had to use the temporary loos in the car park.

'I want those workmen kept sweet, Jenny,' said Greg, who was walking backwards around his office, revolving a pair of green Chinese balls in his hand. 'Walton screwed them right down on the contract. Typical eh? He's told us to keep the tea and biscuits flowing in the hope that they might still do a decent job.'

'Why have *we* got to deal with plumbing contractors?'

'Because we're the nearest thing this company's got to a PR department. Not that Max Clifford ever had to go to Asda in his lunch hour to buy toilet rolls for the temporary bogs in the car park.'

The day was chaos.

Problems arose from factory workers, office staff and visitors alike. Robert Stebbing was accused of eyeing up a factory worker.

'I would never stoop so low!' he wailed. 'I mean, cottaging in a Portaloo?'

Then a visiting client got called a 'jam rag' by someone from the machine shop and had to be mollified with Eric's chocolate Hobnobs.

There were paper towels to replenish and soap dispensers to

fill. 'Take a look at the end toilet in the Ladies,' Greg told Jennifer at lunchtime. 'Seems there's been a bit of a, well, blockage.'

Wally Walton received a lot of complaints. His response was well rehearsed.

'A dripping tap wastes up to ninety litres of water a week. These inserts prevent drips and cut ordinary usage in half too. Type that up and slap it on the bloody khazi doors, Jennifer!'

So it was hardly surprising that Jennifer didn't manage to make her phone call. And by the time she got home, she thought it was too late and would have been rude.

Putting on the Curvz blouse and the black skirt, which she hadn't worn for a little while, she was surprised to find that they both now seemed a size too big.

But even with the extra room in her waistband, she could only swallow two mouthfuls of dinner. Cold pastry and congealed gravy landed in Pepe's bowl. He wolfed the lot in silent disbelief and fell into a steak and kidney pie coma.

'You'll give that dog a heart attack,' said Alicia as they went into the sitting room.

'Oh, don't be ridiculous,' said Jennifer with unusual sharpness, switching on the TV. 'We're not all on the verge of dropping dead.'

Alicia didn't reply and when a medical soap came on, usually one of her favourites, she just sat, staring into her own lap and blinking.

'Do you plan to invite your work chum in for a cup of tea before you go?' she asked suddenly. 'If she is a bona fide chum, that is, and not some Lothario you picked up in the pub the other night.'

'Mum! I've never picked anyone up in a pub in my life, let alone Lothario, whoever he is. Anyway, we're getting straight off. We're going to see a film.'

'Which one?'

'One Flew Over the Cuckoo's Nest.'

'Such an old film. I should have thought it rather dated now.'

'It's a classic, isn't it?'

'You usually go out on a Tuesday. Why have you changed the day?'

God, thought Jennifer. She's a Rottweiler. No wonder I lie so much. 'Don't you want to watch this?' she said. 'They're getting the crash trolley, look.'

They sat on. Outside, there was a distinct lack of toots. Jennifer's ears buzzed with the strain of listening.

'What are you doing with that volume control?' said Alicia. 'I could hardly hear it, even before you started fiddling. Isn't your friend rather late?'

'We'll only miss the trailers. It isn't the end of the world.'

Had Salvatore got the wrong address? Even now, he might be tooting outside some other number ten in some other street. Jennifer stood up decisively.

'Where are you going now?' asked Alicia.

In the cold hall, the pitch darkness beyond the uncurtained window underlined the unlikelihood of anyone going anywhere, ever.

Jennifer rang Nyesha.

'He's half an hour late,' she hissed. 'Is that allowed, in dating rules?'

'I *told* you he wasn't to be trusted,' said Nyesha. 'An Italian hairdresser? I mean – first you get suckered back in by that ex who I never liked the sound of, then you expect a serial womaniser to keep his word.'

'What if he doesn't turn up? What shall I say next time I see him?'

'Why are you whispering? Your mother can't hear you. Look, who cares what you say to a guy who stands you up?'

'Do you think something's *happened*? Do you think his car's broken down?'

'Perhaps his hairdryer's broken down.'

148

They both laughed. Jennifer began to relax.

Then outside, four short toots were followed by a long one.

'Shit!' said Jennifer.

Back in the sitting room, she grabbed her jacket.

'Surely you'll have missed the beginning of the film by now,' said Alicia. 'Not just the trailers.'

'For goodness' sake!' said Jennifer. 'Who cares? If we have, we'll catch up.'

'Hm. When shall I expect you back?'

'Half past eleven. Nelly will be in to help you to bed.'

'Well, be careful. Now bring me my handbag.'

Jennifer waited impatiently while Alicia scrabbled among old bus tickets, cough candy and lipsticks.

She came out with two two-pound coins and pressed them into Jennifer's hand. 'Treat yourself and your friend to a little drink after the show. On me.'

24. *Dry roasted*

Salvatore's car was low-slung and oyster-coloured, inside and out. The upholstery looked and smelt like real leather. They cruised smoothly along the Ring Road, lights winking and needles flickering, the readout on the digital speedometer the only testament to their speed. Jennifer pressed the two-pound coins and all the guilt that went with them into her purse and concentrated on watching buildings, trees and streetlamps flash by in an accelerating mural.

Salvatore was wearing one of his practically transparent shirts, and gold gleamed at his sleeves and collar. His aftershave made Jennifer's eyes water.

'I sorry I late,' he said, as they slowed for traffic lights. 'Something come up at work I can't 'elp.'

Jennifer was grateful for the apology. 'No problem. I was able to watch TV with Mum, keep her company a bit longer.'

He looked at her. 'Is nice, how you do,' he said. 'Look after the Mama. You are kind person.'

She felt his words as a direct salve to her guilt. 'Am I?' she asked. 'Does it really seem that way to you?'

Instead of a reply he leant over and kissed her on the cheek. She went on staring out of the windscreen as if nothing had happened. But as he slid a CD into a slot and Katie Melua's voice poured into the car, heat from the kiss seemed to percolate through her body, all the way down to her toes.

Inside the pub, which turned out to be the Frog and Newt,

the landlord raised his eyebrows when he saw Jennifer and Salvatore together. He nodded at Salvatore and held two small glasses up. Salvatore nodded.

Whatever the stuff was, it smelt foul, but wanting to be up to the game, she downed it and felt its burning track down her throat. Then she went to get a table while he brought her a gin and tonic. She was glad of the gin when it arrived, crisp and refreshing. Salvatore sipped a second of the little drinks, which he said was grappa.

'This isn't very local, for you, is it?' she asked. 'To the salon, I mean.'

He spread his arms across the back of the plush bench. 'Is nice. They know me 'ere.'

She was conscious of his body, close to hers. It was a taut body. No need to yank bits of it this way or that and hoist other bits up or down.

'How did you first come to Leeds?' she asked. It was something she had often wondered about.

'Is long story. I come to work in restaurant. Is very hard. Now I am hairdresser.'

She waited expectantly, but he did not go on. 'You must miss your family?' she enquired.

'No' really. My life is 'ere now. Is better in Leeds than in Napoli.'

She couldn't imagine this. 'But what about the weather?'

'Sunshine is no' the only thing in life. Where I come from, is very poor. Traditional society. There is no work. You living with you Mama until you thirty.'

'Even in this country,' said Jennifer, 'where we don't have anything like such strong family bonds, it can still be difficult to break away from home.'

He smiled politely, but she could tell he wasn't really interested. She tried hairdressing again. 'It must be great to have that skill, of bringing out the best in someone's face.'

'Sorry,' he said. 'Excuse, please.'

And he sprang off to the bar.

He came back with two packets of dry roasted peanuts, another grappa for himself and another gin and tonic for her, even though she had made little impact on the first one. Her mother's money wasn't going to get spent: she didn't think Salvatore would like the idea of a woman buying him a drink.

'I'm not really hungry,' she said, as one of the packets landed in her lap.

'Eat, eat. You need to build your strength. For what come later.'

He tipped a whole packet of nuts into his mouth.

She stared. Did he mean what she thought he meant?

And then he winked. In the hands of a lesser man – someone like Eric perhaps – the wink would have been easy to shrug off. All it would have said was, 'I want to shag you senseless whether you like it or not.' But in Salvatore's hands, the wink said, 'I know you better than you know yourself, you dirty bitch. If you want the shag of a lifetime, come home with me.'

With weak fingers, she opened her nuts and pinched a few up into her mouth, where they went round and round.

'What colour knicker you wear tonight?' asked Salvatore.

A spray of chewed nut came out of Jennifer's mouth.

Salvatore appeared not to notice. 'Only I spend a bit time this afternoon thinking about it. Black? I ask myself. Red? And then I think: Salvatore, this is Jennifer you are speaking of. Jennifer, who come every week with the Mama. Jennifer who is pure like the vestal virgin. I tell myself, it 'as to be white.'

Fear fluttered in Jennifer's stomach. It wasn't too late to be firm. It wasn't too late to steer the conversation firmly back to a more acceptable topic.

'Fluorescent pink,' she said.

His laugh made the landlord look round. 'Ah! Is surprise! I like very much,' said Salvatore. 'I like very much to see the pink

152

knicker on you.'

His voice dropped to a whisper as he took her hand. 'But also, on the floor.'

On the way to Salvatore's, Jennifer pulled herself out of the dreamlike state of capitulation she'd been in for the past half hour and forced herself to think about Alicia. It was already gone ten, which meant she was unlikely to be in much before midnight, even if nothing much happened back at Salvatore's. What if Alicia lay awake worrying? And then, what if she stayed awake and asked her point blank where she'd been? In that event, Jennifer would have to tell the truth.

'What you say?' Salvatore's voice made her jump. 'Mama. You say Mama.'

'Sorry, I was talking to myself.'

He brought the car to an abrupt halt on a grass verge. 'You are worry about you Mama. What is problem? You want phone her?'

Jennifer sighed. 'No. I worry about her too much.'

Salvatore turned the engine off. 'Is no such thing as worry too much where the Mama is concern.'

'She thinks she's ill,' said Jennifer. 'And in a way, she is. But not in the way she thinks she is.'

Salvatore frowned. 'Explain, please.'

'I'll try,' said Jennifer. 'I don't fully understand it myself.'

Understand or not, for the first time that evening she had his full attention. It was cosy in the car, gently buffeted by the wind-rush of other cars passing. She talked uninterruptedly for what felt like a long time, going back over Dr Ganguly's retirement and its implications, something she hadn't realised she was still worried about until she heard herself talk.

Salvatore frowned a lot and said 'tcha!' Perhaps it was disloyal to confide in him. But the story didn't seem to damage Alicia's reputation in his eyes. When she finished, he shook his head slowly. 'This doctor, I think maybe he is crazy one. You mother, she is nice. She 'ave dignity.'

Even though she didn't believe him, it was a cheering reaction. 'Thanks, Salvatore.'

'She is woman of 'igh standards. She is old-fashioned lady.'

'Yes, she's certainly that,' said Jennifer.

'I like very much. I take you 'ome to 'er.'

'Oh!' said Jennifer.

He turned the key in the ignition and the engine started with barely a sound.

'Look,' said Jennifer, hurriedly. 'There's no need for a complete change of plan. I mean, her illnesses probably are at least *partly* in her own mind. Don't you think? It isn't good to pander to her too much. It might even make things worse. Besides, our neighbour will be there now. Doing her Horlicks. Helping her to bed.'

Salvatore stroked the steering wheel thoughtfully. 'Neighbour is not same. Is not family. Family is important. One thing I learn when my father die.'

'But I won't stay out too long.'

He looked doubtful.

She sighed. She had obviously set something in motion, and now there was no stopping it. 'Oh well, if you think it's best. Perhaps it is getting rather late.'

That was when he turned and looked into her eyes. His face was serious in the moonlight. 'On second thought, I think is best you come 'ome with me. And I take your mind off.'

And then his mouth was on hers. The kiss was over almost before it began. He turned back to the wheel, started the car and launched them both back onto the Ring Road. Jennifer was left breathless and wanting.

Salvatore lived in a purpose built block of flats on the edge of Gledhow, a district you could either reach via the upmarket 'village' of Chapel Allerton, or the downmarket dump of Potternewton. His block lay opposite a ribbon of woodland, known for bluebells, woodpeckers and the fact that in the late seventies, the Yorkshire Ripper drove a prostitute past it before murdering her. Tonight the lampposts cast an orange mist that made it look deep and dark. While Salvatore garaged the car, Jennifer stood gazing at the wood, and wondered at its secrets.

Two young couples came out. One of the men, trendily dishevelled, aimed his remote at a soft-top sports car parked out front.

'Are they your neighbours?' asked Jennifer when Salvatore emerged.

'Pah!' he said, shepherding her into a dimly lit communal hallway.

His flat was on the top floor. The living area was open plan, with a black carpet and a dining table and chairs that looked to be made of glass. The white leather sofa looked big enough for a small family to move into. Overall the room, totally clutter free, looked more like an art installation than a home.

'Very striking,' she said, trying not to sound out of breath from the stairs.

'Thank you. What you like drink? I have the Bombay gin. Or the Chianti.'

'Either is fine.'

She sat down. No curtains or blinds obscured the sight of the dark, silent sea of the woods, moving gently in the night breeze. It had begun to rain; rivulets varnished the window.

'What a view,' she called. 'How long have you lived here?'

'One year. Two.'

He was taking a long time in the kitchen.

'Just going to the loo.'

He didn't respond.

The bathroom was more homely than the sitting room. Blue fluffy mats stood around the toilet and basin. Turquoise seahorses trod water on the tiles above the bath. On impulse, she opened the bathroom cabinet. A tube of Savlon contorted itself next to a jar of Vaseline. Boxes announced innocuous painkillers. This ordinariness reassured her.

Emerging into the hall, she saw that the living room was darker. She hesitated for a moment before walking in.

The lights were off and the room was filled with golden leaping candlelight and the scent of lavender. She glanced at the windowsill and saw an aromatherapy burner. On the glass coffee table, a bottle of red wine gleamed in the soft light. These things were striking but they were not the main thing. The main thing was Salvatore, who was sitting on the sofa, completely naked.

She stood, rooted to the spot.

He patted the cushion next to him. She moved slowly towards the sofa. Time had gone funny: each second stretched, indefinitely. She couldn't take her eyes off his body. He looked sculpted, the candlelight showing all his muscles in relief. His face looked carved, perfect. Held by his smiling eyes, she sat down carefully at the far end of the sofa and did not look anywhere near his lap.

'Take off the shoes,' he said.

Obediently she slipped off her lace-ups, and paired them neatly. He pushed a glass of wine across the table towards her. He stood up. She thought her heart might stop. But he was only going over to the music system, where he crouched, looking through CD's. His buttocks were muscular, with two perfect dints.

She took a large gulp of her drink, knowing this was only a temporary reprieve. Unless he was a naturist, which she doubted, at some stage in the evening when he'd finished selecting music or perhaps when he thought she'd had enough to drink, he was going to make love to her. She closed her eyes. It wasn't too late to stand up and snap the light on and tell him she had changed her mind about the whole thing.

But she did nothing. And soon she sensed his soft footfalls across the carpet, felt the weight of his body on the cushion beside her. She kept her eyes closed. And then came his touch. His arm around her shoulders, the press of his warm, naked side against her clothed one. The murky scent of his underarm. And as he kissed behind her ear and began moving his lips down her neck in tiny increments, the idea that there might once have been a moment when she might once have told him to stop was gone forever.

A mere fifteen minutes later however, he was separated from her, sitting at the other end of the sofa lighting a cigarette.

He inhaled deeply then blew the smoke out in a long plume. 'I sorry. As never 'appen to me before.'

He flicked ash into a granite ashtray that looked as if it might need two men to lift it.

Jennifer felt at a complete loss. It had all been going so well, or so she'd thought, until she'd put her hand down between his legs and found there was nothing solid to grasp hold of.

'Is it me?' she asked.

He shook his head, but not convincingly. She sat, skin cooling.

He lit another cigarette from the butt of the first one. Still, he said nothing. She began to feel deflated, her nakedness an embarrassment. She looked around for her blouse and bra and couldn't see them.

She located her knickers, though, in a tight twist between two of the sofa cushions. A worry gripped her. What was the etiquette of the situation? Was it best to pick up her clothes discreetly and leave, or did one hang around in case the man was willing to have another go?

After another few minutes of his silent smoking, she decided on the former.

'Gosh, is that the time?' she said. 'I'd better be going.'

He grunted.

'Once it gets to midnight,' she added, 'Mum will worry.'

He stubbed his cigarette out and stood up. 'You want call cab? I am over the limit to drive you.'

He had become polite now, almost formal.

'Thanks,' she said.

It was a relief when he went out into the kitchen with the glasses and bottle. She moved quickly around as if released from a spell, collecting her blouse and bra from behind the sofa, quickly putting them on.

Dressed, she flicked the main light on. The window once again became a black rectangle in a white wall.

He didn't come back into the sitting room and soon the taxi was pipping discreetly outside.

She put her head around the kitchen door. Still naked, he had washed the glasses and was going around the surfaces with a cloth.

'I'll be off then,' she said.

'Okay. I see you.'

' 'Bye then.' She'd hoped for a kiss. 'Don't worry. About, you know.'

A cool look came into his eyes. She headed for the door.

25. *Chicken Salad*

The minute Jennifer answered the phone on her desk the next morning, the girl from the catering franchise appeared and stood waiting for her lunch order.

'I'll have to ring you back,' Jennifer told Nyesha.

'Don't do this to me,' said Nyesha. 'I've been on tenterhooks all morning. What happened?'

'All right. Hang on,' said Jennifer. 'Chicken salad, please.'

The girl took Jennifer's five pound note and fumbled unsuccessfully in her purse belt for change. While Jennifer waited, hand over mouthpiece, the girl took the belt off and emptied its contents onto her desk. She began slowly counting out one and two pence pieces.

Jennifer gave up. What did it matter what the girl overheard anyway? She wasn't going to go into graphic detail. 'We went for a drink,' she told Nesh.

'And?' said Nyesha. 'I take it this time there was an "and"?'

Now Derek had got up from his desk and was advancing clutching a piece of paper.

'I can't tell you about that right now.'

'I'll ask questions. You just answer "yes" or "no". You can do that much, can't you?'

Derek had arrived and was standing playing his pen on his teeth.

'All right,' said Jennifer.

'Did you and the hairdresser get blazing?' asked Nyesha. 'Did you hit skins? Were you banging boots?'

'Where do you get these weird rap music expressions from?' asked Jennifer.

'Where every other self-respecting woman of colour gets them. Off the Internet.'

'All right. Sort of,' said Jennifer.

At the other end of the phone, Nyesha yelled, but not to her. 'She did it! The sister went windsurfing on Mount Baldy.'

The girl gave up pretending to pick up low denomination coins. Derek lowered his piece of paper and stared.

'Shush!' said Jennifer. 'People can hear you at this end. And who are you talking to?'

'Ginny. Don't worry – she's been rooting for you. And Carlotta. She bet me ten quid the lonely hearts thing would bring rain to the parched desert floor. Which it has, hasn't it? If it wasn't for all the pre-date hairdos you'd never have ended up in the arms of the Italian stallion.'

'I suppose you could see it that way,' said Jennifer. 'But don't bank on spending your winnings just yet.'

'Why? What happened? Was there some kind of technical hitch?'

Now Greg was heading across to her desk, glowering at Derek.

'Yes. Look, I'll have to go, Nesh.'

'No you don't!' said Nyesha. 'Just a few more questions. Come on, girl. I'm your counsellor in times of trouble, right? You owe me.'

It was fair enough. While Greg arrived and stood at a slight distance, perhaps so as not to be counted in the same breath as Derek, Nyesha made a series of graphic but inaccurate guesses as to what had gone wrong in the bedroom. Eventually she guessed right.

'Did he have trouble with his Admiral Winky?'

'Uh-huh,' said Jennifer.

'Did he pitch his tent at all?'

'Yes, at the beginning,' said Jennifer.

'But the lift went up to the trouser department and came straight back down before anyone got in?'

'Exactly that,' said Jennifer. 'Though I don't think we should really be discussing it like this. Anyway, he said it had never happened to him before.'

There was a snort at the other end of the phone.

At the same time, Jennifer saw Greg's eyes flare in alarm. 'Ah. Um, right,' he said. 'Catch you later.'

He turned on his heel and hurried away.

Derek was also looking bothered. 'Best be getting on. Can't stand here gassing all day.'

And he was off, forgetting to leave his bit of paper.

Now the franchise girl was looking at Jennifer with sympathetic eyes. 'Poor you. I'm usually trying to get the lads to put their hammers back in their toolboxes, not the other way round.'

'Sorry, girl,' said Nyesha. 'Everyone's shaking their heads at this end. You did realise we were on speakerphone? Seems like performing with Flacido Domingo is out of their experience too.'

The next day was Saturday. Alicia sent Jennifer out to buy incense cones, saying she wanted to perfume her hair with them, an idea she'd got from *Herbalist Today*. Jennifer had hoped to forget about Salvatore for a few days, but at the shops she was plagued by the sight of bottles standing to attention, products rising proud from shelves. Even toilet rolls stood in erect columns, tall and sturdy.

Up in the little home office later, she typed the words 'erectile dysfunction' into the search engine then trawled through article after article. An hour later, she'd read up on everything from smoking to heart disease; high cholesterol to hormone disorders. Nowhere did it say that sometimes a man just didn't find a woman attractive enough – which was no doubt the truth in Salvatore's case.

The whole relationship thing was disappointing. First the dating debacle, then Bobby, now this. Perhaps she wasn't destined to be in a relationship just now. Perhaps she wasn't destined to be in a relationship, period. The question hung, depressing and familiar.

That afternoon, knowing she could find solace in practical tasks, she decided to finish her papier-mâché animal. She made gesso in the kitchen, whisking in Plaster of Paris from a cracked, powdery sack that gave off little white puffs every time she touched it. In the shed, her brush rasped across dry paper as she covered the names and signatures of her lonely hearts suitors in an opaque shell.

Later, when the gesso had dried, she added paint: Titanium White, Bone Black, a touch of crimson. She rolled tiny pieces of white clay into pellets for toenails and stuck them on. This was a male animal so two plastic beans came next and a cone of paper with a tassel on the end. Then, with rain pattering on the corrugated plastic roof of the shed, she stood back to admire her creation.

It was a dog; a bull terrier with more than a touch of lawnmower about him. With his thick neck, huge hinged jaw and lopsided patch over one eye, he looked a real bruiser. He was nothing like a real dog. And yet somehow he was exactly like one. When Jennifer picked him up, he was as light as a feather.

Pepe normally reacted to Jennifer's animals the way he reacted to snow, by not seeing them. But when the new dog came in, he sprang up, backed into the sofa and barked fit to bust. Alicia clapped her hands over her ears.

'Shush, Pepe!' said Jennifer.

But his barking took on a stubborn, mechanical regularity.

Jennifer put the paper dog down on the floor. 'He's not real, you silly dog!'

The elderly poodle ran out of the room, nails skittering on the kitchen lino as he headed for the safety of his basket. It was a gratifying reaction.

'What on earth *is* it?' said Alicia.

'It's a dog, of course,' said Jennifer. 'I'm going to put him on display in here.'

Alicia eyed the dog's testicles. 'But it's hideous! What if Narendra comes round? To say nothing of my *Times of our Lives* ladies.'

'I'm sure they've seen it all before, Mum. Don't you think?'

'Not in *my* living room. Why can't you make your pieces *attractive?* I mean, it's verging on the obscene. Just looking at it is enough to give you a hiatus hernia. And dogs aren't striped.'

'It's not supposed to be realistic. That's the whole point.'

'I'm sure it'd look very well in your bedroom.'

'Nelly keeps my toad in her sitting room.'

'Yes, well she's probably just being polite.'

It was obvious that Alicia didn't like the papier-mâché dog any more than Pepe did. But Jennifer was getting fed up of giving in over everything.

'The dining room. That's my final offer,' she said. 'Your ladies never go in there.'

Alicia rearranged her crossword on her lap and pressed her lips together.

It wasn't exactly a yes. But it would do.

26. *Custard cream*

On Monday morning, a selection of 'seconds' bottles arrived from BK Packaging. They needed modifying before Jennifer could figure out whether her plan was going to work. But Eric said the lads in the Machine Shop owed him a favour, and if there was any cutting to do, she should look no further than him. Jennifer smiled and kissed him on the cheek.

'Steady on, lass!' he said, his eyes enormous in his spectacles, like goldfish that swim round the front of the bowl.

The cut-out bottles, when added to the artist's impression, scale elevation drawings, prices and specifications on Jennifer's desk, brought the pile of stand design documentation to teetering point.

This meant that the time had come to present the idea to Greg. After what Robert had said, Jennifer had been putting it off. But she couldn't do that for ever. Putting on her overall for protection, she grabbed the pile and set off.

When she reached the top of the stairs and found his door closed, she sighed with relief at the temporary reprieve.

She had been standing there for a few moments before she realised that the faint sounds she could hear behind the door were shouting. As she waited, there was a pause, then another volley. One of the voices was a woman's.

Suddenly the door opened.

'It was only ever meant to be a wee bit of fun. Why do you men always take things so seriously?'

Jocasta Jardine stalked out. She took in Jennifer's posture.

'Have you been listening to our conversation?'

'No! Of course not!'

'Hah! D'you think I floated up the Clyde in a barrel? Why else would you stand with your ear pressed against the door?'

'All right, so I was *trying* to listen. That doesn't mean I succeeded. These doors are solid oak.'

'Well, if I hear my business being parroted round the factory, I'll know who to blame, eh?'

She walked off down the corridor.

Jennifer poked her head round the door. Greg, his desk a mess, was staring into space. He looked exhausted.

She felt sorry for him. 'Is everything all right?'

The question seemed to annoy him. 'Of course it isn't. Not that it's any business of yours. Come in, if you're coming.'

She went in, but her pile of documentation didn't quite follow. Papers slid and plastic bottles bounced. Mumbling apologies, she bent down to pick them up.

Greg eyed her. 'For fuck's sake! What is this: your entry for the Turner prize? Or perhaps you're going all out for a Blue Peter badge? And how have you managed to get that overall so filthy? Haven't you heard of Persil?'

'Sorry,' said Jennifer, regretting all sorts of things and all at once.

He looked at her more kindly then, and seemed to force himself to speak more civilly. 'It's all right. Spit it out. I won't bite.'

'Okay. Well, it's about the stand metalwork,' she said.

He frowned. 'Haven't you sorted that out yet?'

'I'm in the process of doing so. As you said, the sales force don't like it. And Eric said the stand as a whole looked dated. So I thought we might try something completely different.'

But Greg's face had darkened. 'Eric? Eric from Packing? Since when was the Marketing Department led by the shop floor?

I've to take advice from a short-arsed, short-sighted porn addict now, have I?'

Jennifer stood clutching the slippery, awkward armful of bottles and papers. 'No, not at all. I only mean … .'

But it was too late for explanations.

'I suggest you go back to your desk and get on with your work, which is after all what you're paid for, not going around the bloody factory getting vox pops from every Tom, Dick and Harry about how the Marketing Department should be spending its non-existent exhibitions budget.

Or else get yourself off to B&Q, buy whatever you need to tart up that stand and get on with it. I've got other things to do besides watch you turn my office into a children's activity corner. Why have you brought all that stuff in here, anyway? I hope it's nothing to do with our stand design?'

Jennifer's decision was swift, and definite. 'No, it's nothing at all to do with it. It's just some junk I'm clearing out of the stockroom.'

Even though, rationally, Jennifer wasn't expecting Salvatore to ring, she was unsettled for the next few evenings.

'You seem to be getting very sensitive to noise,' said Alicia, while they were having their ten o'clock cuppa. 'I shan't be able to hear the TV at all if the volume gets any lower. How about a visit to Narendra? I mean it could be something serious.'

'It's okay, Mum. It'll pass.'

'Do you get a ringing in your ears?'

'Unfortunately not.'

Jennifer nibbled the edge of a custard cream. On Friday, Alicia had a hair appointment. The thought of facing Salvatore if they hadn't spoken beforehand was dreadful.

'Mum,' she said. 'Do you think it's time we tried a different hairdresser?'

Alicia's mouth was an 'o' of surprise. 'But why?'

'For a change.'

'But darling, Salvatore is such fun. A friend, by now. And I have so few outings to look forward to.'

'Someone else might be fun too. What about Simon? The one we went to last spring, when Salvatore was in Italy. You liked him.'

'I rather got the impression that Simon was one of *them*.'

'So? Anyway, how do you know Salvatore isn't one of them, as you put it?'

Alicia smirked. 'A woman just *knows*.'

Jennifer decided to change the subject. 'Did I tell you,' she said, knowing full well she hadn't, 'that work have asked me to design an exhibition stand?'

'Oh.'

'It's for a big electronics show in Zurich. In the New Year.'

Alicia sipped her tea. 'They want *you* to design their stand? I knew they were a cheapskate company, but that's ridiculous.'

'Thanks, Mum,' said Jennifer. 'Your faith in me is touching.'

Inevitably, Friday morning arrived. Alicia looked extra smart in a mint green dress she'd inherited from a recently deceased *Times of our Lives* friend and when she tossed her hair, it gave off a scent somewhere between cow dung and roses. Jennifer, on the other hand, was having a bad face day. She decided she would not actually enter the salon but leave her mother at the doorstep.

But it seemed her feet had other plans. They reached the threshold and at the moment they should have turned back, they kept on walking, across the black and white checked lino floor and up to the leatherette banquette. Her eyes, more obedient, remained riveted to the floor.

Having said that, she somehow knew exactly where Salvatore was standing (at the desk), how he was standing (lolling) and what he was wearing (airtight trousers). Behind him stretched the empty salon, a theatre with no actors or audience.

Her mouth was dry. She would have to look up soon and she had no idea what expression she would have on her face when she did so.

Then she heard a loud cry of appreciation. He was swooping towards them, all nods and smiles and glimmering eye contact. 'Jennifer! 'Ow are you, my darling?'

He took her hand. And she realised that something extraordinary had happened. Since she'd last seen him, someone had sewn thousands of tiny magnets into her skin, that responded to him and no one but him. She felt his presence like a force field. His warm dry touch coursed through her veins like gin.

'Alicia! Your hair it a smell like a garden,' he said. 'And you looking very beautiful today. Like the Queen.'

He put his lips close to Jennifer's ear. 'I with you soon, my darling.'

Jennifer sank down onto the banquette, grinning inanely while Salvatore sorted Alicia out and passed her into Tony's hands. Then he slid onto the banquette next to her and took her hand in his own.

'You stay. While I do the mother. Then I do your 'air and we 'ave a little talk.'

'Oh, God. I'd love to but I've got to go to work.'

'Work?' said Salvatore, as if it were a concept he'd never heard of. 'Don' worry, we do it quick. Tony 'e wash your 'air straight after the mother. Yes?'

It was already eight thirty. These days Jennifer didn't usually linger more than five minutes, so she could be at work for nine. But somehow it was hard to worry about that now.

In front of the mirror, the feel of his hands on her head made her close her eyes in pleasure. He didn't talk during the cut, but when he'd finished, bent to whisper in her ear. His breath was hot and humid on her ear.

'I am so 'appy you come in. I am thinking about you.'

'You are?'

'You think I 'ave forgotten you?'

He reached into her lap and covered her hands with his own strong brown ones. She thought she was going to stop breathing. She thought she was going to explode with desire. He brought one of her hands to his lips. She managed to look at him.

He returned her gaze. 'What you do next Tuesday night?'

Tuesday, thought Jennifer. That's perfect. 'Nothing,' she said, casually, glancing at Alicia waiting in reception. But she seemed oblivious. The flap of her handbag held a mirror, and she was turning her head this way and that in front of it.

He touched the tips of his fingers to hers. 'You are now, my darling.'

Back in reception, Alicia eyed Jennifer then insisted she be dropped back home, despite the fact that in recent weeks she'd agreed to go home in a taxi. Jennifer gave in, deciding she was already so late for work that an extra fifteen minutes would make no difference.

When they were on the Ring Road, Alicia put her hand on her daughter's arm.

'I wanted to have a word, dear. Now, what was Salvatore doing, groping around in your lap?'

'Oh! I don't remember. A hairpin, perhaps.'

Her mother looked unconvinced. 'Darling, you *must* be careful with Italians. They aren't like British men. He's our friend, I know. But you must set limits. *He* won't set them, believe me. And he won't respect you if you don't. Their women won't let them anywhere near, you see. It's the Church. That's why they come to England.'

'Mum, Salvatore didn't come here for that reason. He came to start a new life. To run his own business.'

'There's no need to get hot under the collar, darling.'

'But it's as though you think he's untrustworthy.'

Alicia raised her eyebrows. 'I don't know what to make of

169

you, dear. The other day you were saying you wanted to change hairdressers. Now you're defending him to the hilt. As to your question, no, I don't think he's untrustworthy. I do trust him. But within reason. And in his place.'

'What do you mean, in his place? Like a servant?'

'No, dear. Like a man.'

Was there a hint of tacit acceptance in Alicia's advice? That was a question Jennifer asked herself again and again over the next few weeks.

There might have been.

Nevertheless, as a month went by and Jennifer saw Salvatore on all four Tuesdays, it still felt impossible to come clean with her mother. The nature of their relationship would certainly have been difficult to admit to. Salvatore picked her up just after the *Times of our Lives* minibus had left and they sped through the early autumn streets to his flat to down a few glasses of wine and go straight to bed.

Jennifer began to feel like a sexual being again. Her orgasms happened quickly, as if they'd been queuing like fans at a stage door.

Unfortunately, his didn't. His manhood was up, then down again, wilting before her like a seedling in a downpour. She tried to talk to him about it. But the cool look came into his eyes and her attempts faltered. As if to compensate, he focussed more and more on her pleasure, trying to squeeze as many climaxes into their allotted two hours together as the director of a Hammer Horror movie.

He liked to try it in different places: in the toilet; on the kitchen table amidst breadcrumbs and jam; in the stairwell, where anybody might have interrupted them.

One evening, he introduced a courgette into their love play. She accepted this, hoping it might inspire him. But the offending body part remained limp, even when she offered her mouth for the task.

Jennifer kept thinking he would end the relationship.

But so far he hadn't.

She knew you couldn't call it love. And yet, at the end of each Tuesday evening, when she collected her clothes from wherever they lay – dangling from the doorknob, draped over the oven door or flung across the communal banisters – called a taxi and arrived back home breathless in time to hear Alicia's account of Edna's abortive efforts at macramé, or Mrs Harrison's attempt to embezzle money from the tea and coffee fund, or how Mr Green had congratulated her on not having 'let herself go' like some of the others, Jennifer felt like the cat that had got the cream.

The black skirt was now definitely hanging off her. She made it pack its bags and leave for Oxfam.

Nyesha, however, wasn't keen on the idea of Salvatore.

'Remind me what you like about this guy?' she asked. 'Do you enjoy going out and doing things together? Does he make you laugh? Are you soul mates? Can you talk to each other?'

Jennifer considered. 'No. No, no and no.'

'What's the big attraction then?'

'Sex,' said Jennifer.

'And?'

'I'm sure there *is* an 'and',' said Jennifer, not wanting to be shallow. 'I just don't know what it is.'

But the conversation with Nyesha bothered her. Her friend was right. Sex wasn't enough to base a relationship on. The following Tuesday, as she lay on the rumpled sheets of Salvatore's bed, she decided they needed to talk.

Few personal items were in evidence in Salvatore's bedroom: nothing stood by the bed except a box of tissues and a digital alarm clock. Perhaps if you'd slid open a wardrobe door, a jumble of jumpers and trousers would have tumbled out. But in front of that door, everything was antiseptically neat and tidy. The mirror above his bed reflected this. It also reflected them: her pale spreading acreage next to his neat brown allotment.

'Why don't we ever go out together?' she asked.

He pulled a face. He was lying flat on his back, while she propped up the headboard. 'Many reasons, I think.'

'Such as?'

'I am too horny. I would not be able to keep my hands off your body in public.'

'We could always, um, do it first. Then go out somewhere afterwards.'

He pulled a face. 'But where you want go that is better than 'ere? What is point of meal, drink, pictures when what we really want is what come after?'

She pulled the sheet over her cooling body. 'The point is to enjoy each other's company in a different way. They're showing *Il Postino* at the Hyde Park next week.'

The Hyde Park was an independent cinema in the student area that had never been modernised. You sat on hard, torn velour seats, surrounded by ornate Victoriana. It had surely been the last cinema in England to dispense with usherettes. Jennifer loved it.

'It's an Italian film,' she elaborated. 'About a postman. About Pablo Neruda actually.'

He frowned.

'The poet,' she added.

He nodded vaguely. There were surprising gaps in his English.

'So, shall we go?' she persisted.

He rolled over to the edge of the bed and sat up. 'How long is film?'

'An hour and a half.'

'And how long the mother stay, at the old biddy group?'

'Oh, two hours. Two and a half, if you count getting there and back. We'd have time. But even if we didn't, it wouldn't matter.'

He put on his slippers. 'But the way we make it now, you don't 'ave to tell her you going out. I thought that is what you want, eh?'

Jennifer sighed. 'I did at first. Whereas now … well, I don't want to skulk about forever.'

'But is modern way. Is our little secret. Is more exciting this way, no?'

'Well, yes, but … .'

'Also is difficult for me in the salon. I no want advertise private life, there. If you Mama know, maybe she tell other customer.'

Jennifer shrugged, not seeing what the problem was.

'Anyway, is not right,' said Salvatore decisively. 'Is not right, tell the mother about the sex life.'

'I wasn't going to mention *sex*. Just that we're, well, going out together.'

It wasn't the right expression.

'In my country,' he said, 'you tell the mother you are going out together, as you put it, and next thing she expect is the wedding bells.'

He reached for his dressing gown. 'This poet film is important for you, yes?'

'Well, it's a good film. But a different film would do.'

'Ah. Maybe then I get video, DVD? We watch 'ere.'

It wasn't quite the same. But at least he was making an effort.

He took her hand. 'As for the mother, let us not disturb. I not want everything to be spoil.'

He lowered his head, rather gracefully, and kissed her hand.

'Well, all right,' she said. 'But if you're worried that my mother will disapprove, she won't. She really likes you, you know.'

He put up his hand to forestall her. 'One thing I know. What a woman like for herself, she not always like for her daughter.'

He spoke with such authority that she had to believe him.

27. *Brown stuff*

At work, Wally Walton was busy intensifying the gloom of the shortening days by having energy-saving light bulbs installed all over the factory and office.

He and Greg crossed swords about it. But then, they crossed swords about almost everything these days: they had words about the company's advertising spend, which Walton wanted to slash to a degree that Greg thought spelt commercial suicide; words about the Marketing Department's stationery usage, which Walton deemed excessive, and it almost led to fisticuffs about the hotel Jocasta had booked for Zurich: five star rather than the maximum three stipulated in company Board and Lodging guidelines.

'Joc found it nigh on impossible to book anything in that Swiss shithole,' said Greg one morning in his office. 'Walton's got no idea.'

He was so frazzled these days he'd taken to confiding in her occasionally. It was nice, thought Jennifer, even though it came out of desperation, not fellow feeling.

His shirt collar was loose.

'You've lost weight,' she said.

Greg grunted. 'Is it surprising, the pressure that idiot puts me under? What does he want us to do: doss down under the arches at the Hauptbahnhof? With his environmental concerns, the man might look modern but underneath he's out of the Ark. You better watch yourself. He'll be telling you to send out letters on sheets of bog roll next.'

'Mm,' said Jennifer. 'Greg, are you okay?'

He shot her a look. 'Of course I'm not bloody okay. Your point being?'

His openness had its limits. Fair enough, thought Jennifer. She had problems of her own, anyway.

That morning, BK Packaging's lorry had arrived with its featherweight load of plastic bottles filled with absolutely nothing, and as she had watched Eric slice open the boxes and wipe off the beads of polystyrene that clung to his fingers, she'd realised that dreaming something up on paper was one thing and seeing the actual materials in front of you was quite another.

She had run her hands over the bottles and seen that although there were hundreds and hundreds of them, there was only one of her, to cut and fix them into shape. And now they were here, and she'd spent half the puny stand budget on them, she was committed to a plan that had not been cleared, or even seen by anyone else. She swallowed.

'All right, love?' asked Eric.

'Yes,' she'd said, fighting an urge to confide in him. 'In for a penny, in for a pound.'

In the days that followed, however, the practical aspects of making parts for a display system virtually in secret weren't as bad as she'd feared. She did most of the work after three-thirty, when she had finished her PA duties and Eric had clocked off. Greg was preoccupied with his own problems, glad she had things in hand and not keen to visit Packing. When he did, it was always possible to hide the exact nature of what she was doing.

She enjoyed, as always, working in the spaciousness of the factory area rather than at her desk. There were hubbubs around the clocking off machine every time a shift left. Then, as if a flock of squabbling birds had taken off, everything went very quiet.

She wasn't home till six-thirty but Alicia seemed to accept

this, especially as Jennifer's guilt about Salvatore meant she was attention personified for the rest of the evening.

As for the work itself, it was repetitive and straightforward. So progress was good. Good that is, once you accepted that everything was going to take twice as long as anticipated. Even now she could see there would not be time to build the thing up in all its glory before it had to be shipped.

So the practical side of the enterprise was copeable-with. But as for the emotional side, Nyesha was worried about her.

'I wish I was up there to support you, girl,' she said one night on the phone. 'I don't think it's good for you, living a lie.'

'Living a lie? That's a bit strong.'

'Well, how would you put it? You've been deceiving your mother for months. Add Greg into the equation and it seems half your life is being lived in secret.'

Jennifer had her catchphrase ready. 'I'm operating on a need-to-know basis. I'm prioritising the preservation of other people's peace of mind.'

'What's the difference between that and telling gigantic porkies?'

Jennifer sighed. 'Okay, I do feel bad about Mum.'

She nearly told Nyesha about her recent discussion with Salvatore. But guessing that her friend would be critical, she kept quiet.

'The work thing's okay. What I'm doing there is taking total responsibility for the stand; shouldering the whole burden. I am stand manager, after all. And Greg's under a lot of pressure just now.'

'Hmm. That's probably okay if things go right. But what if they go wrong?'

Jennifer glanced at the spider plant on the windowsill. Its baby plants had stopped growing for the winter and hung suspended around it. 'They won't go wrong, Nesh,' she said. 'They can't afford to.'

November arrived and with it, Alicia's MRI scan. At the hospital Alicia, frail in a pale green gown laundered to within an inch of its life, was slotted into the futuristic white tunnel of the scanner, wearing something that looked like a space helmet. Jennifer, despite being pretty sure the scan was a waste of time, was unable to swallow the lump in her throat. But they were back in the car and on their way home within the hour.

'Now it's just a question of waiting for the results,' said Alicia cheerily. 'And keeping our fingers crossed that it's not a brain tumour.'

'Brain tumour?' said Jennifer, alarmed. 'Who said anything about a brain tumour?'

The sight of her mother's bony ankles sticking out of the white machine plagued her for the rest of that day.

Then came a night that seemed to hold its cursor over the bad side of things, press 'select text' and highlight them in bold. It was a Tuesday.

At his flat, instead of the red wine or Bombay gin that they usually drank together, Salvatore produced a bottle of brown stuff. Jennifer accepted a glass of it because he said it was traditional, but it was worse even than the grappa. In fact, it made her throat feel as if someone had attacked it with a flamethrower.

Then he wanted them to have a bath together. He had set up little loudspeakers on the edge of the bath. The room was full of steam. He produced an oil burner from the airing cupboard. 'Rosemary. To stimulate and invigorate.'

Jennifer didn't particularly want to be stimulated and invigorated. She'd rather have jump cut to the later part of evening, after sex, where they lay together on the bed with him stroking her hair. But when Salvatore was set on a course of action, a combination of their language difficulty, his persuasiveness and her desire to please made it difficult to resist.

She undressed while he turned tactfully, rearranging towels

on the rail. She knelt in the water, felt trickling rings of heat around her thighs. He folded her clothes neatly. Rihanna sang from the speakers.

He spoke about the benefits of steam. The pores, he kept saying, the pores. He scooped her hair up, fastening it with a large pink clip, like in the salon. He talked about Italy and the tin bath of his childhood. Not very much water, he said. Not very hot.

She lay down. The heat was making her woozy. Hot water seeped into her hair. She gazed at her body, a sky of cumulus clouds covering an undulating desert.

'Is time you were wash,' he said, wiping a flannel down her arms, then across her breasts and belly. 'Now the face. Eyes closed.'

But when she shut her eyes, everything swayed. She had to open them again.

'Is okay.' His voice was kind now. 'I wash your back. Turn around. Kneel.'

She levered herself round in the confined, slippery space. But she bruised her knees on the bath and her change of position made the room tip and heave again, and she had to fight to stabilise it.

Salvatore took his clothes off and got into the bath behind her. The water rose and surged through the overflow. Jennifer felt the flannel on her shoulders and back. And then she felt something that was pretty unfamiliar these days: his hardness. He was pressing himself against the back of her legs. Oh, she thought, pleased despite her wooziness.

His hands separated her buttocks, making a coolness between them. He pressed himself between her buttocks. She waited for his fingers, which would no doubt snake round in a moment. But the nudging between her buttocks grew more insistent. One hand gripped her shoulder; the other clutched her around the waist.

178

Then suddenly, a dry prickly pain shot through her.

It was a shock. 'What are you doing?'

But he pushed again, making her wince with pain. He was, she realised, going up her backside. Perhaps not far, but he felt enormous, all wrong.

'Salvatore,' she said. 'Don't do that. It hurts.'

But he had begun to move gently. 'Please, my darling, please. Is first time I am inside you. Is precious thing.'

His tone was soft, reverent.

It was true. He was having no problem with his erection now. For that reason and that reason alone, she let him continue. Her forehead dripped, whether from water or sweat she didn't know.

'Try to get used,' said Salvatore. 'Think of the shirt leefters; they do this every day.'

But it was like having a cactus shoved up her bottom. She bore it for a few more seconds, but it was really too much. 'Ow! You've got to stop!'

'I nearly there!' he cried.

Then he gave a thrust like razor blades, cried out, and withdrew.

She subsided into the bath water, and lay there in a sort of stinging, throbbing relief.

'I sorry,' he said now. 'I sorry if I hurt you. I am very excite.'

'It's all right,' she said.

But as she gathered herself up out of the grey, tepid bathwater, she wanted nothing more than to be at home in her own bed, with a cup of cocoa and her furry cat hot water bottle.

'I dry you,' he said. 'In the bedroom.'

'I can dry myself, thank you.' It came out abruptly.

His face was concerned. 'Darling! You are upset! I make better, I promise.'

In the bedroom, he had her lie down while he fished a large hairdryer out of the wardrobe. Soon a strong, warm breeze was playing over her toes and ankles, the note changing as the dryer tilted. The warm wind moved up to her calves, her knees. Currents flowed across her belly and breasts, her hands. He played the dryer up her sides, across her shoulders, over her neck. Then he turned her onto her front and began to brush her hair.

Despite everything that had happened in the preceding half hour, she felt herself drift away on a carpet of sensation.

When she woke, he was standing by the bed in his black towelling dressing gown, holding a tiny brown tulip shaped cup. Coffee. Her eyes flicked across to the bedside clock. The red LED digits said 21.30.

'You drink then I call taxi. You will still be back before the mother.'

28. *Five a day*

The next day at work, as Jennifer slotted things into each other down in Packing, her nether regions were on fire. Sitting down was out of the question.

At last work was over and she was able to call in to the doctor's surgery. She didn't have an appointment, and the receptionist told her she was in for a long wait, so she sat, or did what passed for sitting, in the crowded waiting room.

There was a strong scent of patchouli as someone sat down next to her; a familiar voice saying hello. Through a fug of discomfort, she saw a denim jacket and jeans with a thermal layer of dark blue showing through the rips.

'Andy!' She remembered him saying his parents lived nearby. It was lovely to see him. Or would have been, if she had any energy.

'How's things?' he said.

'Well … .' She glanced around the room, which was completely packed and very quiet. It seemed they always met somewhere where conversation was difficult.

He grinned. 'Fair point.'

The room waited. More patients were called. People re-crossed their legs, straightened their jackets, picked up and put down magazines.

Andy's turn came. 'I'll wait for you outside?'

'Don't bother. I've got to wait for a cancellation. I might be ages.'

'No sweat, I've got time.'

When she finally went in, Dr Ganguly's face was tired and kindly. 'Something troubling you?'

Jennifer sat down gingerly. 'I ...,' she began.

He held up his hand to forestall further confidences and jabbed at his computer keyboard. 'Just get you up on the screen. Damn this new system: Government gimmick! Ah, buggeration.'

He turned from the screen. 'We'll leave that for the moment. I'm all ears.'

On the examination table, he separated her buttocks for less than a second. The ping and snap of rubber gloves was a signal to get dressed again and she climbed down from the examination table trying not to gasp.

He tried to type again, swore, then pulled a prescription pad out and wrote on it. 'Prescribed you some cream,' he said. 'Apply to the affected area twice daily.'

He pushed the green leaf across his desk towards her. 'Any idea what's caused it? Been under a bit of stress lately, perhaps? Tend to strain a bit on the, umm ... .'

His fatherly eyes, tank top and maroon paisley tie were conspiring to make it impossible to tell him what the real cause was. But a horrible trapped feeling was coming over her, very familiar. Surely she could tell him the truth? She took a deep breath.

'It isn't that,' she said. 'I've got myself into a situation.'

'Go on.'

'It was nice at first, but I don't feel fully in control ... I think I have to try and stop.'

His intercom crackled, making them both jump. He flicked the switch. 'What is it, Fiona? I have a patient with me.'

'Call on line two, Doctor. I'm sorry, but she's most insistent.'

'Who is?'

'Mrs Spendlove.'

Jennifer gasped. What was her mother doing, ringing now?

'Tell her I'll call her back in five,' said Dr Ganguly.

He turned again to Jennifer, glancing at the clock as he did so. 'Now, dear. You were saying you'd lost control.'

Jennifer managed a nod. Did her mother *know* she was there? But how could she?

'What is it then, your particular downfall? Chocolate? Crisps? Peanut butter sandwiches?'

Jennifer was startled. 'What? Well, all of those I suppose. But I ... .'

I thought as much,' said Dr Ganguly, with satisfaction. 'You've struggled with your weight for some time, haven't you dear? Sugary foods are seen by many as addictive, especially chocolate. And of course they can cause the most terrible constipation.'

He eyed her body. 'You've taken an important step in coming here today to ask for help. Very important.'

Already, he was pulling a leaflet from somewhere. 'Complex carbs, that's the answer. Simple carbs interfere with the blood sugar and create cravings. More fruit and veg is what you need. Five a day and all that. Tip-top thing, fibre. Reduces cravings for the wrong sort of foods *and* lends the bowels a helping hand.'

He had begun to sound like an evangelist quoting his favourite passages from the Bible. Jennifer found herself picking up the leaflet, opening it and nodding. But her untold secret seemed to swell inside her, making it hard to breathe; making her feel she might faint from the sheer weight of her own silence.

It was a relief to get out of the surgery and into the cold evening air. Andy was lurking in the car park, jigging from foot to foot to keep warm.

'How'd it go?' he asked.

She grunted. 'Thanks for hanging around.'

'No prob. Thought we could walk to the chemist together.'

He had no 'side'. What you saw was what you got. Anyone more different from Salvatore was hard to imagine.

The headlamps of the last rush hour cars sped towards them as they walked towards the distant lit windows of the chemist.

'How did the rest of the dating thing go?' she asked, for the sake of saying something.

She expected him to say it had been a washout. But he grinned awkwardly.

'Oh, all right. Not bad, as it happens. I met someone.'

'Really? Well, that's good news.'

'Her name's Pez.'

'Pez. Right. What's she like?'

'She's cool.'

'What does she do?'

'Oh, this and that. She's working on a catering contract at the moment. It's not what she really wants to do. She wants to make films.'

They had arrived at the chemists. In the sterile lighting, they handed their prescriptions in and stood by a display of hair accessories.

Jennifer ran her fingers over the blunt plastic teeth of an Alice band.

'What about you?' asked Andy. 'What went down with your other dates?'

Jennifer sighed. 'It all feels like something that happened in another lifetime. But I'm okay. I'm sort of seeing somebody. At least for the moment.'

'Right. Lucky bloke. What's his name?'

'Oh … he's an Italian hairdresser.'

'Nice. Maybe the four of us could like, get together? Go for a pint and a curry, yeah? Pez struggled with the lonely hearts thing a bit, as a way to meet. It might help her to know another couple who met the same way.'

Jennifer tried to imagine them all in the Frog and Newt:

184

Andy and Salvatore bonding over a shot of Grappa while she and Pez, whoever she was, sipped Pinot Grigio and discussed Art.

'Maybe,' she said.

He smiled with what looked like genuine pleasure.

But as they collected their prescriptions and walked out into the wintry dark, she felt like crying.

29. *Chocolate decorations*

Jennifer's physical recovery from Salvatore's idea of bath time fun only took a few days. But a fortnight on, her emotions still felt as muddy as the bathwater. At times, she hated him. Then, at other times, she longed to see him, to talk about things, put it all right.

When it was time to take Alicia to her next hair appointment, her hands sweated on the steering wheel.

She supported Alicia across the pavement. The salon was decked with early Christmas decorations. A large tree in the window was hung with multicoloured lights that blinked on and off.

She hoped that if Salvatore mentioned another date, she would manage to be noncommittal, to suggest they leave it till after Christmas. That was what she knew she should do.

'Darling, you're hurting me,' complained Alicia. 'I'm an old lady, you know. I mustn't be *gripped*.'

In the salon, it was Tony who came forward to greet them; Tony who sat Alicia down at the mirror then led her to the washbasins. Salvatore waved distractedly from the back, where he seemed to sorting through a box.

Jennifer stood by the reception desk for a few minutes, staring at a poster for hair mousse.

Out of the corner of her eye, she saw Salvatore finish with the box then go over to the cupboard where they kept the mops and brooms and rummage there.

She hadn't anticipated this. Wasn't he going to come over?

It seemed not. He disappeared into the backstage area of the salon and did not re-emerge. Tony finished washing Alicia's hair and began to towel it. The Christmas lights went through their sequence: blue, white, red and green, then began again, merciless.

Jennifer wrote out the cheque for Alicia's hairdo – it was always the same amount, after all – and propped it against the till. She thought of leaving a note. But what would she say? As she stood, she saw Tony lead Alicia to the mirrors. Salvatore would come back in a minute to do Alicia's hair.

But suddenly Jennifer didn't want to be there when he did.

She snatched up her bag and hurried to the door, nearly falling over the step in her haste to be gone, back to the safety of her little pink-roofed car.

The week passed quietly. At work, progress was slow and steady. At home, a reality TV show was on every night, its well-worn formula as soothing as Temazepam. Jennifer had been intending to tell Alicia about the Zurich trip this week, but she was in a good mood at the moment and it seemed a shame to destroy the peace.

As for Salvatore, if their relationship was over in his eyes, Jennifer hoped he would respect her enough to ring and tell her. But the phone didn't ring. And then it didn't ring again. She should be relieved, of course. She could imagine all too well what Nyesha's opinion of him – and her – would be if she ever told her what had happened.

But one evening she found herself sitting on the stairs with the phone in her hand, having failed to swallow even a mouthful of dinner. It didn't make the least bit of sense – ringing him perhaps for the purpose of being told never to ring him again, but she wanted things to be clear.

He picked up straight away. 'Pronto!'

She heard soul music murmuring in the background. Resolutions buzzed in her mind. Ask him straight. If he doesn't answer, repeat the question until he does.

'Salvatore,' she said firmly.

''Oo is this?'

'Jennifer. This is Jennifer.'

'Ah, Jennifer. How are you?'

'How are *you*?' she said.

Oh, no, she thought. I'm already acting as if his welfare is more important than mine.

'Must not complain,' he said. 'What can I do for you?'

She launched into it. 'Look, last time I came into the salon you were offhand. I thought perhaps you didn't want our relationship to continue. That's fine by me, in case you were wondering. It isn't as thought we've got that much in common. But I thought closure would be good. That's why I've rung. So we can both know where we stand and move on.'

She was glad he couldn't see her face.

But he let out a groan. 'Darling! I not wish finish our friendship, of course no! Is only, sometime is very busy at salon. I cannot give attention when the hat is drop. Is busy time of year, the Advent. Is why I have not make date for this week. We fully book. Evenings, too.'

This wasn't the line she had anticipated. She felt thrown.

'I know Christmas is a busy time,' she said. 'But … the salon didn't look busy the other morning. And couldn't you have said hello? We could at least have had a conversation.'

Not that their relationship ran on conversation.

There was a pause at his end.

'I sorry,' he said. 'It was mistake of me. Listen, I go now. I have people here, Mario and other friends. But I ring you soon. We have nice chat. Next week, okay? Please don' worry. Ciao, bella. Bye-bye Jennifer.'

The phone call had been a mistake, she thought as she put the phone down. Now instead of a dull fatalistic feeling, she had a dull fatalistic feeling laced with hope.

Nevertheless, it was predictable that next week would come and go without a phone call. And when it did, Jennifer couldn't exactly describe herself as surprised.

At work, with the exhibition more or less sorted – site services booked; official show photographer engaged, and five thousand fluffy white 'bugs' being tagged with the company's logo at a printer's somewhere in Germany – it seemed a good time to at least try and look forwards, not back.

The stand, product of countless hours of thought and labour, was packed into five crates, the lids hammered down ready for shipping. The exact date when they would make the crossing to Europe on a three thousand tonne container ferry was unknown, but as they rose on the forks of a lifting truck and passed over the tailgate of the shipping company's lorry, the entire project passed out of Jennifer's hands for the time being.

Perhaps it was a bit like leaving one's child at the school gates. She stood with Eric watching. The crates had looked huge indoors but they looked small in relation to the gigantic artic.

'I hope the boat doesn't go down somewhere in the middle of the English Channel,' she fretted.

'Nah. Safe as houses, sea freight. Shame you and me can't go with it, though. Hitch a lift.'

'But you're going to Australia for Christmas. You'll be well away.'

'Aye, but I'm going with the wife, aren't I?'

'Charming!'

They walked companionably back up the factory. Ahead, the swing doors were propped open, showing clearly the dividing line where the factory ended and the General Office began. At Jennifer's desk, Greg was standing, looking at his watch.

'Will he let you make another one of them stands?' asked Eric.

'I don't know, Eric. I suppose it depends what he thinks of this one.'

She crossed the floor and sat back down at her desk, wondering what time the artic would reach the M1.

'You're getting Derek's work back, I'm afraid,' said Greg. 'And since Jocasta's threatened to go to the Union over the sales quotations issue, you're going to have to take those back on board too. Not much I can say about it, with your work on the show finished.'

'Fair enough,' said Jennifer.

But as she tore the wrapper off a ream of A4 and shoved it into the printer, her desk and indeed her entire life seemed claustrophobic all of a sudden, and unbearably small.

Over the next fortnight, the caterer's cakes and scones became hard to resist again.

Down in London, Nyesha had a lot of clients to wine and dine in the run-up to Christmas, so communications with her fell into a hiatus, although Jennifer talked to her voicemail extensively.

Jennifer saw Salvatore again at the salon. He smiled and was polite. There was nothing you could fault him on technically. But he was acting, all of a sudden, as though their relationship had never happened. It was a turn of events that Jennifer hadn't expected, and she had no idea how to deal with it.

The only way seemed to be total avoidance. On the way to Sainsbury's at the weekend, Jennifer asked Alicia if she'd mind getting a taxi to and from the salon from now on.

Alicia's reaction was unexpectedly positive. 'Very well, darling, if it will help. I know your job is more demanding than it used to be.'

'What? You mean you don't mind? Gosh.'

'I do sometimes wonder if it's too much for you, looking after me.'

Jennifer let go of the steering wheel. The car mounted the curb and ran along the grass verge. She brought it quickly back down onto the road.

'Good heavens,' said Alicia. 'Your driving gets worse and worse. Do you think you ought to take a refresher course? I mustn't be *tilted*, you see. Narendra says it's bad for someone of my constitution.'

'Yes, yes. But what were you saying?'

Alicia rearranged her handbag on her knee. 'Well, that little conversation we had a few weeks ago. About your need for more, um, *freedom*. Yes, that's the best expression. On reflection, I over-reacted. In my defence, I've always found you rather recalcitrant, darling, rather unwilling to 'let me in' as they term it nowadays. One senses when one is being kept in the dark, you see. One lives in fear of a nasty shock. But it has been pointed out to me that I may not be *encouraging* you in the right way.'

They were now in Sainsburys' car park. Jennifer brought the mini to an abrupt halt in a parking space. 'Pointed out to you? Who by? Nelly?'

'Never mind who. That's hardly relevant. What I'm trying to say is that from now on, I'd like you to feel free to come and go as you choose – within reason, of course. You seem tired these days. You've lost weight – not that it wasn't high time, mind you. But getting out and about might help. Nelly and I can always come up with an arrangement to cover.'

She waited for a response. 'Well, aren't you going to say anything?'

'Sorry, Mum. But I'm completely gobsmacked.'

'Darling! Please don't use that expression.'

'Sorry.'

Alicia patted her daughter's knee. 'I expect you're worried there might not be a young man out there who will take an interest? But remember dear, however unhopeful your current situation looks, it won't last forever. Something wonderful may be just around the corner. Or something terrible that will make you realise just how lucky you were, only you couldn't see it at the time. Or a combination of both – something that makes you re-evaluate everything.'

She sniffed, searched for the lace-edged hanky in her pocket, and dabbed rather ostentatiously at her eyes. 'Oh, none of us knows what the future holds.'

And she gave a little smile, and patted her daughter's arm some more. Jennifer stared. It was hard to be certain, but she had seen films where people behaved like this. And if her memory served her right, it was called 'mothering'.

30. *Mince pies*

At work, the Christmas decorations went up. Jocasta made Derek throw out the green plastic scarecrow that passed for a tree and splash out on a real Douglas fir. It stood proudly in reception, its fat blue-green branches bristling with festivity.

Christmas cards multiplied on desks until they reached a critical mass and had to be Blu-tacked onto walls, hundreds of little flaps opening onto nothing.

The sandwich girl began selling mince pies and Jocasta began coming to work in a rust-red trouser suit and a silky halter neck top that made Greg's eyes pop out of his head. He fought back with a skintight shirt. Jocasta parried with black patent leather boots. Greg's final and decisive thrust was to razor-cut his hair to within a millimetre of its life. Rumours about their relationship flew all around the factory, but no one had any real evidence.

Jennifer felt uninterested in Christmas. At home, the tree Ernie had bought a week ago was still living in the garage in a bucket, leaning against the breezeblock wall like a drunk at a bus stop.

At work there were free turkey and cranberry sandwiches served by Wally Walton and the Production Director, both wearing Santa hats and beards. Afterwards, the marketing team drank a bottle of Cava in Greg's office and then suddenly the year was over as far as the company was concerned and Jennifer was driving home.

In her bag was her new passport, which had arrived that

morning. With Eric in Australia, the stand shipped and the PA duties omnipresent, the exhibition stand seemed a figment of her imagination. But the passport proved it was real, and she must prepare Alicia and Nelly for her trip.

She found Nelly behind the garage with a wastepaper basket, studying the list of recyclables stuck to the lid of the brown wheelie bin. She listened to Jennifer's request with a frown. 'You're sure you'll need me, love? I mean, don't get me wrong. Ernie and me could use the money. We could always use the money. But in the circumstances?'

'What circumstances?'

Nelly peered into the wastebasket then began to rummage about in it.

'What circumstances, Nelly?'

Nelly's face took on a rabbit-in-the-headlights look. The contents of the waste paper basket landed in the wheelie bin with a clunk. 'Oh, nothing. There. That'll have to do, light bulbs or no light bulbs. I can't be expected to fanny about trying to save the planet at my age.'

Alicia's reaction half an hour later was also puzzling. She seemed to see the news in terms of Jennifer, rather than herself. 'Darling, that sounds like a wonderful opportunity. A chance to really *shine* in your job and show them what you can do. And you'll see real snow; be in the middle of a proper winter.'

As she got to the end of her sentence, her eyes filled with tears.

'Well, yes. But I'm thinking of you,' said Jennifer. 'The arrangements we need to make. Work's willing to pay for as many extra hours as we need from Nelly. She can stay overnight if you're worried about being alone in the house in the dark.'

The lace-edged hanky came out again. Alicia blew her nose then pushed the hanky firmly up her cardigan sleeve. 'Don't worry about details, darling. Your trip isn't for another few weeks, is it? Goodness knows what will have happened by then.'

This behaviour was unsettling. 'Mum. Are you all right? You don't seem quite yourself.'

'Perhaps not,' said Alicia. 'But don't worry about it.'

'But .... .'

'But, nothing. Now if you don't mind, I'd like to catch the six o'clock news.'

There was nothing for it but to sit in front of the TV and try to ignore the sniffs, sighs and discreet nose blowings that accompanied George Alagiah's description of recent events in Helmand Province.

Christmas morning arrived, frosty and crisp. Jennifer, determined to make an effort, lugged the tree in from the garage and threw some tinsel at it. She exchanged presents with Alicia and put a turkey leg in the oven for herself and a nut roast for her mother, who had announced that she was going vegetarian. As a concession to the festive season, neither item was date expired.

After they had eaten, and Jennifer had drunk a whole bottle of Chenin Blanc, they sat in front of the Bond film with a large box of Cadbury's Milk Tray.

Boxing Day morning was similarly excessive. When Jennifer went into the kitchen to wash up after lunch, she could only just bend to fish the Marigolds out from under the sink.

As she was stacking the last plate in the draining rack, the phone rang. She peeled off the pink rubber hands and left them to their own devices.

On the other end of the phone, the stifled sound of a man crying jolted her out of her tranquillised state.

'Who is this?' she asked.

The man made a series of incoherent sounds. Jennifer caught a strangled attempt to say her name. So it was someone she knew. Whoever he was, he was in a terrible state.

'Take a deep breath,' she said. 'Then tell me who you are and what's happened.'

Andy's house was in a warren of Victorian back to backs, a sodden pizza box the only thing growing in the tiny front garden. Jennifer walked up the steps and rang the bell, turning her back on the drizzle. He came to the door in grey tracksuit bottoms. Above the drooping neck of his jumper, chest hair and stubble threatened to meet. His eyes were puffy.

'Sorry,' he said. 'I was cool until you answered the phone. It was the sound of a friendly voice that got to me. I've been here on my own all over Christmas.'

The sitting room led straight off the street and was freezing despite the gas fire being on full blast. The curtains were half closed and Julie Andrews mouthed on the TV while Morrissey moaned from the music system.

Andy went into the galley kitchen to put the kettle on. Through the bead curtain that stood for a door, Jennifer saw smeared plates shovelled into the sink. Two big saucepans stood on the cooker; one encrusted with something brown, the other with something white.

She perched on the sofa arm. 'It's certainly quiet out there. I think we're the only two people in the whole of Woodhouse.'

On the main road, normally so congested, the traffic lights had gone from red to green and back again unwitnessed.

'Yeah. Like a ghost town,' he said.

'Students gone off to enjoy the contents of their parents' fridges I suppose.'

After the phone call, she had unzipped the TV blanket she was wearing and gone into the sitting room where her mother was humming to *The Sound of Music* and looking as if she too had been having a good cry.

'Of course you must go if you have a friend in need,' she'd said, giving Jennifer one of her new 'I'd-never-dream-of-standing-in-your-way-about-anything' looks. 'And take her or him a nice slice of Christmas cake while you're at it. We have so much. It's wrong not to share it.'

It was so cold in the sitting room that they had to go up to Andy's room. It was a mess, strewn with CDs, books, newspapers and flaccid black clothes. But the mess reminded Jennifer of Bobby's room at his old student house and she found it comforting. The present receded, and was replaced by a more carefree time.

The bed was two double mattresses on top of each other. Jennifer sat on it while Andy turned a fan heater on. He sipped his tea experimentally, then confiscated hers quickly and reached a pack of Newcastle Brown down from the wardrobe. He pulled two cans out from the plastic webbing.

She hesitated then snapped the tab. She felt the fizz of beer on her tongue, the sharp edges of metal. 'It's Pez, isn't it?' she said.

He sat down next to her. The mattresses were so springy she nearly toppled over. 'I've blown it,' he said.

'Oh, Andy. Surely not?'

'We had a row. And now I haven't heard from her for, like, three days. We were meant to be spending Christmas together. Listen, I'm not imposing on you, am I? It's just, everyone else I know in Leeds seems to be away.'

She could see he was near to tears again; that having once given in to them, it was now hard to hold back.

She put her hand on his arm. 'First, it's totally fine that you rang me. It's doing me good to get out of the house: I was beginning to forget there was a world outside our front room. Second, holidays are stressful. Aren't they one of the main times couples fall out? Doesn't mean you won't get back together.'

He didn't reply. The fan heater was drying her eyeballs. Outside it was getting dark already, even though it was only half past two. It had been one of those days where it had never really got properly light, as if the sun had woken up, taken a quick look around, then decided to go straight back to bed.

She withdrew her hand, feeling awkward. 'What was the row about?'

'We'd said how we wanted to always be honest with each

other, never lie.'

Oh God, thought Jennifer. Say no more.

He went on. 'She said however big or small a thing was, we had to tell each other the truth, no matter how bad it made us feel. And then she asked about my other lonely hearts dates.'

'And?'

'I didn't tell her anything saucy. Well, there wasn't anything saucy to tell. But the numbers freaked her.'

There was a stack of bowls near the bed, spoons sticking out like Dalek's arms, a pool of beige milk in the top one.

'I didn't know you went on that many dates,' said Jennifer.

'Seventeen.'

'That's not that many. Anyway wasn't she flattered? That you picked her?'

Andy studied his feet. 'I suppose she would've been. If that had've been what happened. But she was the only one who didn't reject me.'

'Oh, Andy. I know you've, well, got no job. But you're a nice guy. Good-looking, too.'

It was true, she thought. His skin wasn't brilliant, and his physique a bit scrawny, but he had a kind, strong face. And he was very nice.

'One girl actually said to me, "there are three things I look for in a man: money, power and status".'

Jennifer couldn't help laughing. Then a thought struck to her. 'You didn't *tell* Pez you'd been rejected seventeen times, did you?'

'Sixteen,' said Andy. 'Look if you're going to be honest, you're going to be honest, right? But then she's up and getting dressed and calling a taxi at two in the morning.'

Jennifer shook her head.

'Told you I'd blown it,' said Andy. 'I've never had a girlfriend as cool as Pez. And now it's over before it's even begun.'

The pathos of this made him clutch his knees.

His sadness was hard to witness. Jennifer moved closer again and put her arm round him. 'When she calms down and thinks about it, she'll realise that other people's opinions don't matter.'

He hardly seemed to hear.

'It's *her* opinion that counts,' said Jennifer.

She took his hand and peered into his face, wanting to insert optimism into him, so that he would feel better.

He looked at her. They held each other's gaze.

And then something happened. A question rose in the space between them. She felt uncertain, looked to him for the answer. There was another moment of strange, pregnant, hesitation and then he leant forward and touched his lips to hers. His lips were soft.

Jennifer had never had any inkling of fancying Andy. She could appreciate him in theory, or on someone else's behalf, but that was as far as it went. She was surprised then, to find herself moving into his kiss. And as the kiss went on, confident and wholehearted, she was surprised to feel little flares of interest rising from the depths of her being.

Things moved quickly, then. They tipped back onto the bed. His glasses came off. She saw the mustard and brown whorls of the carpet close-to. She saw that his back and shoulders were smooth and toned and that he looked better naked than clothed. She dug her nails into his buttocks. He had no trouble with his hard-on, and she had no trouble welcoming it in. She felt the sheet work itself into a pole under her back. They laboured and ground against each other with an almost mechanical seriousness, as if they were part of the manufacturing plant back at the factory.

Before he came, there was a moment of stillness, like the second before a dive. She was borne along on a torrent of feeling, like a small boat taken by the current. Yet when she came, she found herself laughing, because sex had never in her life been so quick or enjoyable or straightforward. Afterwards, he lay on top of her, and she felt his heart beat as if it was her own.

'That's never happened to me before,' she said shyly, when they had got their breath back and were sitting up against the wall, the ventilation grille letting a trickle of icy air onto their hot backs.

'What hasn't?'

'Sex working like it's supposed to.'

He grunted and put his glasses back on. They had a John Lennon appeal, she realised. She noticed that his boxer shorts, by the bed, were brand new and printed with little penguins in Christmas hats and scarves. She looked quickly away. Those had probably been a present from Pez.

She reached for her bag. 'I brought you some Christmas cake. Well, it's from my mum really. In conjunction with Sainsburys.'

She put it on his lap. It lay there in its aluminium foil, a silver ingot, and he didn't touch it.

'Right,' he said.

She could feel him withdrawing from her, in tiny increments. It hurt. 'So, what now?' she blurted.

'Now in general or now this afto?' he asked, flatly.

She bottled out. 'Now this afto.'

The park was wet, windy and litter-strewn, the wooden exercise apparatus that stood around its perimeter dark and sodden. The weather made it difficult to talk. And the way Andy was walking, head buried deep in the hood of his Parka, made it more difficult still.

Jennifer sighed. 'Was that a bad idea? What we just did.'

'Didn't know it *was* an idea,' he said.

She glanced at him, feeling the painful tug of invisible threads joining them together, threads that had not been there before. They were walking level with the skateboard park now. A lone skater practised his moves, wheels smacking wood. Trees dripped.

'What's your hairdresser going to say?' he asked.

His gloomy tone said it all.

Jennifer shrugged, deciding abruptly that she had had enough of words for the afternoon. Better just to walk.

So they did, past the University buildings then alongside the main road with its traffic lights changing from red to green and back again, untroubled by traffic. Jennifer started another lap without consulting him.

He followed. It was getting dark properly now; the temperature dropping. Jennifer had no gloves and no pockets. She blew on her hands and worked them into their opposite sleeves. But the walking was good. She would have liked it to go on forever, round and round silently, without saying anything. In the silence, she could imagine communion.

When they had walked for almost an hour, they came parallel to the main road again. Across it, the café where they'd first met was closed, its chairs stacked up on the tables.

'It's getting late,' he said. 'Better be getting back.'

She didn't challenge this and they crossed the road to her Mini. She turned to him. His face was dear to her. It had always been dear to her. She just hadn't recognised that before.

She took a deep breath, bracing herself for what had to be said. 'In the New Year ... .'

He frowned.

'When you get back with Pez,' she said.

He looked at her suspiciously.

'Don't fall for it again,' she said.

'Fall for what?'

'The old honesty trick. '

There was a note of relief in his laugh. It hurt, but she smiled anyway and moved into his hug, a chaste shoulder-to-shoulder job.

'Thanks for coming round,' he said. 'I feel loads better.'

'Sorry,' he added. 'I didn't mean ... .'

'I know what you mean. Don't worry about it. Just have a good New Year.'

In the damp cold of the Mini, the thud as he banged on the roof in farewell was loud. It seemed a metaphor, a knock on the head for any last dreams of romance she might be nurturing.

31. *Holey cheese*

On the second of January, everyone went back to work. And everyone looked glad.

'Nice Christmas?' people asked. 'It was okay,' came the reply. The unspoken corollary, 'I'm glad it's over.'

In Reception, the Douglas fir was parched, a downpour of needles pattering onto the carpet every time anyone went anywhere near it.

Jennifer took down Christmas cards and tried to believe she would be in Zurich ten days from now. But even when Robert Stebbing paid her a visit to drop off some business cards, she couldn't raise much interest.

'The Bahnhofstrasse is meant to be one of *the* best shopping streets in the world,' he enthused from his perch at the end of her desk. 'Do they have January sales over there? You might be able to pick up a Patek Phillipe watch at half price.'

Noticing her gloomy look, he changed tack. 'You never *did* tell me about your master plan.'

'I made a sort of cover. To disguise the fact the metalwork needed renovating.'

Robert gave her a quizzical look. 'A sort of cover? Now, why do I think there's a little more to it than that? Could it be to do with an order for several hundred scrap plastic bottles? I had to *prise* that out of Brian Kelly, mind. Dear friend and valued customer though he is, the man is yawn-inducingly professional.'

Jennifer smiled. 'I was planning something quite extravagant, it's true. But I can't see it happening now. It seems a crazy dream, not something you could actually do in real life. I'll probably go back to Plan A and just use the stand as it is.'

Robert looked disappointed. 'You mean you might not go through with it? But you *must!*'

'You don't know what it is.'

'But if someone of your aptitude has thought of it? You've done the training, dear. What's more, you've got the talent. I gather your papier-mâché sculptures are to die for. Can't you give me just the teensiest clue? I might be able to help. Brian Kelly doesn't need to know, nor anyone else for that matter. Any confidences will stay within these four walls, I assure you.' He glanced rather unconfidently around the large open place office.

Jennifer fiddled with a piece of Blu-tack. 'Robert, I'd love to tell you. But I can't, because I haven't told Greg. And I should have done. I should have got his blessing. And his input. I've been such an idiot. How good can any idea be when it's conceived totally in isolation? And that's what mine has been. I suspect it's totally inappropriate. I suspect it just won't fit in, among all those smooth surfaces and clean lines.'

Robert jumped to his feet. 'Of course it won't fit in. Surely that's the whole point? Switzerland is so *boring*. I mean, Heidi? Yodelling? Holey cheese? What's all *that* about? So, their public institutions are transparent and their trams run on time. Big deal. In my experience, a little English eccentricity goes a long way in a place like that. Your creation will stand out.'

'Yeah. Like a sore thumb.'

'No! Like a beacon of creativity, a paean sung loud and long at the altar of individuality. A shout to the heavens – Look at me! Look at me!'

'You're very kind, Robert,' said Jennifer, wishing she could have even half the faith in herself that he had. 'But that's the very thing that worries me.'

The rest of the day was busy. It was the Monday phenomenon doubled, trebled and quadrupled as everyone in offices all over the country started facing up to all the things they had put off until after Christmas. It was quite nice, getting back in touch with all those people whose telephone voices Jennifer knew, but whose faces she would have struggled to identify.

But one, she had no trouble picturing. He rang mid-afternoon.

'Salvatore.'

'Darling! I am sorry. I have neglected you very badly. And now, I am thinking, Jennifer she is very angry with me.'

Jennifer glanced at the cursor on her computer screen appearing, disappearing. She didn't feel much of anything, unless it was empathy with the Douglas fir, starved of sustenance to the point where its needles dropped off.

'Is just, my uncle he die at Christmas,' said Salvatore. 'In Napoli at the Molo Beverello. Is only fifty-two. Is tragedy.'

Jennifer felt suspicious.

'Is run over by tourist bus,' said Salvatore. 'His man bag also is crushed beneath the wheels. My mother, she is devastated.'

What if it were true? Jennifer sighed. She ought to give him the benefit of the doubt. 'Salvatore, how terrible. I am sorry. Have you been to his funeral?'

'No. Is day after tomorrow. In Napoli. I fly in the morning.'

There was a pause. Then he told her the salon was going to be closed for a while.

'Tell you Mama I sorry,' he said. 'I will see her in a fortnight. And there is one more thing, my darling. Is my birthday. On January thirteen. I am having party. Just a few very special friends. I want you to be there to drink champagne amongst. Is important to me.'

'Oh,' said Jennifer.

She didn't need to think up a lie. Her flight to Zurich left Leeds Bradford International on the eleventh.

'I'm going to be in Switzerland then for work, I'm afraid,' she said. 'At an electronics show.'

There was an incredulous pause. 'You go abroad with work?'

'Yes, we're exhibiting there. I've designed an exhibition stand.'

'You? You are joking me?'

'Nope.'

'Perhaps is something you can sort out?'

For a moment she didn't know what he meant. But he went on. 'Perhaps your boss, he find someone else who can do? I back January tenth. I call you then, my darling, to firm up.'

'Salvatore, there's really no point in you calling.'

'Now, I go. Is much to do. Tony also he is very upset. Uncle Roberto he meet many time. Till I see you, bella Jennifer. Ciao. Bye-bye.'

He was incredible.

She was glad when the day was over. As she came out of the factory, half an hour later than usual, the dark had a set-in feel to it, as though it was ten o'clock at night, not five-thirty in the afternoon. Frost glittered on the tarmac. Even though the shortest day was a fortnight ago, the nights still seemed to be drawing in.

Nevertheless, she recognised the figure lurking by the car park entrance. It must have been the way he was jigging from foot to foot. She walked over, pulse and step quickening. Had he reconsidered after all? Suddenly the night didn't seem so dark, the cold so bitter.

Andy was bandaged up in scarf and gloves, his breath visible.

'Hi!' she called, rather breathlessly. Maybe they could go for a drink together, a nice glass of Merlot somewhere by a pub fire. 'I didn't know you knew where I worked.'

'Right,' he said, glancing nervously towards the side door. 'Uh, well I didn't.'

The penny dropped, taking her hopes with it. 'You're not here for me.'

'Well, no.'

He had the grace to look embarrassed. 'Sorry, Jen.'

'It's fine,' said Jennifer, although it wasn't.

His eyes darted towards the side door, then away again. Did Pez work here?

Suddenly Jennifer didn't want to know. 'I'll be off. Mum will be expecting me.'

But the side door of the building had already opened and a slim figure in a long black coat was hurrying towards them, breaking into a trot across the frosty ground. The catering franchise girl must have spent some time in the Ladies because her lips and nails, which had been normal earlier, were dark purple. She grinned and pecked Andy on the lips. 'Neat! I didn't know you two knew each other.'

'Only in a previous life,' said Jennifer, as Pez slipped her hand into Andy's. 'And now I really must be going. You two have a nice evening.'

Yeah,' said Andy.

'Cool,' said Pez. 'See you, Jen.'

They looked good together: it was impossible not to see that. In some remote and almost inaccessible part of her being, Jennifer was pleased for them.

But the flame of empathic happiness was too tiny to warm her as she made her way slowly across the dark car park to the cold, lonely interior of her little car.

32. *Tofu*

Another week passed. And then suddenly, as if someone had snatched whole bags full of time from under her nose when she wasn't looking, it was the day before Jennifer's flight. She'd planned to do a full day's work, but Greg came by her desk mid-afternoon.

'Don't you have knickers to pack or something? Get yourself off home and get some rest under your belt – you'll need it.'

Her journey home, beating the rush hour, was pleasingly quick. As she turned the corner at the end of the street, she planned a long hot soak in the bath before tea. She was brought up short by the sight of Dr Ganguly's black Honda Civic in the drive. As she pulled up behind it, her headlights illuminated a film of frost on the roof and boot. He must have been there for some time, then. In her mind, red alert went off. She scrambled out of the car and ran for the kitchen door.

She grappled with the handle, taking a moment to realise it was locked from the inside. She suddenly remembered her mother's strange mood swings of late and realised that she had forgotten to ask about the MRI results. She banged on the glass, hopping from foot to foot. 'Mum! Mum!'

Pepe began barking hysterically.

The blurred form of Dr Ganguly loomed behind the glass. 'One moment, dear, while I find the key. Not in the door, you see. My doing. Your mother needs to be more careful about intruders.'

He fumbled the key into the lock. At last the door was open. She pushed past him and his attempts at explanation, ran through the hall and pounded up the stairs. Pepe, thinking it was a game, raced after her.

As she flung open the door of her mother's bedroom, she prepared herself for rumpled sheets, an ashen face and perhaps a life-support machine, whatever that looked like.

But the counterpane was smooth, the room fresh. A tiny vase of snowdrops twinkled on the windowsill. There was no one there.

Jennifer ran back onto the landing. 'Where *is* she? What's *happened*?'

Pepe was doing shuttle runs up and down the hall.

Dr Ganguly had shambled to the bottom of the stairs. 'Jennifer, Jennifer, calm down. Don't upset yourself. Your mother's down here.'

Jennifer thundered back down the stairs and burst into the sitting room.

Alicia was on the sofa. She was wearing her best blouse and brooch and sipping a cup of tea. The dint in the cushion next to her suggested that up until a few moments ago, Dr Ganguly had been sitting next to her.

'Darling! You're home early. How lovely. Did I hear you shouting just now? I expect you'll tell me all about that in a moment.'

'You're not ill.'

Alicia's smile faltered. 'Being ill isn't the only thing we old people do, you know.'

'But Doctor Ganguly's here. And the door was locked. I thought ... .'

Dr Ganguly entered the room and Jennifer realised that Alicia was no longer listening to her, but had transferred her attention completely and utterly to him. He smiled and bent down to fondle the dog's topknot. The dog gazed at him with adoring eyes and tried to lick his hands.

Jennifer stared. 'What's going on?'

'I'm sorry about the door, dear,' said Alicia. 'But Narendra and I needed a moment's guaranteed privacy. He had something rather important to ask me.'

'What? – Does he want you to have an operation?'

'I expect you could manage a cup of tea, dear. Narendra, you'll find another cup in the cupboard above the sink. Oh, and I had Nelly buy you some sugar cubes. They're in the bread bin.'

'What a blessing when one's peccadilloes are so accurately remembered,' said Dr Ganguly as he left the room.

'Is it about the Patients' Voice, then?' asked Jennifer.

'No, dear.'

Jennifer sank down into a chair. 'Does he want to put you in a home? Is that it?'

Alicia smoothed her skirt. 'Not exactly, dear. Not in the way you're imagining, anyhow. What he *does* want, and believe me, I wasn't expecting this at all … .'

She paused for dramatic effect, a private smile playing on her lips. 'What he does want, the dear darling man, is for me to marry him.'

Jennifer's mouth fell open.

'And I've said yes,' said Alicia, as though this was an even greater surprise.

Dr Ganguly came back in. Jennifer suppressed the memory of him putting on rubber gloves and asking her to climb onto the examination table.

'Oh no dear, not that cup!' cried Alicia. 'Nelly does the gravy in that. I meant the right-hand cupboard, not the left. One of the ones with daisies around the rim.'

Dr Ganguly went out again, seeming pleased to resume his steady trundle from one place to another.

Alicia smiled. 'We've set a date, you'll be pleased to know: Valentine's Day.'

'What? In six weeks' time?'

'Yes. Isn't it just the most romantic thing you ever heard? A whirlwind affair.'

'Jesus. But even if you want to, surely you won't get in anywhere at such short notice. And what sort of place are you thinking of? A church? A mosque?'

Alicia's smile faltered. 'Leeds registry office, I expect. By the way dear, Narendra's a Hindu, not a Muslim. And do you have to blaspheme every time you open your mouth?'

'Is that why you wanted nut roast on Christmas Day?'

'Of course not. Narendra won't expect ... but even if he does, I'm sure I can get to like it. There's that quiche they do in Tesco's, with the feta cheese and the red peppers. And I gather one can work wonders with tofu these days, provided one marinates it properly. As for the spiritual side of things, I think I'd take to that rather well. We do meditation down at the centre, you know. The teacher often compliments me on my posture.'

Jennifer was silent.

'You might try to be just the teensiest bit happy for me, darling,' said Alicia.

Jennifer thought of a new objection. 'But what about his children? I mean he's got three, if those photos on his desk are anything to go by. How will they feel about their Dad marrying a Western woman?'

Alicia drew her shoulders back. 'Narendra assures me that daughters and son alike will be delighted to see him married again. To see him taken care of. But even if they weren't delighted, do you really think that would stop us?'

Jennifer blinked.

'Don't get me wrong,' said Alicia. 'I'm not saying one doesn't consider one's children at all. But much as you and I love each other, darling, we're not joined at the hip. We have our own lives to lead. And those lives might take us anywhere. Darling, has my news upset you dreadfully? You don't seem yourself.'

'What do you mean, take you anywhere? Are his family in India? Will you be going to live in India?'

Alicia's cheeks, masked by foundation and powder, did not change colour. But a flush began on her neck. 'Don't be silly, darling. We'll be going there for the honeymoon, naturally, but that will only be a short trip. Weeks, not months. Well maybe two months. Three at most. But we won't be going out there to live – not at the outset, anyway.'

'Christ on a bike!'

Dr Ganguly came back into the room, plus china.

'Ah, that's better,' said Alicia. 'Now if you'd do the honours, Narendra dear, I'm sure we could all do with a top up. Jennifer and I will continue our chat later.'

Jennifer couldn't bring herself to offer congratulations or say anything that might prompt the newly betrothed couple to talk about their wedding.

Dr Ganguly had to take up the conversational baton. He told them about the new doctor who was replacing him at the surgery. Then he got onto the subject of Zurich. 'Now, there is a city that is really worth seeing. Not your average tourist spot, of course. If you want to see the Alps, you must go to Geneva. But if you are after the real, working Switzerland, Zurich is the right destination: fondue, cheese, meat; outstanding restaurants; piano music, tinkling from dawn till dusk, and everywhere, crystal chandeliers.'

It was a relief to finally show him out and go back into the sitting room, where Pepe had taken up the vacant place on the sofa, lying with his head in Alicia's lap.

'Isn't he just the dearest man?' said Alicia. 'I just know it's going to be the happiest marriage ever.'

'I thought you didn't allow him up on the sofa.'

'Sit down, dear.'

'I can't talk about it anymore now. Other people have lives too. I've got to get ready for Zurich.'

'I know you're busy, dear. But at least let me fill you in on the basics.'

She began with the photographer, a man called Lawrence who worked for the local paper. 'My husband-to-be has already done tons of research, you see. Of course, none of this need concern you imminently.'

'Imminently? I should think not. I've enough on my plate as it is.'

'Yes, you're away at a key time. But I know you arranged Zurich ages ago.'

'I didn't "arrange" Zurich. It's a major electronics show, attended by companies from all over the world, that's always held in January.'

'Whatever. But the thing is, we don't want you standing around like a spare part. We want you *involved*.'

'What, do a reading or something?'

'No, dear. We want you to be Matron of Honour.'

Jennifer's heart sank. But her mother had already produced a printed page. 'Here you are. A breakdown of your duties in the weeks leading up to the Big Day. Narendra's receptionist Fiona – such a nice girl – got it off the Web.'

She jabbed certain items. 'You won't have to bother with the business about the dresses. But I'd like you to deal with the flowers. And help me with my hair and make-up on the day. And distribute the slices of wedding cake at the reception. And have the first dance with the best man. Anyway, it's all down here.'

Jennifer, picturing a best man of Dr Ganguly's age, who might have to hang on to her on the dance floor to keep himself upright, felt her heart sink even further.

'Look, surely you don't need people to fill all these traditional roles, if it's in a registry office? Couldn't I be Best Woman, or something?'

Alicia bridled. 'Matron is the correct term. If the bride is not in the first flush of youth.'

'But no one would mind if we did it differently,' said Jennifer.

'Or,' said Alicia, in the manner of someone playing an ace card, 'if the bridesmaid herself is also of mature years.'

'I'm only thirty-two, Mum,' said Jennifer faintly, but her mother had already moved on, to talk about cake and icing, and a marzipan bride and groom.

33. *Danish Pastries*

The alarm went off at four-thirty. Jennifer had slept with the curtains open and the full moon shone on her suitcase which sat by the door. Up before the central heating, she shivered as she stepped out of her pyjamas and looked back longingly at the snug nest of her bed.

She didn't feel good. Nevertheless, she lugged her case to the top of the stairs then pushed open Alicia's door. The room was dense with sleep. In the shaft of light from the hall, her mother's skin looked papery, hair thin on sponge rollers, like nearly used reels of cotton. Her breathing ticked in her throat, a slow clock. They had said their goodbyes last night. Now Jennifer blew a kiss and felt a sob rise unexpectedly to her throat. She swallowed it back.

Downstairs, she said hello to Pepe then shut him back in the kitchen and rang for a taxi. Then she stood waiting, touching her fingers to the cold glass of the hall window and making three black ovals in the condensation.

Salvatore had rung late last night, fresh from his Naples trip.

'Darling! Is me! I am safe home!'

'How did the funeral go?'

'It went all right. Is sad. Is not what I am ring to discuss.'

'You're ringing to discuss your party.'

'Is so. You change your mind, yes?'

When she said nothing had changed, he began wheedling. She told him she had to go.

There was a shocked silence.

And then, before he could begin on another tack, she hung up. She was surprised how easy it was.

There was no other traffic on the roads so the ten-mile journey passed quickly, despite eerie stops at traffic lights where there was no sound except the taxi's engine.

Inside the small airport though, there was a mini rush hour. Jennifer joined the queue at the check-in desk, nudging her case forward in the second, knee-high queue of baggage. Candy-striped, it stood out among the other travellers' black and silver.

In the departure lounge café, people shunted trays along chrome railings, past heaps of glistening Danish pastries.

When new instructions appeared on the departures board, and a cone of people funnelled in the direction of the gates, Jennifer followed them. Everyone looked so cool, as though the early morning hop to Gatwick was second nature to them.

On the other side of the huge plate glass windows, men in emerald green overalls and earmuffs waved their arms around.

As all the travellers sat down again on orange plastic seating, Jennifer noticed that every one, male or female alike, was locked in contact with some device or other, be it a laptop, an iPad or a mobile phone. No one smiled, chatted or even made eye contact.

Jennifer looked down at her own green Primark bag, with its pitiful tube of Fruit Gums and Joanna Trollope novel.

In a few minutes, she would have to stand up, hand over her boarding card and take her place on the plane. But it felt like a charade. She didn't cut it in the business world. She didn't cut it in Salvatore's world, and the world she and Bobby had once lived in was dead and buried, like a bygone civilisation. Even the world she knew with Alicia was on the way out. Her mother was entering a new life of Indian food and trips to the subcontinent.

Jennifer realised with a sickening twist of loneliness that she no longer truly belonged anywhere, anyhow, to anyone.

'Good God! What are you doing back here?' said Alicia from halfway down the stairs. Nelly was on her starboard side. 'Was your flight cancelled?'

'No,' said Jennifer, putting her case down and shutting the front door behind her.

Pepe wound himself round her legs, but she ignored him. It was still only just past eight o'clock in the morning, but she felt she had been awake forever.

'Then what?' said Alicia.

'I don't know,' said Jennifer, wanting just to crawl up the stairs and into bed.

'What do you mean, you don't know? How can you not know?'

Alicia seemed to have lost some of her new found beatitude. Nelly patted her arm. 'Now then, Mrs S, don't go getting all worked up. It does you no good. I'm sure Jennifer has her reasons. Let's get you down these stairs and in front of a nice cuppa. We'll sort the rest out later.'

But Alicia had no intention of sorting the rest out later. As soon as she was seated in the dining room, she turned to Jennifer again, bristling as though her daughter's failure to get on the plane was a personal affront.

'Now, suppose you tell me what all this is about?'

Jennifer sat down. Fuck *off*, she said, in her head. She stared at the tablecloth, a red, embroidered one from a car boot sale.

'Well?' said her mother. 'You get everyone running around after you, making arrangements – which we all do willingly, since you've given us to believe this is an important opportunity for you – and then, with suitcases packed, flight tickets bought and presumably hotel rooms booked, you throw the towel in at the last minute and let everybody down. Why?'

I *so* don't need this, thought Jennifer. Refusing to look at her mother, she picked up the teapot.

This seemed to incense Alicia. 'Put that blasted thing down!

217

Don't just ignore your own mother. You owe me an explanation.'

Jennifer's resentment rose up like a tsunami inside her. She banged the teapot down so hard onto its Houses of Parliament mat that the lid jumped off. She sprang to her feet again. Her wrists felt weak. Her breathing had gone wrong. It took moments to understand that the shouting she could hear, that was making her mother flinch and stare, as at some dreadful road accident, was coming from her own mouth.

'If anyone has any explaining to do, it's *you*!' she was yelling. 'You don't imagine you're in *love* with him, surely?'

'What on earth has all this got to do with Narendra and me?' asked her mother.

'Just because he's asked you, doesn't mean you've got to say yes. You don't have to do what he says, even if he is your doctor.'

'I know I haven't *got* to. I *want* to.'

Jennifer paced up and down. 'You think he's lonely since his wife died. Well, being sorry for someone doesn't mean you've got to marry them.'

'I am not marrying him because I feel sorry for him.'

'Is it the money, then? Are you worried in case you end up in a nursing home, and have to sell the house to pay for it?'

Alicia threw her hands up in exasperation. 'For goodness' sake! Have you no romance in your soul? You sound like some nineteenth century paterfamilias. You'll be asking me if I'm pregnant next.'

Jennifer felt some of the fight go out of her. She sank back down in her chair. 'So why *are* you getting married?' she pleaded.

'That's rather a personal question dear.'

'I'm not fishing for the gory details.'

Nelly came in with fresh water for the pot, and toast. Both women ignored her.

'I've nothing against him personally,' said Jennifer, still in a pleading tone. 'But why can't you take things slowly? Go out on dates. Go to the theatre, to dinner, little days out in the country.'

Alicia sighed. She looked pained. 'Darling, I'm not sixteen. We old folks don't go on forever, you know. We have to strike while the iron is hot. Make hay while the sun shines. Close the stable door before ... .'

'Yes, yes,' said Jennifer.

'And don't forget,' said Alicia more quietly, 'I've never actually been married before.'

There was a pause.

'Anyway,' Alicia went on, 'I fail to see what any of this has to do with your extraordinary *volte-face* about Switzerland.'

Jennifer felt incredulous. 'You lied to me, Mum. You deceived me.'

As she said the words, as she actually came to the nub of what had wounded her, the sadness of it swept away the last of her anger, a river in spate carrying a log downstream. She burst into tears.

Alicia had the grace to look ashamed. 'Darling, I ...'

'After everything I've done for you,' sobbed Jennifer. 'All the sacrifices I've made.'

Alicia looked at her hands.

'The way I've put my life on hold to look after you!' Jennifer went on.

Alicia gripped the edge of the table. 'Darling. Listen to me. I didn't mean to keep you in the dark. But I thought it best to operate on a "need to know" basis. I didn't want to tell you anything until there was something *to* tell.'

Her hands fluttered up. 'Oh dear, I'm not putting this very well. But you know what I mean. And I know you've made sacrifices to care for me.'

Her voice dropped. 'But I thought they were sacrifices made of your own free will. I didn't know you *resented* it. You never said. I wish you'd told me before, Jennifer. I thought we were happy together. And you must remember that I didn't *mean* to get ill. It isn't my fault.'

In the midst of her unhappiness, Jennifer realised it was now or never. All the fantasies she had ever entertained about what might happen when she finally confronted her mother with the unvarnished, no-holds-barred truth came flooding into her mind. Ambulance sirens wailed, doctors ran down corridors with the tails of their white coats flapping and heart monitors flat-lined.

And Jennifer took her chance. 'But you're not really ill, are you, Mum?' she wailed. 'There's nothing physically wrong with you. That's the whole point.'

There was a pause, during which her Alicia stared at her daughter with a look of complete incomprehension on her face. But the ceiling didn't fall. The mirror didn't crack from side to side. And, if the post that dropped through the letterbox was anything to go by, the world outside had gone on functioning the same as usual. In short, in the little room where Jennifer and Alicia sat, in the modest semi on the respectable but shabby housing estate in Leeds, nothing really happened.

Alicia wasn't even angry. 'Oh darling, if only that were true.' she said. 'But you and I both know it isn't.'

Nelly, who had been standing there with her head turning this way and that like someone at a ping-pong match, fished a hanky out of her apron, sat down at the table and began to dab at her own eyes.

'Dear, dear, what a to-do! Who'd have thought it? And all over a silly little trip to a silly little country that didn't even have the guts to stand up and fight with us in the Second World War.'

It wasn't every day that the parameters of the known world shuddered. It wasn't every day that one went to the far edge of one's experience and came back to find that nothing had really changed.

But this was such a day, and everything that happened after Jennifer had said the unsayable had a strange, luminous quality.

As she helped Nelly clear away and wash up the breakfast things, even the cups and plates seemed ringed with light. It didn't matter that her words had had almost no effect on her mother. What mattered was that she had, at last, said them.

'Are you all right, love?' Nelly asked her gently. 'Staring at the washing up brush like that. Why don't you just leave all this to me? Surely you need to be phoning someone about something, with your not getting on that plane and all.'

'What? Oh God, you're right,' said Jennifer.

She was still feeling disorientated when she rang Greg's mobile.

The voice at the other end said the call could not be connected, so she dialled his home number in London, where he was meant to be touching base before the trip to Zurich.

It was his wife who answered, a woman whose curt manner could have brought even Buzz Aldrin back to earth with a bump.

'He's not here. He's on a business trip. Switzerland.'

'Yes,' said Jennifer, her voice still gluey from crying. 'But his flight's not till the day after tomorrow.'

A pause. 'Who is this?' asked the wife.

'I work beside him.'

Another pause, pregnant this time.

Jennifer thought she mustn't be making herself clear. 'Look, let me explain,' she said. 'I was meant to be going out there first. He was following me the next day. But something's come up now and I can't make it. I'll spare you the details. But he's going to be very upset. So I need to let him know as soon as humanly possible.'

There was a sharp intake of breath at the other end of the phone. 'You're her, aren't you? You're the one. Oh, how dare you. How dare you ring here!'

'What? No! You've got the wrong end of the stick. I'm not her. Of course I'm not her. Not that there is a 'her,'' said Jennifer. 'In fact, I haven't the faintest idea what you're talking about. I just need to get a message to my boss. Please can you ask him to call me?'

'Listen to me. I've got news for you: you can have him. And don't think I won't make him pay. As for you, you little whore, I hope you roast in hell.'

She hung up.

'Oh dear,' said Jennifer, to the silent handset.

She went upstairs to her bedroom, drew the curtains, got undressed and got into bed. But she couldn't sleep. Too much had happened and her mind reeled. She lay, staring at the ceiling and letting time pass without her.

That evening, Nyesha rang. She was totally unsympathetic. 'I know you're freaked out about your Mum's wedding, but why can't you go to Zurich?' she asked.

'Everything feels too fucked,' said Jennifer.

'Tsk!' said Nyesha. 'What's happening to you, girl? You never used to swear.'

'I just couldn't go through with it,' said Jennifer. 'The world felt so unfriendly all of a sudden. No one at the airport even looked at me. I had to get home.'

'I've never heard anything so pathetic,' said Nyesha. 'Get a grip. Your co-passengers were probably just shell-shocked with having got up so early.'

The moment Jennifer hung up, the phone rang again.

Salvatore's voice was soft. 'Darling. I am ring for apologise. The way I speak you yesterday, is not good. I happy you still here because I want wish you the successful trip. I want tell you, is okay miss my birthday. We celebrate together when you are back.'

'Thanks,' said Jennifer said. 'But I'm not going. Listen, I'd better not stay on the phone.'

'Not go Switzerland? But why?'

'It just didn't work out.'

'But how, not work out? What happen?'

'I don't know,' she said. 'All sorts of things. Mum.'

'The Mama? Why?'

Jennifer hesitated. 'Oh well, I suppose you'd better know. We'll need you to do her hair and make-up. If you do that kind of thing, for that kind of occasion.'

'Porca Madonna! She is dead?'

'No,' said Jennifer. 'It's far more shocking than that.'

34. *Cava*

Salvatore opened the door singing, glass in hand. He was dressed in a flowing white silk shirt and tight black trousers, a cross between a wine waiter and the Marquis de Sade.

'Darling! You are arrive!'

'Happy Birthday,' said Jennifer.

On the phone last night he'd listened to her in a way he hadn't done since their first date. He'd talked about his Uncle's death and about how a funeral sometimes made one reassess one's priorities. Jennifer still had no plans to give him a second chance. But she'd decided that a party among people she didn't know might do her good. It would get her out of the house, for one thing: despite the events of the day before, her mother still had only one real topic of conversation – her wedding.

'So, who's actually coming to the party?' she asked now.

She had never met any of his friends, though he talked of a hairdressing colleague called Mario.

'A chosen few,' he said. 'The inner circle.'

'I'm honoured,' she said, rather falsely. She didn't feel honoured. In fact, now she was here, she didn't feel much of anything. It struck her as strange that she had been so besotted with a man with whom she had so little in common. An image of Andy came to mind, but she pushed it quickly away. It was no good replacing one lost cause with another.

Salvatore ushered her towards the sitting room. The flat was quiet, though the soft glow of candles spilled out into the hall.

But in the sitting room, on the white sofa with a can of Special Brew idling in his hand were no suave Italians, only Tony. Jennifer's heart sank.

'All right?' said Tony.

Salvatore guided her to the sofa. 'Sit 'ere, darling. To keep company for Tony. While I get drink.'

Jennifer tried to make the best of it. 'How are you, Tony?' she asked.

'All right. Bit knackered. Been down the gym.'

'What were you doing down there?'

'Weights and stuff.'

The conversation lapsed. Tony swigged lager. The TV and DVD seemed to be missing from their usual spot in the corner. Jennifer started on a bowl of potato chips.

Salvatore came in with glasses and a bottle with a foil top. 'Ey! Why you not talking? Is not very party!'

The cork shot out and the mouth of the bottle smoked like a gun. Jennifer took off her jacket. She was wearing a new pink blouse from Per Una, whose size 18s she could now squeeze into, despite the Christmas excesses.

But no compliments were forthcoming from anyone.

'Jennifer, why you look so stiff?' asked Salvatore. 'Drink a bit the champagne. 'Appy birthday Salvatore!'

It was not champagne, Jennifer noted, but Cava. She raised her glass in a toast anyway.

Tony drained his in one. 'Cheers, boss.'

Salvatore refilled their glasses and put a CD on the player.

'Have you been to the gym today, as well, Salvatore?' asked Jennifer.

'I train him. I teach him play badminton and work with weights.'

Tony pulled a face. 'He's a fuckin' slave driver.'

'Ey!' said Salvatore. 'What I tell you about the swearing?'

He came back and sat on the sofa arm next to Jennifer and

began fiddling with her hair. She pulled away. Surely he didn't think they were still an item?

But he only moved nearer. 'I happy you 'ave forgot the work shit. A woman, building an exhibition, doing the man's work. Is not good.'

Jennifer pulled away from him again. 'It does happen. Lots of women work in the field these days. Look, is anyone else coming tonight? Mario and his wife, for instance?'

'Work in the field,' Salvatore chortled. 'Milk the cow. Spread the muck.'

Salvatore and Tony laughed, too long and heartily for Jennifer's liking. Then Salvatore said he was sure Mario and his wife would arrive soon and much to Jennifer's relief got up from the sofa arm and bobbed up and down refilling the bowls of nuts and crisps. He seemed reluctant to let anyone's glass go down to less than three-quarters full.

When he eventually sat down again it was in an armchair. Lady Gaga gave way to Jessie J, who gave way to Amy Winehouse. Salvatore only liked women singers. No one said much, which made the drinking seem very applied. Jennifer thought she would stay another fifteen minutes, then go.

'You want watch film, darling?' asked Salvatore suddenly. 'I remember you tell me you like.'

Jennifer felt compromised without knowing why.

'What your favourite film, Tony?' asked Salvatore.

Tony named several films Jennifer had never heard of.

When Jennifer was asked, the only film she could think of was Shirley Valentine, which had been on over Christmas.

'What kind of film is this?' asked Salvatore.

'It's the story of an English woman,' said Jennifer reluctantly. 'And a Greek man.'

'Ah! Is good! What happen?'

'Well, she goes on holiday to a Greek island and, er, meets him and ends up going to live there. She falls in love with the place.'

'She make love with many Greek men?' asked Salvatore.

'No. Her husband comes out to find her and doesn't recognise her.'

Tony looked scornful.

'That's the point of the film,' said Jennifer. 'She's changed so much, you see. She becomes unrecognisable to the people from her old life.'

'This is crazy film, eh?' said Salvatore, squeezing her shoulders.

'It's a metaphor,' said Jennifer.

Tony sniggered.

Salvatore jumped to his feet. 'Okay. Is time we see my film. Is special film. I hire for you, Jenny.'

'Is it *Il Postino*?' asked Jennifer. 'What about Mario and his wife? They'll miss the beginning.'

'They will catch up,' said Salvatore.

Tony stood up too.

'Where are we going?' asked Jennifer.

Salvatore smiled. 'Film is set up. Next door.'

'What, in the bedroom?'

'Darling! You want I carry whole thing through to sitting room? That machine, it weigh a bloody ton.'

In the bedroom, Salvatore's flat screen TV had been installed between the bed and window. The digital clock winked from the bedside cabinet.

Jennifer decided she would stay for the start of the film, as he seemed to have gone to so much trouble. She was shocked that she felt so little towards him now, slightly guilty about it. He didn't seem to have cottoned on.

They sat on the bed, with him in the middle.

But the film was not *Il Postino*.

It was even lower budget.

It was set in an office. Jennifer watched a woman with

cascading blonde hair and a low-cut red blouse welcome a man to his new job and tell him the boss was a disciplinarian. It was in a foreign language, maybe Dutch, and badly dubbed. The music was terrible.

'That leather skirt wouldn't last ten minutes in a real office,' said Jennifer. 'What with the printer toner and stuff. And all that sitting down. It'd get pulled out of shape.'

'Shush!' said both men, watching with surprising intensity considering that nothing was happening except that the woman was fingering a paperweight and sucking the end of her pen. Another man came in, sat on the desk, and began dictating. There was a close up of the woman's mouth, plus pen. Things went on like this, uneventfully, for several minutes. Jennifer's attention wandered. She looked out of the window and wondered what Greg was doing now.

Then from the speakers came a low moan, no translation necessary. Jennifer's attention jerked back to the screen.

With a dull shock, she saw that the woman was now kneeling in front of the man on the desk and that his hands were on the back of her head. And that her head was moving in and out, in and out.

'Oh my God!' she said, staring at both men in turn. They were so engrossed they didn't even hear her.

She stood up.

'Where you going?' asked Salvatore, eyes still riveted to the screen. When she didn't reply he said, 'I pause. I make sure you don't miss. We wait till you come back. '

Jennifer went into the kitchen and switched the light on. In a panic, she took a glass from the draining board and filled it at the tap. The water was cloudy but gradually, from the bottom up, it began to clear.

The truth, when it hit you right between the eyes, wasn't pretty. In fact it was ugly as hell. There could only be one reason why two men wanted to watch a porno with one woman. The whole thing was a set-up. Jennifer took a bracing swig of lukewarm tap water and went back into the bedroom.

The men were sitting in silence, looking at the stalled image on the screen.

'Salvatore,' she said. 'I'm going home. It's been a long day. A long week.'

Salvatore looked shocked. 'What is matter? You not like film?'

It wasn't even worth replying to.

But he followed her out into the hall. 'I sorry, darling. Is Tony, yes?'

'No, it isn't just Tony,' said Jennifer.

'I get rid,' he said. 'Is more relax anyway, just we two.'

'What planet are you on, Salvatore?' said Jennifer. 'Can't you see it's way too late for all that?'

'But is my birthday!'

She turned to face him. 'I couldn't care less about your birthday. You've set me up, haven't you? For a threesome, with Tony. Without asking me, without even caring whether I was interested or not.'

He was taken aback. Then he shrugged. 'What is problem? Is all right when we do other things. You like. In the stairwell. On the kitchen table. In the bath.'

She stared at him. Had he thought she'd actually *liked* the bath episode? Hadn't she made it plain that she hated it?

The moment of self-doubt threw her. Salvatore was still taking. 'This is same thing, I think. We are all adult here. Like-minded. What is problem?'

And then Tony was in the hall with them. 'Where do you think you're going?' he said to her.

'Home,' she said.

Tony stepped towards her. 'I don't think so,' he said. 'That's not in the plan.'

'The plan?' she cried. 'You can forget your bloody plan.'

A nasty look came into Tony's eyes. He grabbed her by the wrist.

Her eyes widened. 'Let go of me!'

His grip intensified. His fingers made a hot, tight bracelet. In some part of her mind, she registered that all those hours he'd spent in the gym had paid off.

She glanced wildly around for Salvatore.

But he had disappeared.

'Salvatore, help!' she cried.

But Tony had her other hand now and was pushing her until the back of her head met the wall. She blinked in shock. This wasn't happening: it couldn't be. Pain shot through her shoulders and she gasped. He was pressing her wrists back against the wall and it was like being manacled. She smelt his sour breath in her nose and mouth. She tried not to breathe, but her breath came anyway, in shallow gasps.

'Salvatore!' she yelled again.

But the word came out in a weak gasp. She twisted her head to one side. She tried to bring her knee up but Tony was too close. He seemed solid as a wardrobe.

More sounds tumbled out of her, weak as air dribbling out of a balloon. Tony's grip grew tighter the more she opposed it. And now his mouth was on hers like a clamp, his tongue pushing between her tight shut lips.

As he came up for air, breath came back to her lungs and a scream ripped out of her throat. 'Shut it!' said Tony, his spittle spraying her cheek.

She saw Salvatore running past them into the bedroom. She screamed again. Tony winced at the sound. One of her wrists came free. She flexed her hand. It felt weightless. Was he letting her go? She pulled away from the wall. She almost smiled. Then one side of her face exploded in stinging pain. He had hit her!

Now her legs went weak. She struggled to remain upright. She closed her eyes and prayed for unconsciousness: that she might not be there to witness what they were going to do to her.

But cool air touched the front of her body. Pain shot through her right shoulder. She gripped the top of her arm. Her hands were free. She opened her eyes. Tony was on his knees, clutching his head. Salvatore stood holding the digital alarm clock, wires trailing out of its back.

Leeds Ring Road at two in the morning was a spooky, anonymous place, its swathe of dimly lit tarmac curving on forever. Sometimes there was a pavement, sometimes just a grass verge. And every step, gaining slowly on industrial parks or empty pubs, seemed only to take a lone pedestrian closer to nowhere.

Between the road and the dark trees, Jennifer trudged, breaking into a jog every time she thought of what had nearly happened to her. Every so often too, she reached into her pocket for the cool smooth lozenge of her mobile, meaning to ring a taxi. But it was no good: she felt she must keep on walking, one eye always on the bright icy disc of the moon above.

'Darling. You think I do not care about you. But is not true. This is not what I am planning,' Salvatore had said, as she'd headed for the front door on shaking legs. 'It all get a bit out of hand. I want make it up to you. I call you next week. Or week after, at any rate.'

Even as she had told him to fuck off, had opened the door and walked out of his life forever, he had still been talking. 'No, no! We can take weekend break. To Italy, maybe. I take you to my home to meet the Mama. Is beautiful in early Spring. Warm. You sleep on it, yes? You not make hasty decision. I call you in a few days when you are feel a little bit better. We take it from there, yes?'

He was unbelievable.

He was one of the worst mistakes she had ever made.

But that didn't mean he was the only mistake.

Right now in Zurich, people were arriving for a show that she was supposed to be setting up.

By the time she let herself in through the back door of home, in a kind of trance, her legs were aching and her feet burning. She had walked so much that she had almost forgotten how to sit down.

Pepe crept to greet her, ears down. Jennifer stood on the mat, letting the dense quiet of the house permeate her. She gazed around the kitchen, the dear familiar kitchen, with the orange mugs on the mug tree and the battered cookery books in their little oak bookshelf. Everything seemed unbearably precious.

She stood, taking it all in.

Then she took off her shoes, padded to the kitchen table, laid her head on her arms and wept.

From somewhere a long way away off, a phone began to ring. It rang and rang, insisting on itself, until Jennifer rose from the depths of a dead sleep to open her eyes. She was still sprawled across the kitchen table and it was still pitch dark. She staggered to her feet and headed for the light switch, cracking her ankle on the table leg and jarring her shoulder, which felt bruised and stiff.

She tried to blink her eyes into some semblance of seeing. The events of the previous evening queued in her mind, to be relived. She resisted them. The kitchen clock said half past seven. But she had surely only been asleep for ten minutes. Upstairs, a light came on.

On the other end of the phone, as soon as her heard her voice, Greg launched into a seamless tirade.

'What in the name of fuck is going on? I've just picked up a message from the show organiser in Zurich to say that nobody's registered yet, or even turned up at our stand. There's crates piled to kingdom come, waiting to be unpacked.'

Jennifer tried to force her brain into gear while Greg shouted. 'Everyone else's stands are going up all around apparently, and ours is still sitting there in the bloody boxes! We've only got tomorrow left before the show opens. I'm waiting for your excuse, Jennifer, and it had better be good.'

'Greg. I'm so sorry, I ... .'

'In fact, come to think of it, why aren't you in prison? Or talking to me from a hospital bed? Or from the secure unit of a mental institution? Because if that was the case, then I might believe you had a legitimate excuse. But no, you're at *home*.'

Jennifer's alarm clock went off upstairs, as if this were a normal day.

'Greg. I've been trying to phone you. I wasn't just going to leave you in the lurch, I was planning to talk you through.'

'Talk me through what?'

She caught sight of herself in the hall mirror. Her cheek was livid and throbbed painfully, her eyes were puffballs and her hair was a lavatory brush. Outside, the sky was beginning to turn light. The clink of milk bottles sounded from the step.

'Talk you through stand build-up.'

'For Christ's sake, Jennifer, I can't build your stand. Nor can the sales team. We need you in Zurich to do it. You're way too young for a mid-life crisis. But if you really must have one, have it in your own time, not mine. For now, get yourself to that airport. And if all the planes are booked, go by train. Go by bus. Crawl to Zurich on your hands and knees if you have to, but get yourself there. And when you get there, I want to see you working like ... .'

This time it was she who interrupted him.

'You will, Greg. That's what I've been trying to tell you, if only you'd let me get a word in edgeways. I had cold feet. I thought you'd be better off without me and my stand design. And maybe you would. But it's time I stood up to be counted, time I stopped letting myself and other people down and found out whether the things I dream of have any value. So I have every intention of coming to Zurich, even if I have to tie myself to the

233

leg of a carrier pigeon and flap there.'

The wind was momentarily taken out of Greg's sails. 'Well, good,' he said. 'Just make sure you do.'

He was unwilling to totally capitulate. 'But let me tell you something. This better not be all talk, Jennifer, I'm warning you … .'

Jennifer cut him short. 'It isn't,' she said. 'See you in Zurich.'

She hung up and stood, listening distractedly to the bland, impersonal sound of the dial tone. She'd made a confident speech. What if she couldn't live up to it?

35. *Crème brûlée*

The Zurich plane roared and rattled, the G-forces pushing everyone back in their seats. Through the thick oval windows of scratched plastic, a neat, tilted design of miniature fields, buildings and roads appeared. Jennifer sipped her gin and tonic, savoured her packet of high quality nibbles and read the paper, handed to her from a salmon pink tower by the door. She had been offered these before the people in the rear section of the plane had even got on.

Her clothes had barely had time to settle back into their drawers. Pepe and Alicia had watched from the sitting room doorway as she hauled her case back down the stairs.

'I'm glad,' said Alicia, 'that you've seen sense and come round to my way of thinking.'

The taxi hooted outside.

Jennifer bent to kiss Pepe's head. Then she hugged her mother. 'Good luck with the wedding preparations.' Alicia squeezed her daughter's hand. 'Thank you dear. And good luck with … whatever it is you're doing out there. Do put some ice on that nasty bruise, once you're on the plane. Fish some out of your gin and tonic. We need it completely gone by the Big Day: I can't have my Matron of Honour looking as if she's gone ten rounds with Lennox Lewis. Who would have thought you'd be clumsy enough to walk into the kitchen door like that? After all the years we've lived here.'

There were still some things it was best not to reveal. Now

the plane levelled out, above a platform of white cumulus clouds that looked solid enough to walk on. Jennifer, deciding to visit the loo, unfastened her seatbelt and headed back down the plane, walking through an atmosphere of hush and spaciousness.

A blue curtain separated First Class from Economy. Jennifer peeped through and saw another world. Children grizzled and emptied packets of peanuts over people sitting behind them. Women's suits creased while you watched and men's legs poked awkwardly out into aisles.

Her gaze swept up and down the plane. And then it snagged. In the middle section about ten rows back, sat Jocasta Jardine. Her eyes were shut and her head was resting on someone's shoulder. Jennifer's eyes travelled west. The man, ginger-stubbled and leather-jacketed, was Greg. And as Jennifer watched, he tilted Jocasta's face towards his and kissed her gently.

Jennifer let the blue curtain fall.

She didn't need an irate wife to guess they were an item. But knowing it in theory was entirely different from seeing it in the flesh. Forgetting the loo, she walked thoughtfully back to her seat.

Her attention was soon diverted by the in-flight meal. Asparagus arrived, so delicately cooked that it melted in her mouth. There followed a rich, deeply flavoured dish of venison in claret. Then came a velvety, sweet dessert that nearly made her swoon. After relishing every mouthful, Jennifer sipped her cappuccino and sighed with pleasure. It was a long, long time since she had eaten so well, if ever.

But she couldn't just sit enjoying herself. A woman had to do what a woman had to do. She stood, removed a squashed nibble from the seat of her trousers, and walked back to the blue curtain.

Greg and Jocasta, holding hands and immersed in conversation, didn't look up as she approached. But when Greg saw her, he flung Jocasta's hand away from him.

Jocasta, in a mint green skirt suit, was cooler. 'Well, look who it isn't. Been in a fight too, by the looks of it. Did they try to stop you getting on the plane?'

Jennifer's hand went to her bruised cheek.

But she pulled it quickly back. 'Just thought I'd come and reassure you that I'm here.'

'Don't expect me to be reassured by that,' said Greg. 'I won't be happy until I see that stand up.'

Jennifer sighed. The gentle, kissing people had obviously gone into hiding.

'Where are you sitting?' demanded Greg.

'Oh, up the front,' said Jennifer.

'Where up the front?'

Jennifer hesitated. Standing at the airline desk, paying for the only seat left, the cost calculation had been sobering: three hours in the air, three pounds a minute. Derek was going to have a fit.

'By the loos,' she said.

Greg frowned over tented fingers and the remains of his economy dinner, but he didn't pursue it. Jennifer couldn't help noticing salad with tinned sweet corn and grated carrot sprinkled over it. In another little dish lay a square of sponge with a dry-looking lid of jam and desiccated coconut.

'You may have got on the plane,' said Jocasta, 'but you'll never get a room at this late stage. When you didn't check in at the hotel, they'll have let your room go. And the rest of the hotels in Zurich are booked up. I should know.'

Jennifer's face fell. She hadn't thought of that.

Greg narrowed his eyes. 'Puppy dog eyes won't get you a hotel room. Turning up on time is generally what cuts it in the business world.'

Jennifer opened her mouth to protest then decided against it. After all, he was right. 'I know. I realise I've made a total balls-up, Greg, on all sorts of fronts. All I can say is I intend to do my very best to put it right.'

Then, with all the dignity she could muster, she turned and walked back to her seat in First Class.

At the curving marble reception desk of the hotel, the queue of guests waiting to check in extended all the way to the quietly lit, murmuring dining room. There, a man in a tuxedo sat at a grand piano playing a piece with no beginning and no end. Outside in the hotel gardens lay a thick layer of snow and fresh flakes wheeled thickly from the sky.

Jennifer inched forwards with Greg and Jocasta while men in suits exchanged passports for key cards. Now the alcohol had worn off, her cheek ached again.

'I hope they can fit me in,' she said.

But when they reached the desk, and the receptionist checked the reservations, it was as Jocasta had predicted: full.

'But we didn't officially cancel our booking,' said Jennifer. 'Surely there should be something available?'

The receptionist looked very bored.

'Told you,' said Jocasta, scooping up her key card.

Jennifer glanced at the clock above the desk. It was half past six. She grabbed a mint from a little bowl on reception to fortify herself. 'Well, I suppose I'd better go back into town and start looking for a hotel.'

'Aye, good idea,' said Jocasta. 'I'm sure this nice wee lassie behind the desk will ring you a taxi.'

Greg glared. 'For goodness' sake, Joc! You said yourself the rooms are likely to be booked up. And even if they aren't, I'm not having a member of my team, no matter how infuriating, going off on her own into a strange city at night. All the rooms here have got two beds, so you two can double up.'

Jocasta and Jennifer stared at one another. For once, Jocasta's composed expression deserted her. 'What makes you think I'm about to share a room with this bampot?'

'No, I'll go into Zurich,' said Jennifer. 'After all, what's a little snowstorm?'

'Ladies,' said Greg wearily, 'we're in the way here. Let's move it.'

36. White chocolates

The hotel bedroom was almost as big as the entire ground floor of 10 Woodlands Avenue. One window was glass and two big double beds stood a few feet apart, united by an outsized padded headboard. Miniature gold boxes rested on each crisp white pillow.

Jennifer opened one to find four white chocolates nestled in pink tissue. Handmade, no doubt. Derek would've had kittens. Jocasta threw her chocolates onto Jennifer's bed. Jennifer wasn't sure if this was a gift or an act of violence. Jocasta also pulled her bed across the black marble floor, away from Jennifer's.

Jennifer sat down heavily. 'Jocasta. I'm so sorry about this.'

Jocasta unzipped her case briskly, threw some underwear into a drawer and hooked a wedge of beautiful suits onto the rail in the wardrobe. '"Sorry" won't get the stand up in time.'

'No. But *I* will.'

Jocasta turned. She spoke coolly. 'Well, you'd better. People's jobs are on the line if you fail. Mine, Greg's, your own. I've invited my best clients – the company's best clients – to come and look at our new products. How's it going to look if those products are standing on a grotty strip of carpet with no walls, no graphics panels and no indication that this is a proper company and not some bunch of haddies from the middle of bum-fuck nowhere?'

She slid the empty case under the bed and walked towards the door. 'I've put my clothes on the right. You can put yours on

239

the left. And now I'm going down to the bar. We might have to share a room, but I for one don't intend to spend a minute more in it than I have to.'

'I don't suppose you intend to sleep in it much, either,' said Jennifer.

Jocasta's jaw dropped. She cast around for a reply but finding none, turned on her heel and went out, trying to slam the door. But it was electronic and defied her, shutting at its own slow smooth pace.

The exhibition site was a complex of vast, rectangular buildings, each the size of an aircraft hangar. The electronics show took up twelve of them. It was massive. In hall eleven, where the company's stand was, huge glass sliding doors opened onto a vast, lit interior. Men with hammers went up ladders and banged things into the ceiling; men with saws hacked off lengths of plank; men with paintbrushes slapped emulsion onto plasterboard walls that were still being fixed into place by other men with drills and screwdrivers. It was buzzing with activity.

As Jennifer walked through the hall to her stand, she saw no other women at all. She also saw that while some stands looked like show homes, others were still deserted squares on the floor. It was very hard to believe there were only thirty-six hours to go till opening.

But nothing she saw on the way there quite prepared her for the sight of her own stand: a large piece of floor covered with filthy carpet tiles and crates, piled well above head height. It was draughty too, being next to the emergency exit door. Jennifer reached into her bag for the hotel chocolates and stood stuffing them into her mouth one after another.

It was a brief moment of respite. She walked up to the towering pile, which seemed the size of a block of flats. After the dressing-down from Jocasta, she'd called a taxi and come straight here, shoving her case under the bed in lieu of unpacking. But the unpacking job that faced her now was immense. How on earth was she going to do it on her own?

Down the aisle, two men carried a big Perspex panel, marked with a big cross of masking tape. One of them said something and they both laughed. Jennifer wished she had someone to laugh with. That she didn't was her own fault.

She stood, trying not to panic. But one of the Perspex men had noticed her. Panel propped safely against a wall, he came over. Everything about him was broad – his chest, his face, his walk.

'Bonsoir madame,' he said. 'Vous avez une problème?'

She would have liked to throw herself into those capable-looking arms and cry on those strong shoulders. Instead she fished in her memory for the French that would explain her predicament.

Twenty minutes and a trip to the organisers' office later, a man with a crowbar was helping her prise the lids off the crates, and a man with a forklift was helping her stack the ones she didn't need so they took up less space.

Feeling rather better, Jennifer peered into the two crates housing the display system. There, as she'd expected, were layer upon layer of metal pieces swathed in bubble wrap and hundreds of plastic bottles covered in papier-mâché moulding. There was also a brown paper parcel, with her name written on it in thick black letters.

Energised by this sight, she tore off the wrappers. Inside was her overall, washed and starched and ready for action. A piece of paper fluttered to the ground. *I had the wife give it the once over for you. Now give them Germans summat to look at! Love Eric xxx.*

It was exactly the vote of confidence Jennifer needed. She donned the overall, rolled up her sleeves, and began to address herself to the gargantuan task of assembling her stand.

Jennifer worked through the night. Workers arrived at other stands; workers knocked off. But Jennifer went on, lost in a trance of handling the materials she loved.

She slotted and fitted and glued until a glimmer of natural light began to show itself around the edges of the emergency exit door and then, as one of the breakfast franchises opened and the vinegary smell of boiling wursts wafted across, she stood back to survey her handiwork.

The basic structure was erected across half the floor space. And the back left hand quarter of the stand was finished.

She sighed with relief. The stand, to her mind, was going to look fantastic. Of course, it was impossible to predict whether Greg, when he eventually arrived on site, would like it or not. But at least now he could see what he was meant to be liking or disliking.

Her hands were covered in muck. She wiped them on her overall and went to get a coffee and a wurst. Luckily there was no queue. If she'd had to stand and wait, she would probably have fallen over from tiredness.

Back at the stand, she sat on the top of her stepladder to eat. Who would have thought something that looked like a rubber roller could taste so good?

A voice broke through the haze of her ecstasy. 'So this is what you've been doing all night, is it? Lounging around stuffing your face?'

Greg, in jeans and sunglasses, was glaring up at her.

Jennifer shoved the last piece of wurst into her mouth and drained her coffee. 'Hi!'

Greg took his glasses off, revealing bloodshot eyes. 'Is that all you can say? We thought you'd gone off to find another hotel – seems Joc gave you a bit of a bollocking last night, thought she might have gone too far – so we've been round every last crummy god-forsaken hole in this city.'

Jennifer descended her stepladder. 'Really?'

'We even went to the Red Cross hostels and Sally Army type joints. Those places are grim as fuck, let me tell you. But *this* is the last place we thought to find you. What are you playing at? Did you think Joc would stagger in at two in the morning, so pissed she'd just read your note and think 'fair enough' and flop down onto the bed in a coma?'

He paused. 'Though I suppose that isn't a completely unreasonable assumption.'

Jocasta came up behind him. 'Greg,' she said. 'Never mind all that now. Take a look at the thing she's building.'

Over the last few months, Jennifer had imagined a variety of expressions on Greg's face when he finally took in her vision. Surprise was one. Rapture was another. In her worst-case scenario, he looked alarmed for a few seconds before his frown was replaced by a grin of slowly dawning understanding.

What actually happened was that he took one look at the stand towering above his head, let his mouth fall open, made a noise somewhere between a yelp and a sob, and sank to the ground with his head in his hands.

37. *Trio of teas*

Jennifer stood in the queue at the refreshment stall again, grateful that there were a lot of workmen ahead of her, putting in bulk orders for wursts. If she was away from the stand for a while, there was a chance that Jocasta and Greg would talk, and that Greg would calm down.

But when she arrived back at the stand, clutching a trio of teas, Greg was nowhere to be seen.

'I sent him back to the hotel,' said Jocasta.

Jennifer sank down onto one of the red plush thrones that had been unloaded at the stand. 'I didn't think he'd hate it that much. It's not often you see a man cry uncontrollably on his knees like that. Not outside a Sylvester Stallone movie, anyway.'

Jocasta sipped scalding tea. 'You're a fine one to talk about Stallone, with a shiner like that.'

Jennifer fingered her cheek gingerly. The last time she'd looked, its centre had developed to a deep purple, fringed with yellow. She shrugged. It seemed the least of her worries.

'I had you down as a timid wee soul, too,' said Jocasta. 'Not a heavyweight champion.'

'Never mind me. What about Greg?' asked Jennifer.

Jocasta paused. 'Well, he's under a lot of pressure just now.'

Jennifer bit her lip.

'So, what happened?' said Jocasta. 'How did your opponent come off? Bare knuckle fighting over a guy, were you?'

'For goodness' sake!' said Jennifer. 'Will you leave it alone? If it's any of your business, someone assaulted me.'

Jocasta's mouth fell open. At least the smug look was gone. 'What, in the street? A stranger?'

Jennifer touched the bruise again. Tony had hurt her. But Salvatore was the one she blamed more.

'No,' she said, quietly.

Jocasta opened her mouth to say something, but then seemed to think the better of it. The two women observed a short silence. At last Jocasta, frowning, wandered off, across to the finished section of stand.

Jennifer let out a long breath. She was tired beyond tiredness. But she must decide what to do in the light of Greg's reaction. She looked at the still massive pile of metal poles and fixings, and ran over the options again.

There were four. Abandon the show. Exhibit on a bare piece of carpet. Use the metalwork on its own, streaked with green Hammerite and glue that looked like spunk. Or carry on for another twenty-four hours on no sleep doing work that required patience, concentration and strength, and get the stand up but risk ending up in the local hospital suffering from exhaustion.

The idea of sleep was narcotic. She swayed on her throne.

She realised that Jocasta was calling to her from the back of the stand. 'Come here a minute.'

Wearily, Jennifer got up and walked over.

'What is it you're trying to do here?' asked Jocasta.

'Build an exhibition stand,' said Jennifer.

'I know that,' said Jocasta. 'But there's something it puts me in mind of. I've been trying to remember it ever since I saw those drawings up in the stockroom.'

She moved across to a window, a round organic shape like a seedpod, and peered through it. 'Some famous building somewhere. Done by that architect. The weird one.'

She ran her fingers down the gently undulating side of a doorway. 'Gaudi,' she said. 'Yes, that's it. What you're trying to

245

build here is the spit of one of his weird buildings. I went on a tour of them once, on a hen weekend in Barcelona. They looked pretty surreal. I had a wee hangover at the time, which didn't help any. But you couldn't help loving the sheer genius of them. Hey, what's up with you?'

A sob had sprung out of Jennifer's throat.

Jocasta looked alarmed. 'Are you going to tell me what's up or are you just going to sit there greeting like a baby?'

'You can see it!' said Jennifer. 'You understand what I'm trying to do.'

Jocasta stood back, rolling her eyes. 'Jeez. I'm not sure that's a responsibility I want.'

But energy was coming back into Jennifer's arms and legs. She wiped her face with the sleeve of her overall and stood up. 'Look, go back to the hotel if you want to. I'm staying here. I have to get on, if this stand's going to have any chance of getting finished.'

Jocasta drained her tea and crushed the polystyrene cup. 'I was afraid you were going to say that. I suppose we'd better get at it, then.'

'We?'

Jocasta shook her head. 'My head must button up the back. But I can't leave you here to build the entire Casa Batllo in paper all by yourself, can I?'

Having a workmate like Jocasta was a shot in the arm. She worked with production-line speed and reliability, slotting lengths of tubing together and handing them up to Jennifer on the stepladder as if she was born to it. When the two engineers arrived at eleven o'clock to begin installing the scanning electron microscope, Jennifer could hardly believe how much she and Jocasta had achieved.

'I really appreciate your help,' she said as they walked over to the refreshment stand. 'I'd never have got this far on my own.'

'No bother,' said Jocasta. 'I'm enjoying myself. It makes a change from blethering on the phone.'

When they got back, Jocasta having said she'd rather starve than eat something that looked like a peeled tadger, she told Jennifer to sit down and rest for twenty minutes. With the bedlam of the last day before show opening going on around her, Jennifer sat on one of the red thrones and fell into a deep sleep.

She was woken by Jocasta shaking her, none too gently. Feeling as if she had just come round from a coma, she staggered to her feet. 'Sorry. I must have dropped off for a moment.'

'Two hours,' said Jocasta. 'But I need you back now. I couldn't work out how those towers are meant to look on the top. Your plan's rubbish.'

Jennifer, half asleep and disorientated, looked around her. All the crates had gone. The scanning electron microscope was in situ, with one engineer bending over it and one lying underneath. The floor space had only a small amount of metalwork left on it, heaped like a collapsed robot. And the stand itself stood finished up to head height, all internal walls in place. Finishing the top two metres would involve building four small towers and one big one. It would be fiddly and time-consuming. But as Jennifer peered blearily at her watch, she saw it was still only three o'clock in the afternoon.

'You've done loads,' she breathed. 'My God, Jocasta. There's a chance we're going to make it.'

Jennifer let herself thankfully in to the loud silence of the hotel bedroom. She had only managed one glass of celebratory champagne in the bar with Jocasta before her eyes had closed of their own accord and she'd fallen forwards in a doze, nearly cracking her head on the table.

She was too tired to wash or clean her teeth so she got straight into her red flannel pyjamas and then into bed. But there was one thing she wanted to do before she slept. It was still only ten to ten in England: she would just catch Alicia before she went to bed.

At the other end of the phone, her mother was chirpy. 'How was your flight, dear? Is the hotel nice? And how's it going with the, er ... .'

'Exhibition attendance organisation.'

'Yes, yes. These management-speak titles make everything sound so grand, don't they?'

'It's been hard work. I've only just come off site.'

'Dear, dear. I hope you're not letting these people to take you for granted. Bill them for the overtime, won't you? Now, when are you back? The twentieth, isn't it?'

'The nineteenth.'

'I must get Narendra to write it up on the calendar.'

'Mum, can I ask you something?'

'Of course, darling.'

'When you said someone had advised you to encourage me more, was it Dr Ganguly?'

'Yes, dear, it was. The darling, darling, man.'

'Ah,' said Jennifer. 'I'm beginning to get used to the idea of you two getting married.'

'Are you, dear? Well, that's wonderful.'

'And how are you? Are you coping without me?'

'Coping? To tell you the truth, between Narendra and Nelly fussing around me like a pair of mother hens, I've hardly had a moment to myself since you've been gone. I'm relieved when they go home. Now, I'd better go. It won't do to miss the news. There's been a nasty murder here, you know. Just a few miles down the road. Well, five miles actually, so not worryingly close. And do take care, darling. I know what these foreign men are like, especially the Swiss. Give me a nice, old-fashioned Englishman any day.'

'Like Dr Ganguly, you mean?'

'Yes dear, exactly like him.'

Jennifer smiled as she put the phone down. She was glad her mother was in good hands. It occurred to her that Dr Ganguly was perhaps better equipped to deal with her mother than she was. She lay back on the cool, crisp pillow and was asleep in seconds.

The exhibition hall was transformed. A reception desk, complete with three glamorous women in pink suits, was installed at the entrance. Halogen lights winked subtly from the gantries, making metalwork sparkle and paintwork glow. From the stands themselves, corporate videos schmoozed and the smell of fresh coffee wafted. The aisles heaved with visitors in thick winter coats. Reddened faces loomed, breathing alcohol fumes already, even though it was only eleven.

Jennifer was nervous as she flashed her exhibitor pass and walked in. Early that morning, dimly aware of the sounds and scents of Jocasta getting up, her own body had felt heavy and immobile, a sandbag. Next time she woke, the sun was bright on the snow, and the bedside clock said ten past nine.

Jocasta had told her the night before not to rush onto site. So she ate a leisurely bowl of Birchermuesli in the hotel dining room, in an atmosphere so hallowed she was conscious of every chink of cutlery and every swallow. It was here, amidst tablecloths reflecting the blue-white brilliance outside that she began to imagine all the things that might have gone wrong with the stand.

During the tram journey, her mental list had grown.

Now, fifty paces away, she had narrowed it down to the three most likely: the authorities had sawn off the tower, challenging as it did the show height restrictions; the legs had collapsed; a leak in the exhibition hall roof had made the papier-mâché go soggy.

She didn't want to find out. But as she rounded the corner, and faced her creation, she saw immediately that there was nothing to worry about. It was all still in one piece, springing up from the leaf-patterned carpet like a bizarre clump of mushrooms in an enchanted wood.

Although the back wall was ordinary plywood and the side and inner walls Perspex, the careful application of paper pulp had made all lines curved, all corners rounded.

The uprights, thanks to the contours of Brian Kelly's bottles, looked like leg bones. The doorways gaped like shocked mouths and the turrets pointed eccentrically upwards, like wiggly rockets. The orchids had arrived and been positioned here and there, their sinister blooms adding a startling yet appropriate note. And the speckled, multicoloured surface made up out of a hundred Leeds firms' misprints made the other stands look, as Jocasta would say, dull as fuck.

Furthermore, it was heaving with people. The small group of Japanese businessmen she had dreamed of back in the factory was clustered around the scanning electron microscope where the engineers, trussed in unaccustomed suits, were giving a demonstration. Down the aisle, a competitor's stand stood conspicuously empty, despite its two storeys and scattering of scantily clad women.

Jennifer grinned with pleasure and relief.

Greg noticed her and motioned that he wanted a word.

While she was waiting for him, Jennifer slipped onto the stand and straightened the sales leaflets then hung Jocasta's coat behind the rear wall and stowed a tool bag that had been cluttering up the seating area. She surveyed the stand again and smiled.

Seeing it in all its glory, Greg would surely have come round. She thought ahead to the conversation that was about to take place, where he would thank her for having had the vision to create such a marvellous piece of Art. Because Art was what it was, he would say, and as such it towered spectacularly above all their competitors' efforts.

She hummed as she applied the portable vacuum to some

spilt coffee grounds. Then she felt a hand at her elbow.

Greg propelled her into the aisle. 'Right. Let's have you off the stand. It may be big, but it isn't roomy – despite your breaking the exhibition height restrictions – and we need all the space we can get for customers. And you look a mess.'

Jennifer looked down at her suit. In the hotel bedroom it had seemed fine, but in the bright lights of the exhibition hall, it looked appalling. Her shoes still bore white rings from walking the grass verges of Leeds Ring Road. Having said that, her outfit was no worse than Greg's and he stank of stale sweat. Best not to point that out.

'Frankly,' said Greg, 'the most useful thing you can do from now on is make yourself scarce.'

'Haven't you come round to the stand at all?' asked Jennifer. 'Even a bit?'

Greg glanced nervously over his shoulder. 'Come round to it? You must be joking. I've never seen anything so unsettling, so redolent of the inside of the human body in my life. It's so bulging, so … intimate. It's almost alive. Christ, it's got eyes!'

And then he was gone to talk to a man in a cowboy hat and all Jennifer could do was slip away, disappointed, into the throng of visitors that drifted endlessly up and down the aisles.

She spent the next hours eating German apple cake with whipped cream in one of the little café franchises and walking about checking out competitors' stands. High tech minimalism was overwhelmingly the norm. And the more she gazed on steel surfaces and sleek aluminium poles, the more she lost confidence in her own stand. She began to see it through Greg's eyes. It was simply too odd. Next to the gleaming clinical palaces of chrome, aluminium and glass, it looked dirty and a bit sordid.

Having said that, when she returned to it at four o'clock it was as busy as ever. Customers milled in and out of it and posed for their photos on the red thrones. Two men with clipboards stood at a little distance, making notes. Hoping Greg would be mollified by her two carrier bags of competitors' literature, Jennifer went onto the stand again and set about replenishing the coffee machine.

This time it was Jocasta who steered her back into the aisle.

'Come on, Barbara Hepworth. He's told us to eject you on sight.'

'Really? Oh, Jocasta!'

Jocasta glanced to where Greg was bollocking one of the engineers. 'Ach, dry your eyes. Look at the man. The scanning electron microscope isn't working properly so he's going ballistic over everything just now.'

'But what were those men with clipboards doing? Are they going to penalise us for breaking the height regulations?'

'Stop fretting, will you. Why don't you go back into Zurich? Go shopping, or something. You could get yourself some new shoes for a start. And your clothes don't fit. They're way too big and they're creased to buggery.'

Jocasta was wearing her tight blue pinstripe, nothing beneath the jacket but a pink camisole. 'It's all about image at these shows,' she said. 'You can't get away with Marks and Sparks, let alone Netto, or wherever that suit came from.'

Jennifer found it hard to focus on something as trivial as her appearance, when her whole raison d'être seemed to be in the balance.

Jocasta checked the time on her mobile. 'Give it half an hour and I'll come with you. The Bahnhofstrasse is cried to be one of the best shopping streets in Europe. Go on, it'll be a laugh. And it'll make you feel better.'

'I doubt that. And surely I should be helping here?'

'Smarten yourself up and you will be helping.'

Jennifer was about to say she couldn't afford it when she remembered Dr Ganguly's arrival, and the fact that her mother would soon be off her hands.

'But you'll get to know the full, unexpurgated extent of my vital statistics,' she said, in a last attempt to change the course of Fate.

'I've already seen you in your jim-jams,' said Jocasta. 'They don't leave much to the imagination, believe me.'

Jennifer had the sinking, anticipatory feeling that came from knowing something unpleasant was about to happen, sanctioned by being for her Own Good.

The Bahnhofstrasse was wide, with trams hurtling between elegant avenues of trees. Despite the spaciousness of the pavements, the place had a bustling feel.

Jocasta, with breathtaking professionalism, steered Jennifer between shoppers and commuters and in and out of boutiques. She scooped outfits from railings, ordered assistants to fetch larger or smaller sizes and twitched changing room curtains aside, barking out orders to stand up straight, pull those shoulders back and don't even think about tucking that shirt in to those trousers.

But an hour went by without any purchases being made. All the outfits Jennifer liked, Jocasta thought dreary. All the outfits Jocasta liked, Jennifer thought outrageous. Eventually, when Jennifer emerged from one changing room in yet another baggy top and voluminous pair of trousers, Jocasta's patience ran out.

'How did you manage to smuggle those monstrosities in there? You shouldn't try to cover yourself up like that. It makes you look enormous.'

'I am pretty big.'

'You're not. Every heard of body dysmorphia? Have you weighed yourself recently?'

Jennifer shook her head.

'Well, I reckon you've lost about a stone and a half over the last few months,' said Jocasta, 'and you're still dressing like a beached whale. There's just no reason any more to go around wearing a marquee. And black doesn't suit you. It's too harsh for your skin colouring.'

Jocasta stalked over to a rack, brought back a dress and thrust it under Jennifer's chin. 'You should be wearing stuff like this. It brings out the colour of your eyes, your hair. Look in the mirror.'

The colour was bold, a burnt orange. But Jocasta was right. Next to it, Jennifer's skin glowed rather than paled and her eyes smouldered rather than fizzled out.

'It's a great colour,' said Jennifer. 'But I can't imagine wearing it all over me. I'd feel like a chicken tandoori.'

'For God's sake! But all right. We'll see if they've got a top in the same colour.'

She beckoned the hovering shop assistant. 'Translate,' she said to Jennifer. 'But don't try anything funny. If she comes back with another maternity top, I'll no be best pleased.'

But when the last plate glass doorway disgorged them into the icy night air, Jennifer was gripping a clutch of bags. She'd bought two pairs of trousers, one pair charcoal grey ('At least they're not black,' said Jocasta) and the other kingfisher blue ('At least they're not tight,' said Jennifer).

She'd bought a tandoori top to go with the grey trousers and a black velvet one to go with the blue ones. Matching nail varnishes – Hot Brick and Ocean – were in the bag too, and a pair of green, thin-soled Italian ankle boots that would probably not go with anything, but were too beautiful not to buy.

More to the point, when she'd stood in front of the mirror dressed in these outfits and listening to the cooing of Jocasta and the shop assistant, even she had seen a relatively handsome woman looking back at her.

'Not a bad wee haul,' said Jocasta as they headed for the tram stop.

Then she stopped so abruptly in front of another boutique that a commuter, rushing past on the pavement, had to swing his briefcase to one side to avoid hitting her.

'I nearly forgot,' she said. 'Time you got yourself properly measured.'

Jennifer looked up at headless dummies in lacy bras and knickers.

'A decent bra'd make your new clobber look great,' said Jocasta. 'It'd even improve your old stuff.'

'Oh, I don't think so. Anyway, we haven't got time.'

'It'll only take five minutes.'

Jennifer hesitated.

'I'll not come in the changing room,' said Jocasta. 'I promise.'

The shop assistant was slim, young and very pretty. She lulled Jennifer into a false sense of security by letting her choose some bras in whatever size she pleased and take them into the changing cubicle.

But a few minutes later she was back, asking whether any of them fitted. When Jennifer admitted that they didn't, the assistant yanked the curtain aside, whipped her tape measure out, and strapped it around Jennifer's breasts with all the firm precision of a doctor performing a painful but necessary procedure.

A mere ten minutes later however, Jennifer was dressed and standing at the cash desk.

All three bras the shop assistant had produced had fitted, and Jennifer was buying them all. And one of them, a pink and black confection of lace and little satin ribbons, she was keeping on.

She tapped her pin number into the machine. 'Thank you so much,' she said in German. 'I thought it would be awful, being measured. But you made it a pleasure.'

The young woman smiled as she tenderly wrapped Jennifer's overstretched and greying bra in pink tissue paper, and slotted it with the others into a stiff paper bag with string handles – the hallmark, as Jennifer now knew, of quality shopping.

'It is nothing. Two thirds of women, they are the wrong size

255

bra wearing.'

'See?' said Jocasta, on the way out. 'You're not a wee freak after all.'

As they queued for the tram, Jennifer kept glancing down at breasts that seemed, for the first time in their lives, to be in exactly the right place: halfway up her chest. With breasts like that in harness, it seemed suddenly as if she might go anywhere and do anything.

38. *Litres of lager*

The Bier Keller was a dimly lit cavern of warmth and noise, filled with long wooden tables at which inebriated men in short-sleeved shirts held up empty beer steins for refilling. Trays of sausages whizzed past, carried by waitresses in yellow pigtail wigs and dirndl skirts.

Jennifer, in the tandoori top, was sitting next to Greg. She'd hoped he might notice her new outfit, and appreciate her effort to shape up to the company image, but he'd done no more than throw a grunt in her general direction before turning to talk to an engineer.

Jocasta was peering at the menu, chalked up on a blackboard. 'Sausage, sausage, sausage. Or if you're feeling really adventurous, sausage.'

'They've got fondue,' said Jennifer.

'Aye. The sparrow's approach to food. We'll be working at it for two hours and we'll still have eaten bugger all. Still, it's preferable to sausage, so let's go for it.'

A waitress plonked six slopping litre steins of lager in the middle of the table then vanished before anyone could object. Not that anyone wanted to. Exhibiting was thirsty work and the ice-cold lager slid down beautifully.

Eventually another waitress came with a small cauldron of boiling oil, raw steak cubes, sauces, and long forks. Sausages of various colours arrived for the men. An engineer sliced into something white that looked like giant bait. Between eating, which in Jennifer and Jocasta's case took seconds and only occurred every five minutes, lager went on disappearing down throats faster than the river Limmat under the Quaibruecke Bridge outside.

Perhaps it was the alcohol, but eventually Jennifer found herself tugging at Greg's sleeve. 'Talk to me, Greg, please,' she said.

Greg turned. 'Are you drunk?'

'No.'

'Well, you look it. And you sound it.'

'Greg, please don't hate me. I'm so sorry about what's happened.'

Greg sighed.

Jocasta, in an uncharacteristic display of tact, got up and inserted herself into a gap between engineers further up the table.

'All right,' said Greg, turning on the bench to face Jennifer. 'If you want to talk, tell me this: how long did it take you to cook up your little plot?'

'I wouldn't call it a plot,' said Jennifer. 'More a plan.'

Greg ran his hand over his head. 'Plot, plan, what's the difference? Jennifer, can you not see things from my point of view? When a man, new to a high-profile job and working on a shoe string budget, persuades his MD to show a product that isn't ready to be launched at an overseas exhibition, do you really think he's going to like his staff taking risks with the peripherals? Ridiculous, unnecessary risks that stand to jeopardise the whole project? A project vital to a company trying to retain its cutting edge in an ever more competitive marketplace? To say nothing of retaining its high calibre technical staff.'

Behind him, one of the high calibre technical staff appeared to be trying to light one of his own farts.

'Then there's the issue of your squandering company time. Whole weeks of scheming, scuttling off down to Packing and sticking little bits of paper together. I didn't know you had it in you, Jennifer. Was the whole factory in on it?'

'No, of course not! Not even Eric knew, not really. I made the papier-mâché pieces after he'd gone home.'

Greg didn't look mollified.

He went on, in a lower, more intimate voice. 'Furthermore, do you think that I, personally, appreciate being kept in the dark? Do you think that with everything falling to pieces around me, I'm in the right frame of mind for surprises? Do you think I like being deceived?'

Jennifer studied the edge of the table. She hadn't thought of it like that.

Elsewhere in the bar, the party atmosphere seemed to be intensifying. It made their little tableau seem even more sombre.

'I know I've done wrong, Greg,' said Jennifer. 'But oh, I wasn't *trying* to deceive you. You've got to believe me. I only didn't tell you because there wasn't time to make a model and I didn't know how to put it over in a way you'd accept.'

'There wasn't a way I would have accepted.'

'I realise that now. Believe me, if I'd known how much you were going to hate it, I'd never have gone ahead. But I had no idea you'd feel so *strongly* about it. I thought it was something you weren't that interested in.'

Across the room, people had begun to clap and whistle.

'Despite all of the above,' said Jennifer. 'Hasn't it broken the ice? With one or two customers at least?'

'Irrelevant. Attention doesn't necessarily turn to orders.'

'No, but it's better than no attention at all, surely?'

Greg didn't get the chance to reply. A group of men in lederhosen and feathered hats had run in at the far side of the restaurant, followed by women in red aprons and check dresses. By mistake, Jennifer caught the eye of a man with an accordion. He bounded across the room towards her, bringing the troupe with him.

'Oh no,' said Jennifer.

The troupe surrounded the table. Excess embroidery loomed. The accordion player struck up a rousing tune, standing so close that Jennifer could feel the draught from his instrument. The men in lederhosen slapped their thighs; the women plucked undefended men up to dance.

Jennifer, not knowing what else to do, studied the wave-like motion of the accordion man's fingers on the pearly worn keys, a rhythm hard to marry with the sound. The whole thing went on forever. Then at last, with a final, straining chord, it was over. The fiddle player produced a red rose and handed it to Jennifer, to enthusiastic applause from all the other diners in the place. She blushed as she accepted it, not daring to look at Greg.

The troupe dispersed. Jennifer turned, wanting to go on with their conversation, wanting to explain the difference between deceiving someone and operating on a 'need to know' basis. But as she tried to get Greg's attention, it seemed the room was no longer behaving itself.

Things that should have been still – the walls, the tables – had a suggestion of movement about them. She twisted around, looking for Jocasta, and couldn't see her. But the bench bucked suddenly as if on a rough sea. And then the tabletop flew up and hit her across the face.

It hurt. And yet, it seemed simpler to stay there, with her cheek pressed onto the wood, which was sticky and smelt of beer and bleach.

She heard Jocasta's voice, coming from what seemed like very far away. 'What's happened to her? I'm only in the toilet for a minute and I miss all the action!'

Greg's voice, weary. 'Yeah, yeah. Just get her back to the hotel, Jocasta.'

The suburbs of Zurich, rattling by through the tram windows, were very dark. Apart from Jennifer and Jocasta, there were only two people in the carriage: a person of indiscernible gender in a green anorak and an old man dozing.

Jennifer lolled against the window.

Jocasta peered into the night. 'That last station was Ausserdorf. I don't remember anywhere called Ausserdorf. What makes you so sure this is our tram? We've been on it for twenty minutes and I think we're heading away from the city centre, not towards it.'

Jennifer's head juddered against the window.

'Can you no hold on to something?' said Jocasta. 'Sitting like that won't be doing you any good. You look awfully peely-wally.'

She produced a bottle of water, which Jennifer refused. The tram went round a bend. Jennifer's head bounced hard against the window.

'For God's sake,' said Jocasta, 'move away from that window. Christ, the tram this morning didn't travel at this kind of speed.'

'Gonna open the window,' said Jennifer.

Before she could do so, the tram lurched around another bend and decelerated rapidly. Then it stopped. The tram doors opened and stayed open.

'Terminus, terminus,' said the Tannoy.

'Fuck,' said Jocasta. 'This isn't it.'

'Where are we?' asked Jennifer.

'In some anonymous Zurich suburb in the middle of bum-fuck nowhere, by the look of it. With nothing but snow and fir trees for miles around.'

'How will we get back to bum-fuck somewhere?'

'A taxi?'

'That'll cost. Greg will go ballistic.'

'Aye, that he will.'

The light went off, then on again, and there was a judder as the engine was turned off. Jocasta stood up. 'Come on, this tram's going nowhere.'

She held out her arm. Jennifer meant to take it. Instead she dropped to her knees and was spectacularly sick all over the floor.

39. *Crudités*

The difficulties with the scanning electron microscope got worse until it wasn't so much a case of teething problems, as needing a whole new set of dentures.

Demonstrations went wrong and customers walked away, shaking their heads. The engineers shook their heads too, and muttered into their beards about a possible problem with the backscatter detector. When the sliding doors of the exhibition hall swished shut on the last visitor of the day, the engineers stayed and stayed some more, sometimes not getting back to the hotel until after midnight.

Jocasta, on the other hand, always returned to the hotel room at five, insisting she could do no good on site and might as well be relaxing in the sauna, or downing vodka shots in the bar. The timing of her second appearance in the room, in the cold grey early hours of the morning, was less predictable.

As for Greg, he spent his days looking dilapidated and pacing in front of whichever pair of feet was currently poking out from under the microscope. He cadged fags from Jocasta until she snapped at him to get off his wee jaxie and go buy his own.

It never seemed the right moment for Jennifer to try and reprise their conversation at the Bier Keller. Neither was it the right moment tell him about the long, long taxi ride back from the tram terminus or mention the fact that she'd been sick again, on the back seat, and that on top of the one hundred and fifty euro fare, the taxi driver had demanded an extortionate sum of money to cover the cleaning bill. Jocasta had run up to the room to get more money and left Jennifer waiting in the back of the taxi, a hostage.

So Jennifer said nothing. She had plenty of other things to do: wear her new and old clothes, eat Birchermuesli in the silent dining room, put in lengths in the tiny basement pool where she was the only swimmer and put in shifts in the city, visiting the clock museum, said to be the oldest in Switzerland.

And as the days of the show passed, Greg didn't appear to come round in the slightest to Jennifer's stand design, nor acknowledge the hard work that had gone into making it or the fact that other people, including one of the company's top clients, thought it original and funky.

It was unbelievably disappointing and made Jennifer anxious about her future. She swam up and down the pool adding salt tears to the heavily chlorinated waters.

But life went on. So she got showered and dressed and went to Zurich Zoo, where there was a special exhibition of frogs.

The electron microscope limped towards the finishing line. The engineers began to count the hours until they could shut it down, ship it back, and stop thinking about beam astigmatism and turbo pump intake.

The evening before the last day of the show, Greg forsook the Bier Keller and booked a bistro in the French quarter for a farewell dinner.

It had linen tablecloths and an absence of accordions and lederhosen. In honour of this, and despite general uncertainty about the success of the show, everyone had dressed for the occasion. The engineers had ties under their stripy jumpers, Greg wore a crumpled but clean white shirt and Jocasta was in a flowing black crepe de chine trouser suit. Jennifer wore her black velvet top with her blue trousers, the pink and black bra nestling beneath.

Wine that was a speciality of the region was ordered. Over the crudités, the engineers talked about the thermionic emission gun then moved on to the goniometer, which wasn't rotating properly. Jennifer tried to say reassuring things.

'Everyone knows this is a prototype product,' she said. 'If the clients are serious prospects, surely they won't be put off for good?'

They all looked at her bleakly.

Then Greg stood up. 'Has everyone got a drink? You're going to need one. I've got some news for you.'

Jennifer glanced at Jocasta, wondering if she'd had a sneak preview. But she looked as enquiring as the rest of them.

'It's Walton,' said Greg. 'He's flying out tomorrow morning. Should be with us by early afternoon.'

'Shit,' said an engineer.

'Fuck,' said Jocasta.

'Everyone will be affected,' said Greg. 'Though if heads are going to roll, mine will be the first.'

Jennifer took a large swig of wine.

'Whatever happens from here on in,' said Greg. 'I propose a toast. To all of us. Let's draw strength from the fact that we've done our best.'

He held his glass aloft. 'To the team. To our hard work. What more can the old bastard ask?'

Was he including Jennifer in the roll call of people who had done their best? All she could do was hope so.

'Bastard ask,' everyone chorused, not feeling in the least bit reassured.

Two hours later, Jennifer and Jocasta were in their room, having decided to pack now rather than rush the next morning. Jennifer stacked several unread novels in her suitcase next to a pack of Toblerone.

'Oh God,' she said, apropos of nothing.

'You're not still fretting, are you?' said Jocasta. 'Move on. The whole world doesn't revolve around, you, you know.'

Jennifer sat down on the bed. 'But what if I've contributed to Greg losing his job?'

Jocasta let silken underwear pour into her case. 'Well, we're in the right part of the world if he ends up needing psychiatric help. Freud, Jung: didn't they all come from somewhere around here?'

'It's not funny.'

Jocasta stopped what she was doing. 'Look, don't worry about what hasn't happened yet. And as for you, once the show's over, Greg will reflect back on what's happened and see that you meant well. He's not an ogre.'

'Mm.'

'He's just in a bad way,' Jocasta went on. 'It's not just about you and your exhibition stand. It isn't even just about work.'

Jennifer looked questioningly at her.

'Oh, come on,' said Jocasta. 'You've put two and two together by now, surely?'

Despite sharing a room for ten days, there was one thing they hadn't talked about.

'It's not just a fling, between you and Greg, is it?' said Jennifer. 'It has implications.'

Jocasta sat down on her bed. 'Aye.'

They looked at one other.

'His wife's going ballistic right now,' said Jocasta. 'According to Greg she was turning a blind eye, hoping it might blow over.'

'If it's serious between you, it was bound to come out sooner or later.'

'Aye. But how and when these things come out really matters. See the divorce laws: it's tricky. Greg wants decent access to his son when they finally go their separate ways. He wants to look after the boy. Wifey's a serious alky. But if she's the one suing him for divorce, he's less likely to be able to.'

'Greg's got a son? I didn't know.'

'Oh aye. And if there's any real evidence of adultery on his side, the ruling's likely to go against him.'

Jocasta pressed her lips together. 'Of course, the fact that some bampot rung his house just before the exhibition pretending to be me didn't help.'

Jennifer froze. 'What do you mean?'

'I don't know. We never got the full story. Sounds like someone rang and put on a silly voice as if she'd been crying for a week. Saying she couldn't run away with him after all. If only we knew exactly what had been said, but wifey's not telling.'

Jennifer felt sick. 'Did Greg have any idea who it was?'

Jocasta stood up again, and resumed her packing. 'No. Someone who knew about us and wanted to stir things up, he thinks. But that could be any one of a number of people. He's not exactly flavour of the month around here.'

She slid a pair of shoes into a plastic bag. 'If that's what they wanted to do, they succeeded. Wifey downed a bottle of whisky, took the wee boy and left, saying that's the last Greg'll ever see of either of them.'

'Oh my God.'

Jocasta put the shoes into her case and began packing make-up into her cosmetics bag. 'Don't go all pathetic on me. I'm only telling you so's you can stop feeling so bloody guilty. It's not just you, see. Probably not more than one tenth you. okay?'

'Right,' said Jennifer, staring into the half-empty wardrobe. 'Right.'

40. *Raclette*

It was lunchtime on the last day of the show. The atmosphere in the exhibition hall had changed completely. Sales executives, although under instruction not to slack off, were easing off shoes, taking commemorative photos on mobile phones, and planning booze-ups. Everyone was looking forward to four o'clock, when the final customers would leave, stuffing product literature into their bags in a last ditch attempt to justify their trip to the boss. Technicians and labourers would reappear to rip up carpet and flatten walls: to wipe out whole territories.

But for now everything was still intact, and Jennifer, who'd spent the morning in the hotel pool, was sitting in the café nearest the stand, fretting. She was about to tackle a portion of raclette, a Swiss cheese and potato dish, when she saw Greg arrive at the café entrance, looking crumpled.

He spotted her, and wound his way between the tables, then slid onto the seat opposite. Behind them, a waitress was going around shovelling used paper plates and cups into a black bin liner.

'I'm afraid I've a bone to pick with you,' said Greg.

Jennifer waited without saying anything. There were so many bones now it was like a butcher's back room.

He went on. 'It's the matter of Jocasta's expenses. She's very low on cash for someone who came out here with a thousand pounds' worth of euros. She didn't tell me, by the way. I noticed. And she won't tell me how they've been spent. I get the

267

impression she's protecting someone.'

Greg picked up a tablemat and tapped it on the table while he waited for her to speak. 'Well? Spit it out.'

Jennifer looked down. He had her number.

She'd never thought of herself as an out-an-out liar. But it was getting impossible to ignore the way her little falsehoods and her bendings of the truth, added together, all too often turned into something bigger. Blurting her feelings out to her mum had been a start, but there was a lot further to go. Spending Jocasta's money on an unnecessary taxi ride was the very least of it.

'Yes. It is my fault about the euros,' she said.

Then she took a deep breath. She could probably have got away without saying what she was about to say next. Nevertheless, being honest now might help Greg later. And that had to be a priority.

'It's also my fault about something a lot worse.'

While Jennifer was telling him the story about the taxi, Greg clicked his tongue in irritation. But when she moved on to speak about the phone call she'd made to his house, her face hot with embarrassment, he just stared fixedly at the table.

His eyes were open but his face was expressionless. He seemed to have retreated into some remote part of himself, away from her, away from the exhibition hall. The twitching muscle in his right cheek told her he was listening, though. Her voice broke over the phrases 'roast in hell' and 'whore.' In holding this conversation, she was treading in the most tenderly secret part of his life. She knew it and she knew that he knew it, too.

She also knew that if she wasn't finished in his eyes before, she certainly was now. Whoever said telling the truth felt good? It felt awful.

'I'm only repeating all this because you need to know what was said,' she finished. 'Jocasta told me. When I get back to the UK, I'll be handing in my notice. It's the only decent thing to do. And you won't be able to talk me out of it.'

His expression was impossible to read. He looked at her and opened his mouth to speak. But his words were lost in the theme from *Fame*, blasting from his pocket.

He looked down and fumbled, trying to switch it off. Then his eyes narrowed and he clamped the phone to his ear. 'Hello? Hello? Is that … yes … no … yes … oh, Christ! Where are you?'

Jennifer heard tinny shouting at the other end.

'At the stand?' said Greg. 'Already? But I wanted to talk to you first, I wanted to brief you on … yes, of course I'll be there immediately. What? Yes, I'm with her now, as it happens. Yes, she did design it, I'm afraid. We'll be … .'

But the phone had gone dead. And Greg's face had gone grey.

'He got an earlier flight. I couldn't hear half of what he was saying. But he sounded bloody agitated. He wants to see us both. Immediately. We're fucked.'

'I am,' said Jennifer. 'I know that. I hope you aren't, though.'

But Greg was already halfway across the café.

As Jennifer followed Greg through the busy exhibition hall at a brisk trot, she prepared a speech for Wally Walton. 'I have already recognised that this is a resigning matter and taken firm steps in that direction. Greg was innocent of my plan. He knew nothing of it, nothing at all, and when he did find out, left me in absolutely no doubt as to its unsuitability.'

They passed salespeople sitting down in their own hospitality suite to finish off leftover champagne. Jennifer eyed them enviously. The show photographer, carrying a bag of equipment, ran past. A cheer went up on another stand.

'Some company busy celebrating the order of the century, no doubt,' muttered Greg.

They turned the corner. Both of them stopped dead in their tracks. It had been their stand the show photographer was heading for. He was busy setting up his tripod in the aisle. A crowd of people stood about, nodding and smiling. And there was Wally Walton, not fuming as expected, but ruddy-faced and beaming amidst a cotillion of men with clipboards.

He beckoned Greg onto the stand and slapped him on the back.

'Good show, Bond, lad! You bloody bugger, you. So this is what you were up to all those times I couldn't find you. And I thought you were shagging Jocasta Jardine in t'stationery cupboard. More fool me.'

Greg submitted to a vigorous hand pumping. He didn't seem to be taking in Wally Walton's change of mood. 'I can only apologize, Wally, about the teething problems with the SEM. If anyone has to take the rap for this it's me.'

Wally Walton beckoned Jennifer on to the stand. 'Not a bit of it, lad. Bound to get a few teething problems at the outset. Shouldn't put anyone off, not if they're serious customers.'

Greg glanced at Jennifer, now standing next to him. 'There's another thing, Wally. I hold my hand up as regards the stand design. Jennifer did the best she could with little or no guidance from me. I took my eye off the ball. I did not act as a mentor.'

Jennifer stared. Was he standing up for her?

'No!' she said quickly. 'It was my fault, Mr Walton, completely and utterly. I kept Greg in the dark, actively and on purpose. I never even gave him the chance to comment.'

But Wally Walton wasn't listening to either of them. He was waving over a group of men with cameras and holding out his hand to Jennifer as if he intended to shake it. Jennifer had never, in all the time she'd worked for the company, shaken hands with Wally Walton. But here it was. She submitted to the feeling of all the small bones in her hand rearranging themselves.

'Well done, lass. You're a credit to this company. Now turn round and smile.'

As she obeyed him, several flashguns went off. Jocasta, at the stand's perimeter, was giving her the thumbs up. Jennifer couldn't help being pleased that she had on a decent outfit. But she still hadn't the faintest idea what was happening.

She managed to get Wally Walton's attention. 'Well done about what, sir?' she asked.

'Wally from now on, to you,' said Wally Walton. 'But don't tell me you don't know? By 'eck, woman, you've only won our company the Entwhistle-Kreuzendorf-Augustin-de-Coulomb Best Stand Design Award, that's what! That's best design not just for this hall or this show, but for all the stands, in all the shows for the past twelve month. This is a red letter day for our company.'

It was impossible to take in. 'I didn't even know there *was* an award,' said Jennifer.

'Well, there is and you've won it us,' he said. 'And it's not just that. Your stand is a bloody triumph of recycling. It couldn't be more in keeping with t'company mission if I'd designed it meself. And all inspired by the arch recycler himself, Anton Gaudi. Yon Mr Stebbing's just told me you got your bottles from BK Packaging. Sound choice of supplier. Their environmental track record's outstanding. Their stuff's all remanufactured and they run a Green Transport plan. I tell you lass, I couldn't be more made up if the company'd won the Queen's Award for Enterprise.'

'Robert Stebbing?' said Jennifer. 'What's he doing here?'

And there he was, on the other side of the stand, wearing an orange shirt and a green velvet bow tie and orating loudly to a journalist.

'When we at Stebbing Print, Yorkshire division, first learnt of Ms Spendlove's plans, we were only too glad to supply the medium. Gratis, of course. We at Stebbing Print – that's at Seacroft Industrial Estate, Leeds – were absolutely thrilled at the idea of supporting an emergent artist. The fact that we could do our bit for the environment at the same time was a bonus.'

Then he saw Jennifer. Leaving the journalist for a moment, he marched up and kissed her on both cheeks. 'I'm bursting with pride, my dear. Absolutely bursting!'

'You came all the way to Zurich for this?'

'Well, one of our European customers has gone belly-up owing us rather a lot of money, and I had to come over for the creditors' meeting. But that part of the trip was very secondary. And I have someone rather special with me.'

He indicated a tall, pleasant-looking man a lot younger than him, with curly greying hair and square gold-rimmed spectacles.

'Is he your partner?' asked Jennifer. 'He looks nice.'

But Robert had already turned back to the journalist. 'Perhaps even more important than the raw materials was the provision of moral support. We at Stebbing Print – that's just off the Ring Road, only twenty minutes' drive from the M1, A1 and M62 – offered a shoulder to cry on through the inevitable ups and downs of the artistic journey.'

Jennifer noticed that Greg was sitting on one of the gilt thrones and looking stunned. She was about to go over when two journalists approached her, pens and spiral notebooks in hand.

'Ros Draper, The Exhibitor,' said one. 'How did you come up with such a bold, fantastical concept in what is traditionally considered a rather anodyne, conservative milieu? You must have had real vision, not to mention unbelievable courage.'

'It was a case of ignorance being bliss, I'm afraid,' said Jennifer. 'I'd never been to a show before, let alone an electronics one.'

The journalist's pen hesitated over her pad. The other journalist took advantage of the hiatus. 'Jean Jenner, Marketing Today. How much did the stand cost you to build? I mean, it actually looks handmade. So exclusive! Where did you source designers who would work to this unique specification?'

'Oh, I made all the parts myself,' said Jennifer. 'Though I did take some of them home one weekend and let our cleaning lady have a go too.'

Jennifer felt a hand on her arm. 'Our Exhibitions Manager is being a wee bit modest,' said Jocasta. 'Her design was arrived at after literally months of head-scratching research. It was conceived in deliberate contrast with the work you see around you on other stands. Jennifer was aiming to bring some character back into what has become a rather sterile environment. She didn't trust other less experienced artistes, so she made every single piece herself. But then, as I'm sure you know, Anton Gaudi, her inspiration for this work, made many of the pieces of his own creations by hand.'

The journalists, reassured, scribbled furiously. Jocasta hissed in Jennifer's ear. 'Get the idea?'

Then she was gone. Jennifer saw her crouch down next to Greg and gather him into her arms as if she didn't care, for once, who was watching.

The questions went on. Jennifer was quizzed about the ideology behind using waste paper, an interview that Wally Walton interrupted frequently to talk about his factory-wide prohibition on throwing out paper clips and his recommendations for reusing rubber bands.

'I think we might get a piece in an environmental magazine out of this,' he whispered in Jennifer's ear. 'I'll be showing that round the club, I will. They'll have to take me seriously now, with me plans for recycling old golf balls.'

Another journalist asked Jennifer about the origins of the firm and was fascinated to learn that Anton Gaudi had once been to Leeds and had even based his early work on the shapes and patterns glimpsed through the optical microscopes of the time.

'Is that a fact?' said Jocasta, who had reappeared at Jennifer's side.

'Well, no one can disprove it,' said Jennifer.

'Ah,' said Jocasta. 'You're catching on.'

Just then, one of the men with clipboards handed Wally Walton a huge dummy cheque for fifty thousand pounds and all the flashguns went off again. Stepping back out of the dazzle,

Jennifer trod on someone's toes.

Apologizing profusely, she turned and found herself looking up into a kind face, eyes the colour of a stormy sea. It was Robert's friend. He held out his hand.

'Brian Kelly,' he said. 'Delighted to meet you. And let me tell you, I could never in a million years have guessed what you were going to do with all my surplus plastic bottles.'

41. *Free drinks*

Greg, Jennifer and Jocasta showed their boarding passes and walked across the tarmac to the plane. It was a cold day, and bright, the kind of brightness that could hurt sensitive eyes and heads. Greg's sunglasses were in evidence and conversation was being kept to a minimum. As they stepped onto the plane, however, and the stewardess put her arm out to separate Jennifer from the others, Greg delivered the longest sentence he'd uttered all morning.

'What on earth are you doing? She's with us.'

'I'm afraid I'm not,' said Jennifer. 'I'm in First Class.'

'First Class?'

'Yes, First Class. You know – that ridiculously expensive mode of travel normally enjoyed only by the super rich and people blowing their frequent flyer air miles on a treat.'

She smiled and stepped through the blue curtain.

But she could still hear his voice. 'Air miles? You can't have any of those: you've hardly even been out of the country before.'

Ensconced for take-off, Jennifer re-lived, not for the first time, the events of the previous evening. Despite the prize money and Jocasta's protestations, they had somehow all ended up back at the Bier Keller where the engineers had finally persuaded everyone, even Jocasta, to order Weisswurst.

The men had made light work of the fat white sausages, but Jennifer found she could only eat hers with her eyes closed. As this was no basis on which to enjoy a meal, she'd ended up pushing them away uneaten. But here was the strange thing: she'd never got round to ordering a replacement meal.

And that had been to do with Brian Kelly.

The conversation had been standard enough to start with. He'd told her he was a long-standing associate of Robert's and like Robert, had business with the company who had gone bust. She expressed her hope that he hadn't lost a significant sum of money. Then she thanked him for his company's efficiency regarding the supply of the plastic bottles.

But even during this plain exchange, she found herself looking at him with interest. Something had glittered amongst the ordinary words and phrases, like particles of gold on a riverbed.

Quickly, somehow, they were talking about other things: things at once more and less important.

He was a windsurfer, who lived far from the sea and had to be content with windsurfing at a place a stone's throw from the M1 near Wakefield.

He was a cat lover, and his cat was called Fred.

He was a loner, and had started his own company when he was twenty because he didn't like taking orders from other people.

Even then it wasn't so much what he said, as the way he said it: the way he made his sentences fit so snugly with hers. Their conversation felt like a dance, with steps she hadn't realised she knew. And the delight of it lifted everything. Even the accordion music seemed charming. She was glad of every pound she had lost, both on the scales and to Zurich's Bahnhofstrasse.

After the meal, they stood with the rest of the group on the pavement, waiting for the tram. Jocasta held Greg's hand. Robert flirted with the best-looking engineer, the one without a beard. Jennifer's mind teemed with all the subjects she had yet to broach with Brian.

Too soon, the tram was coming up the hill towards them.

'Oh dear,' she said. 'We haven't lifted the lid on our friend Mr Stebbing yet, and the sliding scale of biscuits he offers different customers.'

Somehow she knew exactly what Brian was going to say. 'Then we'll just have to continue our conversation back in England.'

Now, twenty-seven thousand feet above the English Channel, as Jennifer gazed at the in-flight magazine and a photo of a lone male polar bear making its annual journey across Antarctica in search of food, she sensed she'd met a man she could not only feel attracted to but also actually like. Not only like, perhaps ... but that was getting ahead of herself.

The seatbelt sign went off. She closed the magazine with a sigh and stood up. There were still a couple of things to sort out.

Jocasta, in the window seat, was reading the paper. Greg, in the aisle seat, had his eyes closed and his headphones on. Jennifer touched his elbow.

His eyes snapped open, then narrowed as he saw her. He had his headphones off in one second flat.

'Ah, I was waiting for you to appear. Now I grant you've won the company an award, but that doesn't justify your going for an upgrade. The prize money hasn't come in yet – that was a dummy cheque they gave us – and when it does, it isn't yours to spend. And when did you wangle it? – At the airline desk when we thought you were in duty free buying perfume for your mother?' Jennifer sighed. But Greg's face was pale, pinched and stubbly. She saw him, suddenly, not as a boss who had it in for her but as a man badly in need of a long holiday.

'I've had the ticket all along,' she said quietly. 'It was the only seat available when I booked.'

She waved her boarding card at Jocasta. 'Fancy a swop? There's free drinks, slippers, an a la carte menu. Films. A lie-down if you want.'

Jocasta's eyebrows shot up. She scrambled over Greg in her hurry to get the boarding pass. 'Really? Thanks, Jen! Or Greg. Whoever.'

Installed in her new more confined seat by the window, Jennifer sipped tonic water. Ice cracked as Greg poured a miniature whisky into his glass. Outside, the sky was a strong, clear blue, the clouds white and flat, like an unfolded cotton wool pleat. Greg went to put his headphones on again, but Jennifer stopped him.

'Can we talk?'

Greg sighed.

'Look, I know things have been difficult between us,' she began.

He raised his eyebrows.

'All right, very difficult,' she said.

He shifted in his seat. Although he had no trouble expressing his own feelings, he didn't seem keen on other people expressing theirs. But some things had to be faced.

'As you know,' she went on, 'Wally Walton wants me to take on the publicity manager's job for good. The thing is, I haven't definitely accepted.'

He looked surprised. 'I can't see why not, when he's giving you your own office and offering you one and a half times your old salary. Madness to turn that down in the current economic climate.'

In fact, Wally Walton was offering to double her old salary, but she decided not to mention that. 'The money isn't what's bothering me.'

Greg looked as if he couldn't imagine what other consideration there could possibly be.

The stewardess arrived with the hot trolley and handed them plastic trays of food. They peeled the foil lids off their dinners.

'What's bothering me,' said Jennifer, 'is that although I'm in

Wally Walton's good books for the time being, I'm not in yours.'

'His good books are a lot more bankable than mine,' said Greg, tearing open a sachet of salt.

'Maybe. But you and I are the ones who have to work together. I don't need you to actively like me, Greg. But I do want us to cooperate.'

'Sure,' said Greg, vaguely.

'I don't think you understand,' said Jennifer.

A forkful of peas stopped halfway to his mouth.

'Look at it from my point of view,' said Jennifer. 'When a woman, new to a high-profile job and working on a shoe string budget, knows that her MD has promoted her over the head of her boss while still being accountable to that boss, do you think she's going to like it? Do you think she's going to stand any chance of success without his support? Or do you think she's going to fall flat on her face at the first hurdle, when the full extent of her inexperience is revealed and she can't ask for help from a man who's actually a great person and to whom she's incredibly grateful and always will be, for letting her tackle her first really big project, even though he hated the way she did it? To say nothing of the fact that, with his business nouse and her creativity, they might even make a good team?'

Greg stared at her. And then he made a strangled sound.

She was alarmed: was he choking on his roast beef? But no, he was doing something he'd never done in her presence in all the long months since they'd first met. Painful though it was, he was laughing.

42. *A large rainbow trout*

It was Valentine's Day, and they couldn't have asked for nicer weather. At least that was what the beauty therapist kept saying, as she tilted bottles of different coloured fluids into balls of cotton wool and stroked them down Alicia's nose, forehead and cheeks.

Jennifer, Pepe, Alicia and the beauty therapist were in the sitting room at Woodlands Avenue. Clots of early daffodils stood on the windowsill, cream lilies blasted out scent from the coffee table and Alicia's bouquet – pale yellow roses – lay classily in the tissue paper of the florist's box. Pepe, though not attending the wedding, lay by the fire with pale yellow ribbon wound around his collar and Jennifer read the paper on the sofa. Alicia, hair scraped back into a stretchy beige band, was obedience personified.

'This is *fun*,' she said. 'Such a *luxury* to have someone else do what one could do perfectly adequately and probably better oneself.'

The beauty therapist applied streaks of mud to Alicia's face, making her look like a tribal queen. Then she plastered mud into the spaces. 'What *I* say is, a little bit of pampering never did anyone any harm. Now, close your eyes for me. Lovely.'

'Have you decided about your outfit yet, darling?' Alicia called.

'Mrs Spendlove, you really must try not to talk.'

'Not yet,' said Jennifer, engrossed in an article about

windsurfing.

'Oh, darling. I wish you'd get a move on. You are one of the key players in today's drama.'

The beauty therapist gesticulated with a ball of muddy cotton wool. 'You've got to let it dry, or it won't work, and you won't look your best on this day of days.'

'Oh dear! I *am* sorry,' said Alicia, 'But my daughter's procrastination is making me nervous. And I mustn't be made nervous, so my husband-to-be says.'

Her voice softened. 'The darling, darling man.'

Upstairs in Jennifer's bedroom, Nelly's pink silk dress still hung on the side of the wardrobe, shimmering like mother of pearl. It brought glamour to the room, as if a wonderful event had just happened, or was about to. But it had hung untouched for so long that when Jennifer took it down, the dust made her sneeze. The last weeks had seen her lose even more weight. Her promotion had meant a move off the tea trolley route. Greg's new PA was already complaining that she couldn't fasten her trousers.

Standing in tights and slip, Jennifer surveyed the dress. She'd been hoping she might be able to get into it today and had resisted trying it on before now.

In front of the mirror she stepped into it, pulled her stomach in and pushed her shoulders back. This was the moment of truth. The zip went up to waist level and she felt the fabric close in around her hips. The zip went further, to just below her bra strap. It felt snug, but she could still breathe. She reached over her shoulder for the rest of the zip, closed her eyes and pulled. The zip went all the way up.

'Yessss!' she cried.

She opened her eyes to a perfect fit. The waist of the dress sat directly on top of her own waist, its boned bodice encasing and holding her. The colour was perfect wedding-day pink, shimmering with silver and mauve. The skirt rustled over its net petticoat, perfect for dancing. In short, the dress was a vision of frothiness.

But if she was honest, and she tried to be, these days, she had to admit it didn't suit her one jot. It made her look like an outsize Christmas tree fairy – or someone who had been swallowed by a large rainbow trout. Correction: half-swallowed, as her head and bare shoulders were still poking out.

Jennifer sat down on the bed and laughed until she had to wipe her eyes.

Eventually she stood up, took off the dress and folded it. Time it went back to the person for whom it held true meaning: Nelly Sykes.

An hour later, they were sitting in Jennifer's new company car, a white Honda. There were no charity shop purchases in sight. Alicia was elegant in a cream linen skirt suit she'd got from the designer department at Debenhams. Jennifer was wearing the plum trouser suit she'd bought a month ago at good old Marks and Spencer's. It was a size sixteen, had a rosebud lining and flowed in a sea of uninterrupted colour all the way down to her shell pink pointed toes. No one had made any remark about it being 'slimming.'

'Right, bride-to-be,' said Jennifer. 'All we've got to do now is pick Nyesha up then we'll get over to the salon for our hair and make-up. Then it's straight to the registry office.'

'Darling, don't make it sound so much like a whistle-stop tour. It's meant to be the happiest day of my life, remember. You're meant to help me *relish* it.'

'Yes, yes,' said Jennifer, as the engine sprang into life with a purr very unlike the scraping sound the old Mini used to make.

Nyesha, fresh off the London train, was waiting for them outside Leeds station. She was wearing a yellow skirt suit and black sling blacks. Her legs were bare and her hat was the size of a satellite dish.

'You look fantastic,' said Jennifer, as they hugged.

Nyesha surveyed her friend at arm's length. 'Well, you look amazing! Get that cleavage! It's not just that, though. You look, I don't know … .'

'Like someone completely different?' supplied Jennifer.

'No. That's the funny thing. You look more like yourself than I've ever seen you.'

They drove through the one-way system, through the financial quarter of the city then up between the Art Gallery and Town Hall.

Alicia talked about Narendra. 'Of course, in his culture, they exchange garlands, then dance round a fire and feast for days on end. A rose with its stem wrapped in tin foil and a few goats' cheese tartlets must seem neither here nor there to him. Dear me, I haven't left the house with no make-up on for *years*. Don't crash the car, will you, Jennifer darling? I shouldn't want to be seen like this in A and E.'

'What do you think of Jennifer, Mrs G?' asked Nyesha. 'Being sent off to California next month and all.'

'Yes, well it is rather extraordinary,' said Alicia. But she wasn't about to share the day's limelight with anyone. 'I shall soon be doing a spot of jet-setting myself. Narendra and I are hoping to get as far as Sri Lanka, on our honeymoon. He has relatives there apparently. Isn't it marvellous how the whole world opens up once you find the right man?'

'I'll let you know when I've found him,' said Nyesha. 'Talking of which, will there be any hot guys there tonight?'

'I'm none too sure what "hot" means,' said Alicia. 'But if you're talking about the gents from *Times of our Lives*, I suspect 'lukewarm' would be a better adjective.'

They all laughed.

'What about your friends, Jen?' asked Nyesha. 'Andy, for example?'

'He's coming,' said Jennifer. 'But he's taken, by a young

woman called Pez.'

'Good heavens,' said Alicia. 'What sort of a name is that?'

'And what about Greg?' asked Nyesha.

'He and Jocasta are a definite item now,' said Jennifer. 'Anyway I don't think he's your type. There will be a sexy sixty-year-old there with a great tan and newly veneered teeth, though. He got them done in Australia.'

'Australia?' said Nyesha. 'You don't mean Eric, do you?'

The car fell silent as they drove past the main entrance of the hospital and turned right, past Leeds Metropolitan University and the hordes of students surging to and fro along the pavements.

Nyesha tried again. 'What about *your* new man, Jen? Have you met him yet, Mrs G?'

Alicia was examining her teeth in the mirror of her powder compact. 'Who are we talking about now, dear? I lose track, with all the new friends Jennifer seems to have these days.'

'Mr Brian Kelly,' said Nyesha.

'Oh, him. Well, I do keep telling her to invite him round. But he seems rather, well, recalcitrant.'

In fact, he was quite keen. It was Jennifer who'd told him as they sat in the Frog and Newt that there was no need to rush things. 'She's obsessed with the wedding at the minute, recruiting anyone who comes within a five-mile radius. She asked the postman if he'd be her pageboy the other day. You might find yourself giving her away if you're not careful.'

'Are you worried she won't like me?' asked Brian.

'Don't be silly,' said Jennifer. 'No one could dislike you.'

It was more the thought that Brian might look at Alicia, see Jennifer in thirty years' time and run a mile.

'Come to the evening do,' she said. 'She'll be diluted there.'

'You'll meet him tonight Mum,' she said now as they negotiated the Sheepscar Interchange. 'And when you come back from your honeymoon we'll invite him round for dinner.

Anyway it doesn't really matter who comes today, does it? Apart from Dr Ganguly.'

'What on earth are you insinuating, darling?' said Alicia. 'Of course Narendra will be there. Really! A Matron of Honour is meant to offer emotional succour, not undermine at the first opportunity.'

'I didn't mean anything by it,' said Jennifer.

Alicia snapped her compact shut. 'And it's high time you started calling him Narendra. Where are we going, anyway? This isn't the way to Salvatore's. We haven't seen him for *weeks*. Surely he's back from his holiday in Italy by now?'

Jennifer rolled her eyes at Nyesha in the driving mirror.

As it happened, Salvatore had left several messages on Jennifer's Voicemail over the past few weeks, telling her that he had fired Tony and that the incident at his flat had made him think again. His voice held an edge of desperation she'd never heard before. But she had no problem ignoring him.

Nyesha had counselled seeing a solicitor, taking out an injunction. 'Or report it to the police. Get the local paper to do a story on it. It might send his hairdressing business down the pan.'

Jennifer hadn't wanted to. By the empty chairs she saw every time she drove past his salon, the credit crunch was doing the job for her. Either that or the story had got out anyway.

She threw Nyesha a sudden, suspicious look in the mirror.

Her friend winked.

'You didn't!' said Jennifer.

'Didn't what?' asked Alicia.

'Nothing, Mum.'

The drove up Chapeltown Road, past the Polish supermarket and up the hill.

'Listen, I've found us a new salon in Chapel Allerton,' said Jennifer. 'Your stylist is called Linda, Mum.'

Alicia pulled a face. 'Oh, a *woman*.'

'She's meant to be very good. Jocasta recommended her.'

'Ah ... Jocasta! Isn't she the one you used to go to the pictures with? You saw *One Flew Over the Cuckoo's Nest* together, didn't you?'

'Good heavens. You've got a memory like an elephant.'

Alicia smoothed her skirt. 'I can think of more flattering comparisons, dear. Especially on one's wedding day, when one is supposed to be being made to feel like a queen.'

They drew up outside the salon.

Jennifer looked across. It was full of wet-haired women in black capes and dry-haired women with scissors. There wasn't a man in the place. No one in skin-tight trousers, no one leaning on a broom leering. And in the pit of Jennifer's stomach, no feeling other than mild indigestion from having eaten a cheese sandwich too quickly.

'I'm looking forward to this,' said Nyesha. 'I remember Leeds prices.'

'I don't expect this Linda to be a patch on Salvatore,' said Alicia. 'But perhaps you're right. One should be careful on one's wedding day. Narendra says I mustn't be *flirted* with. Except by him, of course.'

She opened the car door.

'Stay there, Mrs G,' said Nyesha. 'I'll come round and help you out.'

In the brief moment Alicia and Jennifer were alone in the car, Alicia turned to her daughter. 'Salvatore always *liked* you. That's why he was nice to me, I'm sure of it. He had his sights set on you.'

'He was nice to you because he liked you,' said Jennifer. 'And anyway, I'd rather have someone with their heart set on me, not their sights.'

'Hah!' said Alicia, throwing Jennifer an unexpected look of appreciation.

And then a strange thing happened. As Jennifer watched her mother ease herself out of the car, she felt a strange glow in the pit of her stomach, a sort of surging tenderness. She'd had the feeling before, of course, just not in the middle of town and not in connection with her mother.

Her mother, holding Nyesha's arm, moved slowly across the pavement.

Jennifer went on watching. She breathed out slowly, but the feeling didn't change. A sense that you treasured a person absolutely in that moment, just as they were. You didn't require them to change. You didn't want to add or subtract anything, so you were, in those seconds, perfectly happy.

It wouldn't last, of course. But as Alicia moved towards the door of the salon, the long moments of tenderness stretched out.